The Dim Lantern

By Temple Bailey

NATAL PUBLISHING LLC
ARS LONGA, VITA BREVIS

CHAPTER I
IN WHICH PHILOMEL SINGS

Sherwood Park is twelve miles from Washington. Starting as a somewhat pretentious suburb on the main line of a railroad, it was blessed with easy accessibility until encroaching trolleys swept the tide of settlement away from it, and left it high and dry—its train service, unable to compete with modern motor vehicles, increasingly inefficient.

Property values, inevitably, decreased. The little suburb degenerated, grew less fashionable. People who might have added social luster to its gatherings moved away. The frame houses, which at first had made such a brave showing, became a bit down at the heel. Most of them, built before the revival of good taste in architecture, seemed top-heavy and dull with their imitation towers, their fretted balconies, their gray and brown coloring, their bands of contrasting shingles tied like sashes around their middles.

The Barnes cottage was saved from the universal lack of loveliness by its simple lines, its white paint and green blinds. Yet the paint had peeled in places, and the concrete steps which followed the line of the two terraces were cracked and worn.

Old Baldwin Barnes had bought his house on the instalment plan, and his children were still paying for it. Old Baldwin had succumbed to the deadly monotony of writing the same inscription on red slips through thirty years of faithful service in the Pension Office, and had left the world with his debts behind him.

He had the artistic temperament which his son inherited. Julia was like her mother who had died two years before her husband. Mrs. Barnes had been unimaginative and capable. It was because of her that Julia had married an architect, and was living in a snug apartment in Chicago, that Baldwin Junior had gone through college and had some months at an art school before the war came on, and that Jane, the youngest, had a sense of thrift, and an intensive experience in domestic economy.

As for the rest of her, Jane was twenty, slender as a Florentine page, and fairly pretty. She was in love with life and liked to talk about it. Young Baldwin said, indeed, with the frankness of a brother, that Jane ran on like a babbling brook.

She was "running on" this November morning, as she and young Baldwin ate breakfast together. Jane always got the breakfast. Sophy, a capable negro woman, came over later to help with the housework, and to put the six o'clock dinner on the table. But it was Jane who started the percolator,

poached the eggs, and made the toast on the electric toaster, while young Baldwin read the *Washington Post*. He read bits out loud when he was in the mood. He was not always in the mood, and then Jane talked to him. He did not always listen, but that made no difference.

Jane had named the percolator "Philomel," because of its purling harmonies.

"Don't you love it, Baldy?"

Her brother, with one eye on the paper, was eating his grapefruit.

"Love what?"

"Philomel."

"Silly stuff——"

"It isn't. I like to hear it sing."

"In my present mood I prefer a hymn of hate."

She buttered a slice of toast for him. "Well, of course, you'd feel like that."

"Who wouldn't?" He took the toast from her, and buried himself in his paper, so Jane buttered another slice for herself and ate it in protesting silence—plus a poached egg, and a cup of coffee rich with yellow cream and much sugar. Jane's thinness made such indulgence possible. She enjoyed good food as she enjoyed a new frock, violets in the spring, the vista from the west front of the Capitol, free verse, and the book of Job. There were really no limits to Jane's enthusiasms. She spoke again of the percolator. "It's as nice as a kettle on the hob, isn't it?"

Young Baldwin read on.

"I simply *love* breakfast," she continued.

"Is there anything you don't love, Janey?" with a touch of irritation.

"Yes."

"What?"

"You."

He stared at her over the top of the sheet. "I like that!"

"Well, you won't talk to me, Baldy. It isn't my fault if you hate the world."

"No, it isn't." He laid down the paper. "But I'll tell you this, Janey, I'm about *through*."

She caught her breath, then flung out, "Oh, you're not. Be a good sport, Baldy. Things are bound to come your way if you wait."

He gave a short laugh and rose. "I wish I had your optimism."

"I wish you had."

They faced each other, looking for the moment rather like two young cockerels. Jane's bobbed hair emphasized the boyish effect of her straight, slim figure. Baldy towered above her, his black hair matching hers, his eyes, too, matching—gray and lighted-up.

Jane was the first to turn her eyes away. She looked at the clock. "You'll be late."

He got his hat and coat and came back to her. "I'm a blamed sorehead. Give me a kiss, Janey."

She gave it to him, and clung to him for a moment.

"Don't forget to bring a steak home for dinner," was all she said, but he was aware of the caress of those clinging fingers.

It was one of his grievances that he had to do the marketing—one could not depend on Sherwood's single small store—so Baldy with dreams in his head drove twice a week to the butcher's stall in the old Center Market to bring back chops, or a porterhouse, or a festive small roast.

He had no time for it in the mornings, however. His little Ford took him over the country roads and through the city streets and landed him at the Patent Office at a quarter of nine. There, with a half hour for lunch, he worked until five—it was a dog's life and he had other aspirations.

Jane, left to herself, read the paper. One headline was sensational. The bride of a fashionable wedding had been deserted at the altar. The bridegroom had failed to appear at the church. The guests waiting impatiently in the pews had been informed, finally, that the ceremony would be postponed.

Newspaper men hunting for the bridegroom learned that he had left a note for his best man—and that he was on his way to southern waters. The bride could not be seen. Her uncle, who was also her guardian, and with whom she lived, had stated that there was nothing to be said. That was all. But society was on tiptoe. Delafield Simms was the son of a rich New Yorker. He and his

bride were to have spent their honeymoon on his yacht. Edith Towne had a fortune to match his. Both of them belonged to old and aristocratic families. No wonder people were talking.

There was a picture of Miss Towne, a tall, fair girl, in real lace, orange blossoms, seed pearls———.

Pride was in every line of her. Jane's tender fancy carried her to that first breathless moment when the bride had donned that gracious gown and had surveyed herself in the mirror. "How happy she must have been." Then the final shuddering catastrophe.

Sophy arrived at this moment, and Jane told her about it. "She'll never dare trust anybody, will she?"

Sophy was wise, and she weighed the question out of her wide experience of human nature. She could not read or write, and she was dependent on those around her for daily bulletins of the way the big world went. But she had worked in many families and had had a family of her own. So she knew life, which is a bigger thing sometimes than books.

"Yo' kain't ever tell whut a woman will do, Miss Janey. Effen she a trustin' nature, she'll trus' and trus', and effen she ain' a trustin' nature, she won't trus' nohow."

"But what do you suppose made him do it?"

"Nobody knows whut a man's gwine do, w'en it comes to gittin' married."

"But to leave her like that, Sophy. I should think she'd die."

"Effen the good Lord let women die w'en men 'ceived them," Sophy proclaimed with a chuckle, "dere wouldn' be a female lef' w'en the trump sounded." Her tray was piled high with dishes, as she stood in the dining-room door. "Does you-all want rice puddin' fo' dinnah, Miss Janey?"

And there the subject dropped. But Jane thought a great deal about it as she went on with her work.

She told her sister, Julia, about it when, late that afternoon, she wrote her weekly letter.

"The worst of it must have been to lose her faith in things. I'd rather be Jane Barnes without any love affair than Edith Towne with a love affair like that. Baldy told me the other day that I am not unattractive! Can't you see him saying it? And he doesn't think me pretty. Perhaps I'm not. But there are moments, Judy, when I like myself——!

"Baldy nearly had a fit when I bobbed my hair. But I did it and took the consequences, and it's no end comfortable. Baldy at the present moment is mid-Victorian. It is his reaction from the war. He says he is dead sick of flappers. That they are all alike—and make no appeal to the imagination! He came home the other night from a dance and read Tennyson—can you fancy that after the way he used to fling Amy Lowell at us and Carl Sandburg? He says he is so tired of short skirts and knees and proposals and cigarettes that he is going to hunt with a gun, if he ever decides to marry, for an Elaine or a Griselda! But the worst of it is, he takes it out on me! I wish you'd see the way he censors my clothes and my manners, and I sit here like a prisoner in a tower with not a man in sight but Evans Follette, and he is just a heartache, Judy.

"Baldy has had three proposals; he said that the first was stimulating, but repetition 'staled the interest'! Of course he didn't tell me the names of the girls. Baldy's not a cad.

"But he is discouraged and desperately depressed. He has such a big talent, Judy, and he just slaves away at that old office. He says that after those years in France, it seems like a cage. I sometimes wonder what civilization is, anyhow, that we clip the wings of our young eagles. We take our boys and shut them up, and they pant for freedom. Is that all that life is going to mean for Baldy—eight hours a day—behind bars?

"Yet I am trying to keep him at it until the house is paid for. I don't know whether I am right—but it's all we have—and both of us love it. He hasn't been able lately to work much at night, he's dead tired. But there's a prize offer of a magazine cover design, and I want him to compete. He says there isn't any use of his trying to do *anything* unless he can give all of his time to it.

"Of course you've heard all this before, but I hear it every day. And I like to talk things out. I must not write another line, dearest. And don't worry, Baldy will work like mad if the mood strikes him.

"Did I tell you that Evans Follette and his mother are to dine with us on Thanksgiving Day? We ought to have six guests to make things go.

But nobody will fit in with the Follettes. You know why, so I needn't explain.

"Kiss both of the babies for me. Failing other young things, I am going to have a Christmas tree for the kitten. It's a gay life, darling.

"Ever your own,
"Jane."

The darkness had come by the time she had finished her letter. She changed her frock for a thinner one, wrapped herself in an old cape of orange-hued cloth, and went out to lock up her chickens. She had fed them before she wrote her letter, but she always took this last look to be sure they were safe.

She passed through the still kitchen, where old Sophy sat by the warm, bright range. There were potatoes baking, and Sophy's famous pudding. "How good everything smells," said Jane.

She smiled at Sophy and went on. The wind was blowing and the sky was clear. There had been no snow, but there were little pools of ice about, and Jane took each one with a slide. She felt a tingling sense of youth and excitation. Back of the garage was a shadowy grove of tall pines which sang and sighed as the wind swept them. There was a young moon above the pines. It seemed to Jane that her soul was lifted to it. She flung up her arms to the moon, and the yellow cape billowed about her.

The shed where the chickens were kept was back

of the garage. When Jane opened the door, her old Persian cat, Merrymaid, came out to her, and a puff-ball of a kitten. Jane snapped on the lights in the chicken-house and the biddies stirred. When she snapped them off again, she heard them settle back to sheltered slumber.

The kitten danced ahead of her, and the old cat danced too, as the wind whirled her great tail about. "We won't go in the house—we won't go in the house," said Jane, in a sort of conversational chant, as the pussies followed her down a path which led through the pines. She often walked at this hour—and she loved it best on nights like this.

She felt poignantly the beauty of it—the dark pines and the little moon above them—the tug of the wind at her cloak like a riotous playmate.

Baldy was not the only poet in the family, but Jane's love of beauty was inarticulate. She would never be able to write it on paper or draw it with a pencil.

Down the path she went, the two pussy-cats like small shadows in her wake, until suddenly a voice came out of the dark.

"I believe it is little Jane Barnes."

She stopped. "Oh, is that you, Evans? Isn't it a heavenly night?"

"I'm not sure."

"Don't talk that way."

"Why not?"

"Because an evening like this is like wine—it goes to my head."

"You are like wine," he told her. "Jane, how do you do it?"

"Do what?"

"Hold the pose of youth and joy and happiness?"

"You know it isn't a pose. I just feel that way, Evans."

"My dear, I believe you do."

He limped a little as he walked beside her. He was tall and gaunt. Almost grotesquely tall. Yet when he had gone to war he had not seemed in the least grotesque. He had been tall but not thin, and he had gone in all the glory of his splendid youth.

There was no glory left. He was twenty-seven. He had fought and he would fight again for the same cause. But his youth was dead, except when he was with Jane. She revived him, as he said, like wine.

"I was coming over," he began, and broke off as a sibilant sound interrupted him.

"Oh, are the cats with you? Well, Rusty must take the road," he laughed as the little old dog trotted to neutral ground at the edge of the grove. Rusty was friends with Merrymaid, except when there were kittens about. He knew enough to avoid her in days of anxious motherhood.

Jane picked up the kitten. "They would come."

"All animals follow you. You're sort of a domestic

Circe—with your dogs and chickens and pussy-cats in the place of tigers and lions and leopards."

"I'd love to have lived in Eden," said Jane, unexpectedly, "before Eve and Adam sinned. What it must have meant to have all those great beasts mild-mannered and purring under your hand like this kitten. What a dreadful thing happened, Evans, when fear came into the world."

"What makes you say that now, Jane?" His voice was sharp.

"Shouldn't I have said it? Oh, Evans, you can't think I had you in mind——"

"No," with a touch of weariness, "but you are the only one, really, who knows what a coward I am——"

"Evans, you're not."

"You're good to say it, but that's what I came over for. I am up against it again, Jane. Some cousins are on from New York—they're at the New Willard—and Mother and I went in to see them last night. They have invited us to go back with them. They've a big house east of Fifth Avenue, and they want us as their guests indefinitely. They think it will do me a lot of good— get me out of myself, they call it. But I can't see it. Since I came home— every time I think of facing mobs of people"—again his voice grew sharp— "I'm clutched by something I can't describe. It is perfectly unreasonable, but I can't help it."

For a moment they walked in silence, then he went on—"Mother's very keen about it. She thinks it will set me up. But I want to stay here—and I thought if you'd talk to her, she'll listen to you, Jane—she always does."

"Does she know how you feel about it?"

"No, I think not. I've never told her. I've only spilled over to you now and then. It would hurt Mother, no end, to know how changed I am."

Jane laid her hand on his arm. "You're not. Brace up, old dear. You aren't dead yet." As she lifted her head to look up at him, the hood of her cape slipped back, and the wind blew her soft, thick hair against his cheek. "But I'll talk to your mother if you want me to. She is a great darling."

Jane meant what she said; she was really very fond of Mrs. Follette. And in this she was unlike the rest of the folk in Sherwood. Mrs. Follette was extremely unpopular in the Park.

They had reached the kitchen door. "Won't you come in?" Jane said.

"No, I've got to get back. I only ran over for a moment. I have to have a daily sip of you, Jane."

"Baldy's bringing a steak for dinner. Help us eat it."

"Sorry, but Mother would be alone."

"When shall I talk to her?"

"There's no hurry. The cousins are staying on for the opening of Congress. Jane dear, don't despise me——" His voice broke.

"Evans, as if I could."

Again her hand was on his arm. He laid his own over it. "You're the best ever, Janey," he said, huskily—and presently he went away.

Jane, going in, found that Baldy had telephoned. "He kain't git here until seven," Sophy told her.

"You had better run along home," Jane told her. "I'll cook the steak when it comes."

Sophy was old and she was tired. Life hadn't been easy. The son who was to have been the prop of her old age had been killed in France. There was a daughter's daughter who had gone north and who now and then sent money. Old Sophy did not know where her granddaughter got the money, but it was good to have it when it came. But it was not enough, so old Sophy worked.

"I hates to leave you here alone, Miss Janey."

"Oh, run along, Sophy. Baldy will come before I know it."

So Sophy went and Jane waited. Seven o'clock arrived, with the dinner showing signs of deterioration. Jane sat at the front window and watched. The old cat watched, too, perched on the sill, and gazing out into the dark with round, mysterious eyes. The kitten slept on the hearth. Jane grew restless and stood up, peering out. Then all at once two round moons arose above the horizon, were lost as the road dipped down, showed again on the rise of the hill, and lighted the lawn as

Baldy's car made a half circle and swept into the garage.

Jane went through the kitchen to the back door, throwing an appraising glance at the things in the warming oven, and stood waiting on the threshold, hugging herself in the keenness of the wind.

Presently her brother's tall form was silhouetted against the silvery gray of the night.

"I thought you were never coming," she said to him.

"I thought so, too." He bent and kissed her; his cheek was cold as it touched hers.

"Aren't you nearly frozen?"

"No. Sorry to be late, honey. Get dinner on the table and I'll be ready——"

"I'm afraid things won't be very appetizing," she told him; "they've waited so long. But I'll cook the steak——"

He had gone on, and was beyond the sound of her voice. She opened the fat parcel which he had deposited on the kitchen table. She wondered a bit at its size. But Baldy had a way of bringing home unexpected bargains—a dozen boxes of crackers—unwieldy pounds of coffee.

But this was neither crackers nor coffee. The box which was revealed bore the name of a fashionable florist. Within were violets—single ones— set off by one perfect rose and tied with a silver ribbon.

Jane gasped—then she went to the door and called:

"Baldy, where's the steak?"

He came to the top of the stairs. "Great guns," he said, "I forgot it!"

Then he saw the violets in her hands, laughed and came down a step or two. "I sold a loaf of bread and bought—white hyacinths——"

"They're heavenly!" Her glance swept up to him. "Peace offering?"

There were gay sparks in his eyes. "We'll call it that."

She blew a kiss to him from the tips of her fingers. "They are perfectly sweet. And we can have an omelette. Only if we eat any more eggs, we'll be flapping our wings."

"I don't care what we have. I am so hungry I could eat a house." He went back up the stairs, laughing.

Jane, breaking eggs into a bowl, meditated on the nonchalance of men. She meditated, too, on the mystery of Baldy's mood. The flowers were evidence of high exaltation. He did not often lend himself to such extravagance.

He came down presently and helped carry in the belated dinner. The potatoes lay like withered leaves in a silver dish, the cornbread was a wrinkled wreck, the pudding a travesty. Only Jane's omelette and a lettuce salad had escaped the blight of delay.

Then, too, there was Philomel, singing. Jane drew a cup of coffee, hot and strong, and set it at

her brother's place. The violets were in the center of the table, the cats purring on the hearth.

Jane loved her little home with almost passionate intensity. She loved to have Baldy in a mood like this—things right once more with his world.

She knew it was so by the ring of his voice, the cock of his head—hence she was not in the least surprised when he leaned forward under the old-fashioned spreading dome which drenched him with light, and said, "I've such a lot to tell you, Jane; the most amazing thing has happened."

CHAPTER II
A PRINCESS PASSES

When young Baldwin Barnes had ridden out of Sherwood that morning on his way to Washington, his car had swept by fields which were crisp and frozen; by clumps of trees whose pointed tops cut into the clear blue of the sky; over ice-bound streams, all shining silver in the early sunlight.

It was very cold, and his little car was open to the weather. But he felt no chill. He wore the mustard-colored top-coat which had been his lieutenant's garb in the army. The collar was turned up to protect his ears. His face showed pink and wedge-shaped between his soft hat and his collar.

He had the eye of an artist, and he liked the ride. Even in winter the countryside was attractive—and as the road slipped away, there came a few big houses surrounded by wide grounds, with glimpses through their high hedges of white statues, of spired cedars, of sun-dials set in the midst of dead gardens.

Beyond these there was an arid stretch until the Lake was reached, then the links of one country club, the old buildings of another, and at last on the crest of a hill, a view of the city—sweeping on
the right towards Arlington and on the left towards Soldiers' Home.

Turning into Sixteenth Street, he crossed a bridge with its buttresses guarded by stone panthers—and it was on this bridge that his car stopped.

Climbing out, he blamed Fate furiously. Years afterward, however, he dared not think of the difference it might have made if his little flivver had not failed him.

He raised the hood and tapped and tinkered. Now and then he stopped to stamp his feet or beat his hands together. And he said things under his breath. He would be late at the office—life was just one—darned thing—after another!

Once when he stopped, a woman passed him. She was tall and slender and wrapped up to her ears in moleskin. Her small hat was blue, from her hand swung a gray suede bag, her feet were in gray shoes with cut-steel buckles.

Baldy's quick eyes took in the details of her costume. He reflected as he went back to work that women were fools to court death in that fashion, with thin slippers and silk stockings, in this bitter weather.

He found the trouble, fixed it, jumped into his car and started his motor. And it was just as he was moving that his eye was caught by a spot of blue bobbing down the hill below the bridge. The woman who had passed him was making her way

slowly along the slippery path. On each side of her the trees were brown and bare. At the foot of the hill was a thread of frozen water.

It was not usual at this time to see pedestrians in that place. Now and then a workman took a short cut—or on warm days there were picnic parties—but to follow the rough paths in winter was a bleak and arduous adventure.

He stayed for a moment to watch her, then suddenly left his car and ran. The girl in the blue hat had caught her high heels in a root, had stumbled and fallen.

When he reached her, she was struggling to her feet. He helped her, and picked up the bag which she had dropped.

"Thank you so much." Her voice was low and pleasing. He saw that she was young, that her skin was very fair, and that the hair which swept over her ears was pale gold, but most of all, he saw that her eyes were burning blue. He had never seen eyes quite like them. The old poets would have called them sapphire, but sapphires do not flame.

"It was so silly of me to try to do it," she was protesting, "but I thought it might be a short cut——"

He wondered what her destination might be that this remote path should lead to it. But all he said was, "High heels aren't made for—mountain climbing——"

"They aren't made for anything," she said, looking down at the steel-buckled slippers, "useful."

"Let me help you up the hill."

"I don't want to go up."

He surveyed the steep incline. "I am perfectly sure you don't want to go down."

"I do," she hesitated, "but I suppose I can't."

He had a sudden inspiration. "Can I take you anywhere? My little flivver is up there on the bridge. Would you mind that?"

"Would I mind if a life-line were thrown to me in mid-ocean?" She said it lightly, but he fancied there was a note of high hope.

They went up the hill together. "I want to get an Alexandria car," she told him.

"But you are miles away from it."

"Am I?" She showed momentary confusion. "I—hoped I might reach it through the Park——"

"You might. But you might also freeze to death in the attempt like a babe in the wood, without any robins to perform the last melancholy rites. What made you think of such a thing?"

He saw at once his mistake. Her voice had a touch of frigidity. "I can't tell you."

"Sorry," he said abruptly. "You must forgive me."

She melted. "No, it is I who should be forgiven. It must look strange to you—but I'd rather not—explain——"

On the last steep rise of the hill he lifted her over

a slippery pool, and as his hand sank into the soft fur of her wrap, he was conscious of its luxury. It seemed to him that his mustard-colored coat fairly shouted incongruity. His imagination swept on to Raleigh, and the velvet cloak which might do the situation justice. He smiled at himself and smiling, too, at her, felt a tingling sense of coming circumstance.

It was because of that smile, and the candid, boyish quality of it, that she trusted him. "Do you know," she said, "I haven't had a thing to eat this morning, and I'm frightfully hungry. Is there any place that I could have a cup of coffee—where you could bring it out to me in the car?"

"Could I?" the morning stars sang. "There's a corking place in Georgetown."

"Without the world looking on?"

"Without *your* world looking on," boldly.

She hesitated, then told the truth. "I'm running away——"

He was eager. "May I help?"

"Perhaps you wouldn't if you knew."

"Try me."

He helped her into his car, tucked the rug about her, and put up the curtains. "No one can see you on the back seat," he said, and drove to Georgetown on the wings of the wind.

He brought coffee out to her from a neat shop where milk was sold, and buns, and hot drinks, to motormen and conductors. It was a clean little place, fresh as paint, and the buttered rolls were brown and crisp.

"I never tasted anything so good," the runaway told Baldy. "And now I am going to ask you to drive me over the Virginia side—I'll get the trolley there."

When at last he drew up at a little way station, and unfastened the curtain, he was aware that she had opened the suede bag and had a roll of bills in her hand. For a moment his heart failed him. Was she going to offer him money?

But what she said, with cheeks flaming, was: "I haven't anything less than ten dollars. Do you think they will take it?"

"It's doubtful. I have oodles of change." He held out a handful of silver.

"Thank you so much, and—you must let me have your card———"

"Oh, please———"

Her voice had an edge of sharpness. "Of course it must be a loan."

He handed her his card in silence. She read the name. "Mr. Barnes, you have been very kind. I am tremendously grateful."

"It was not kindness—but now and then a princess passes."

For a breathless moment her amazed glance met his—then the clang of a bell heralded an approaching car.

As he helped her out hurriedly she stumbled over

the rug. He caught her up, lifted her to the ground, and motioned to the motorman.

The car stopped and she mounted the steps. "Good-bye, and thank you so much." He stood back and she waved to him while he watched her out of sight.

His work at the office that morning had dreams for an accompaniment. He went out at lunch-time but ate nothing. It was at lunch-time that he bought the violets—paying an unthinkable price for them, and not caring.

He had wild thoughts of following the road to Alexandria—of finding his Juliet on some balcony and climbing up to her. Or of sending the flowers forth addressed largely to "A Princess who passed." One could not, however, be sure of an uncomprehending mail service. He would need more definite appellation.

He had not, indeed, bought the flowers for Jane. He had had no thought of his sister as he passed the florist's window. He had been drawn into the shop by the association of ideas—when he entered all the scent and sweetness seemed to belong to a garden in which his lady walked.

He did not eat any lunch, and he took the box of violets back with him to the office, wrapped to prodigious size to protect it from the cold. It was an object of much curiosity to his fellow-clerks as it sat on the window-sill. They all wanted to know who it was for, and one of the abhorred flappers,

who, at times, took Baldy's dictation, tried to peep between the covers.

He felt that her glance would be desecration. What did she know of delicate fragrances? Her perfumes were oriental, and she used a lipstick!

He managed, however, to carry the thing off lightly. He was, in the opinion of the office, a gay and companionable chap. They knew nothing of his reactions. And he was popular.

So now he said to the girl, "If you'll let that alone, I'll bring a box of chocolates for the crowd."

"Why can't I look at it?"

"Because curiosity is a deadly sin. You know what happened to Bluebeard's wife?"

"Oh, Bluebeard." She had read of him, she thought, in the Paris papers. He had killed a lot of wives. She giggled a little in deference to the spiciness of the subject. Then pinned him down to his promise of sweets. "You know the kind we like?"

"This week?"

"Yes. Butter creams."

"Last week it was the nut kind. One never knows. I should think you ought to standardize your tastes."

"That would be stupid, wouldn't it? It's much more exciting to change."

He went back to his work and forgot her. She was one of the butterflies who had flitted to Washington
during the war, and had set that conservative city by the ears in defiance of tradition.

It was these young women who had eaten their lunches within the sacred precincts of Lafayette Square, draping themselves on its statues at noontime, and strewing its immaculate sward with broken boxes and bags, who had worn sheer and insufficient clothing, had motored under the moon and without a moon, unchaperoned, until morning, and had come through it all a little damaged, perhaps, as to ideals, but having made a definite impress on the life of the capital. The days of the cave-dwellers were dead. For better, for worse, the war-worker and the women of old Washington had been swept out together from a safe and snug harbor into the raging seas of social readjustment.

It was after office that Baldy carried the flowers to his car. He set the box on the back seat. In the hurry of the morning he had forgotten the rug which still lay where his fair passenger had stumbled over it. He picked it up and something dropped from its folds. It was the gray suede bag, half open, and showing the roll of bills. Beneath the roll of bills was a small sheer handkerchief, a vanity case with a pinch of powder and a wee puff, a new check-book—and, negligently at the very bottom, a ring—a ring of such enchantment that as it lay in Baldy's hand, he doubted its reality. The hoop was of platinum, slender, yet strong enough to bear up a carved moonstone in a circle of diamonds.

The carving showed a delicate Psyche—with a butterfly on her shoulder. The diamonds blazed like small suns.

Inside the ring was an inscription—"Del to Edith—Forever."

Del to Edith? Where had he seen those names? With a sudden flash of illumination, he dropped the ring back into the bag, stuffed the bag in his pocket, and made his way to a newsboy at the corner.

There it was in startling headlines: *Edith Towne Disappears. Delafield Simms' Yacht Said to Have Been Sighted Near Norfolk!*

So his passenger had been the much-talked-about Edith Towne— deserted at the moment of her marriage!

He thought of her eyes of burning blue,—the fairness of her skin and hair—the touch of haughtiness. Simms was a cur, of course! He should have knelt at her feet!

The thing to do was to get the bag back to her. He must advertise at once. On the wings of this decision, his car whirled down the Avenue. The lines which, after much deliberation, he pushed across the counter of the newspaper office, would be ambiguous to others, but clear to her. "Will passenger who left bag with valuable contents in Ford car call up Sherwood Park 49."

CHAPTER III
JANE KNITS

"Is she really as beautiful as that?" Jane demanded.

"As what?"

"Her picture in the paper."

"Haven't I said enough for you to know it?"

Jane nodded. "Yes. But it doesn't sound real to me. Are you sure you didn't dream it?"

"I'll say I didn't. Isn't that the proof?" The gray bag lay on the table in front of them, the ring was on Jane's finger.

She turned it to catch the light. "Baldy," she said, "it's beyond imagination."

"I told you——"

"Think of having a ring like this——"

"Think," fiercely, "of having a lover who ran away."

"Well," said Jane, "there are some advantages in being—unsought. I'm like the Miller-ess of Dee—

"I care for nobody—

No, not I,

Since nobody

Cares—

For me——!"

She sang it with a light boyish swing of her body. Her voice was girlish and sweet, with a touch of huskiness.

Baldy flung his scorn at her. "Jane, aren't you ever in earnest?"

"Intermittently," she smiled at him, came over and tucked her arm in his. "Baldy," she coaxed, "aren't you going to tell her uncle?"

He stared at her. "Her uncle? Tell him what?"

"That you've found the bag."

He flung off her arm. "Would you have me turn traitor?"

"Heavens, Baldy, this isn't melodrama. It's common sense. You can't keep that bag."

"I can keep it until she answers my advertisement."

"She may never see your advertisement, and the money isn't yours, and the ring isn't."

He was troubled. "But she trusted me. I can't do it."

Jane shrugged her shoulders, and began to clear away the dinner things. Baldy helped her. Old Merrymaid mewed to go out, and Jane opened the door.

"It's snowing hard," she said.

The wind drove the flakes across the threshold. Old Merrymaid danced back into the house, bright-eyed and round as a muff. The air was freezing.

"It is going to be a dreadful night," young Baldwin, heavy with gloom, prophesied. He thought of

Edith, in the storm in her buckled shoes. Had she found shelter? Was she frightened and alone somewhere in the dark?

He went into the living-room, whence Jane presently followed him. Jane was knitting a sweater and she worked while Baldy read to her. He read the full account of Edith Towne's flight. She had gone away early in the morning. The maid, taking her breakfast up to her, had found the room empty. She had left a note for her uncle. But he had not permitted its publication. He was, they said, wild with anxiety.

"I'll bet he's an old tyrant," was Baldy's comment.

Frederick Towne's picture was in the paper. "I like his face," said Jane, "and he doesn't seem so frightfully old."

"Why should she run away from him, if he wasn't a tyrant?" he demanded furiously.

"Well, don't scold me." Jane was as vivid as an oriole in the midst of her orange wools.

She loved color. The living-room was an expression of it. Its furniture was old-fashioned but not old-fashioned enough to be lovely. Jane had, however, modified its lack of grace and its dull monotonies by covers of chintz—tropical birds against black and white stripes—and there was a lamp of dull blue pottery with a Chinese shade. A fire in the coal grate, with the glow of the lamp, gave the room a look of burnished brightness. The kitten,

curled up in Jane's lap, played cozily with the tawny threads.

"Don't scold me," said Jane, "it isn't my fault."

"I'm not scolding, but I'm worried to death. And you aren't any help, are you?"

She looked at him in astonishment. "I've tried to help. I told you to call up."

Young Baldwin walked the floor.

"She trusted me."

"You won't get anywhere with that," said Jane with decision. "The thing to do is to tell Mr. Towne that you have news of her, and that you'll give it only under promise that he won't do anything until he has talked it over with you."

"That sounds better," said young Baldwin; "how did you happen to think of it?"

"Now and then," said Jane, "I have ideas."

Baldy went to the telephone. When he came back his eyes were like gray moons. "He promised everything, and he's coming out———"

"Here?"

"Yes, he wouldn't wait until to-morrow. He's wild about her———"

"Well, he would be." Jane mentally surveyed the situation. "Baldy, I'm going to make some coffee, and have some cheese and crackers."

"He may not want them."

"On a cold night like this, I'll say he will; anybody would."

Baldy helped Jane get out the round-bellied

silver pot, the pitchers and tray. The young people had a sense of complacency as they handled the old silver. Frederick Towne could have nothing of more distinguished history. It had belonged to their great-grandmother, Dabney, who was really D'Aubigne, and it had graced an Emperor's table. Each piece had a monogram set in an engraved wreath. The big tray was so heavy that Jane lifted it with difficulty, so Baldy set it for her on the little mahogany table which they drew up in front of the fire. There was no wealth now in the Barnes family, but the old silver spoke of a time when a young hostess as black-haired as Jane had dispensed lavish hospitality.

Frederick Towne had not expected what he found—the little house set high on its terraces seemed to give from its golden-lighted window squares a welcome in the dark. "I shan't be long, Briggs," he said to his chauffeur.

"Very good, sir," said Briggs, and led the way up the terrace.

Baldy ushered Towne into the living-room, and Frederick, standing on the threshold, surveyed a coziness which reminded him of nothing so much as a color illustration in some old English magazine. There was the coal grate, the table drawn up to the fire, the twinkling silver on its massive tray, violets in a low vase—and rising to meet him a slender, glowing child, with a banner of orange wool behind her.

"Jane," said young Barnes, "may I present Mr. Towne?" and Jane held out her hand and said, "This is very good of you."

He found himself unexpectedly gracious. He was not always gracious. He had felt that he couldn't be. A man with money and position had to shut himself up sometimes in a shell of reserve, lest he be imposed upon.

But in this warmth and fragrance he expanded. "What a charming room," he said, and smiled at her.

Her first view of him confirmed the opinion she formed from his picture. He was apparently not over forty, a stocky, well-built, ruddy man, with fair hair that waved crisply, and with clear blue eyes, lighter, she learned afterward, than Edith's, but with just a hint of that burning blue. He had the air of indefinable finish which speaks of a life spent in the right school and the right college, and the right clubs, of a background of generations of good blood and good breeding. He wore evening clothes, and one knew somehow that dinner never found him without them.

Yet in spite of these evidences of pomp and circumstance, Jane felt perfectly at ease with him. He was, after all, she reflected, only a gentleman, and Baldy was that. The only difference lay in their divergent incomes. So, as the two men talked, she knitted on, with the outward effect of placidity.

"Do you want me to go?" she had asked them,

and Towne had replied promptly, "Certainly not. There's nothing we have to say that you can't hear."

So Jane listened with all her ears, and modified the opinion she had formed of Frederick Towne from his picture and from her first glimpse of him. He was nice to talk to, but he might be hard to live with. He had obstinacy and egotism.

"Why Edith should have done it amazes me."

Jane, naughtily remembering the Admiral's song from Pinafore which had been her father's favorite, found it beating in her head—*My amazement, my surprise, you may learn from the expression of my eyes*——

But no hint of this showed in her manner.

"She was hurt," she said, "and she wanted to hide."

"But people seem to think that in some way it is my fault. I don't like that. It isn't fair. We've always been the best of friends—more like brother and sister than niece and uncle."

"But not like Baldy and me," said Jane to herself, "not in the least like Baldy and me."

"Of course Simms ought to be shot," Towne told them heatedly.

"He ought to be hanged," was Baldy's amendment.

Jane's needles clicked, but she said nothing. She was dying to tell these bloodthirsty males what she thought of them. What good would it do to shoot

Delafield Simms? A woman's hurt pride isn't to be healed by the thought of a man's dead body.

Young Baldwin brought out the bag. "It is one that Delafield gave her," Frederick stated, "and I cashed a check for her at the bank the day before the wedding. I can't imagine why she took the ring with her."

"She probably forgot to take it off; her mind wasn't on *rings*." Jane's voice was warm with feeling.

He looked at her with some curiosity. "What was it on?"

"Oh, her heart was broken. Nothing else mattered. Can't you see?"

He hesitated for a moment before he spoke. "I don't believe it was broken. I hardly think she loved him."

Baldy blazed, "But why should she marry him?"

"Oh, well, it was a good match. A very good match. And Edith's not in the least emotional——"

"Really?" said Jane pleasantly.

Baldy was silent. Was Frederick Towne blind to the wonders that lay behind those eyes of burning blue?

Jane swept them back to the matter of the bag. "We thought you ought to have it, Mr. Towne, but Baldy had scruples about revealing anything he knows about Miss Towne's hiding-place. He feels that she trusted him."

"You said you had advertised, Mr. Barnes?"

"Yes."

"Well, the one thing is to get her home. Tell her that if she calls you up." Frederick looked suddenly tired and old.

Baldy, leaning against the mantel, gazed down at him. "It's hard to decide what I ought to do. But I feel that I'm right in giving her a chance first to answer the advertisement."

Towne's tone showed a touch of irritation. "Of course you'll have to act as you think best."

And now Jane took things in her own hands. "Mr. Towne, I'm going to make you a cup of coffee."

"I shall be very grateful," he smiled at her. What a charming child she was! He was soothed and refreshed by the atmosphere they created. This boy and girl were a friendly pair and he loved his ease. His own house, since Edith's departure, had been funereal, and his friends had been divided in their championship between himself and Edith. But the young Barneses were so pleasantly responsive with their lighted-up eyes and their little air of making him one with them. Edith had always seemed to put him quite definitely on the shelf. With little Jane and her brother he had a feeling of equality of age.

"Look here," he spoke impulsively, "may I tell you all about it? It would relieve my mind immensely."

To Jane it was a thrilling moment. Having poured the coffee, she came out from behind her battlement of silver and sat in her chintz chair. She did not knit; she was enchanted by the tale that Towne was telling. She sat very still, her hands folded, the tropical birds about her. To Frederick she seemed like a bird herself—slim and lovely, and with a voice that sang!

Towne was not an impressionable man. His years of bachelorhood had hardened him to feminine arts. But here was no artfulness. Jane assumed nothing. She was herself. As he talked to her, he became aware of some stirred emotion. An almost youthful eagerness to shine as the hero of his tale. If he embroidered the theme, it was for her benefit. What he told was as he saw it. But what he told was not the truth, nor even half of it.

CHAPTER IV
BEAUTY WAITS

Edith Towne had lived with her Uncle Frederick nearly four years when she became engaged to Delafield Simms. Her mother was dead, as was her father. Frederick was her father's only brother, and had a big house to himself, after his mother's death. It seemed the only haven for his niece, so he asked her, and asked also his father's cousin, Annabel Towne, to keep house for him, and chaperone Edith.

Annabel was over sixty, and rather indefinite, but she served to play propriety, and there was nothing else demanded of her in Frederick's household of six servants. She was a dried-up and desiccated person, with fixed ideas of what one owed to society. Frederick's mother had been like that, so he did not mind. He rather liked to think that the woman of his family kept to old ideals. It gave to things an air of dignity.

Edith, when she came, was different. So different that Frederick was glad that she had three more years at college before she would spend the winters with him. The summers were not hard to arrange. Edith and Annabel adjourned to the Towne cottage on an island in Maine—and Frederick

went up for week-ends and for the month of August. Edith spent much time out-of-doors with her young friends. She was rather fond of her Uncle Fred, but he did not loom large on the horizon of her youthful occupations.

Then came her winter at home, and her consequent engagement to Delafield Simms. It was because of Uncle Fred that she became engaged. She simply didn't want to live with him any more. She felt that Uncle Fred would be glad to have her go, and the feeling was mutual. She was an elephant on his hands. Naturally. He was a great old dear, but he was a Turk. He didn't know it, of course. But his ideas of being master of his own house were perfectly archaic. Cousin Annabel and the servants, and everybody in his office simply hung on his words, and Edith wouldn't hang. She came into his bachelor Paradise like a rather troublesome Eve, and demanded her share of the universe. He didn't like it, and there you were.

It was really Uncle Fred who wanted her to marry Delafield Simms. He talked about it a lot. At first Edith wouldn't listen. But Delafield was persistent and patient. He came gradually to be as much of a part of her everyday life as the meals she ate or the car she drove. Uncle Fred was always inviting him. He was forever on hand, and when he wasn't she missed him.

They felt for each other, she decided, the thing called "love." It was not, perhaps, the romance

which one found in books. But she had been taught carefully at college to distrust romance. The emphasis had been laid on the transient quality of adolescent emotion. One married for the sake of the race, and one chose, quite logically, with one's head instead, as in the old days, with the heart.

So there you had it. Delafield was eligible. He was healthy, had brains enough, an acceptable code of morals—and was willing to let her have her own way. If there were moments when Edith wondered if this program was adequate to wedded bliss, she put the thought aside. She and Delafield liked each other no end. Why worry?

And really at times Uncle Fred was impossible. His mother had lived until he was thirty-five, she had adored him, and had passed on to Cousin Annabel and to the old servants in the house the formula by which she had made her son happy. Her one fear had been that he might marry. He was extremely popular, much sought after. But he had kept his heart at home. His sweetheart, he had often said, was silver-haired and over sixty. He basked in her approbation; was soothed and sustained by it.

Then she had died, and Edith had come, and things had been different.

The difference had been demonstrated in a dozen ways. Edith was pleasantly affectionate, but she didn't yield an inch. "Dear Uncle Fred," she would ask, when they disagreed on matters of manners or morals, or art or athletics, or religion or the lack of it, "isn't my opinion as good as yours?"

"Apparently my opinion isn't worth anything."

"Oh, yes it is—but you must let me have mine."

Her independence met his rules and broke them. Her frankness of speech came up against his polite reticences and they both said things.

Frederick, of course, blamed Edith when she made him forget his manners. They had, he held, been considered perfect. Edith retorted that they had, perhaps, never been challenged. "It is easy enough, of course, when everybody gives in to you."

She had brought into his house an atmosphere of modernity which appalled him. She went and came as she pleased, would not be bound by old standards.

"Oh, Uncle Fred," she would say when he protested, "the war changed things. Women of to-day aren't sheep."

"The women of our family," her uncle would begin, to be stopped by the scornful retort, "Why do you want the women of your family to be different from the others you go with?"

She had him there. His sophistication matched that of the others of his set. Socially he was neither a Puritan nor a Pharisee. It was only under his own roof that he became patriarchal.

Yet, as time went on, he learned that Edith's faults were tempered by her fastidiousness. She

did not confuse liberty and license. She neither smoked nor drank. There was about her dancing a fine and stately quality which saved it from sensuousness. Yet when he told her things, there was always that irritating shrug of the shoulders. "Oh, well, I'm not a rowdy,—you know that. But I like to play around."

His pride in her grew—in her burnished hair, the burning blue of her eyes, her great beauty, the fineness of her spirit, the integrity of her character.

Yet he sighed with relief when she told him of her engagement to Delafield Simms. He loved her, but none the less he felt the strain of her presence in his establishment. It would be like sinking back into the luxury of a feather bed, to take up the old life where she had entered it.

And Edith, too, welcomed her emancipation. "When I marry you," she told Delafield, "I am going to break all the rules. In Uncle Fred's house everything runs by clockwork, and it is he who winds the clock."

Delafield laughed and kissed her. He was like the rest of the men of his generation, apparently acquiescent. Yet the chances were that when Edith was his wife, he, too, would wind the clock!

Their engagement was one of mutual freedom. Edith did as she pleased, Delafield did as he pleased. They rarely clashed. And as the wedding day approached, they were pleasantly complacent.

Delafield, dictating a letter one day to Frederick Towne's stenographer, spoke of his complacency. He was writing to Bob Sterling, who was to be his best man, and who shared his apartment in New York. Delafield was an orphan, and had big money interests. He felt that Washington was tame compared to the metropolis. He and Edith were to live one block east of Fifth Avenue, in a house that he had bought for her.

When he was in Washington he occupied a desk in Frederick's office. Lucy Logan took his dictation. She had been for several years with Towne. She was twenty-three, well-groomed, and self-possessed. She had slender, flexible fingers, and Delafield liked to look at them. She had soft brown hair, and her profile, as she bent over her book, was clear-cut and composed.

"Edith and I are great pals," he dictated. "I rather think we are going to hit it off famously. I'd hate to have a woman hang around my neck. And I want you for my best man. I know it is asking a lot, but it's just once in a lifetime, old chap."

Lucy wrote that and waited with her pencil poised.

"That's about all," said Delafield.

Lucy shut up her book and rose.

"Wait a minute," Delafield decided. "I want to add a postscript."

Lucy sat down.

"By the way," Delafield dictated, "I wish you'd order the flowers at Tolley's. White orchids for Edith of course. He'll know the right thing for the bridesmaids—I'll get Edith to send him the color scheme——"

Lucy's pencil dashed and dotted. She looked up, hesitated. "Miss Towne doesn't care for orchids."

"How do you know?" he demanded.

She fluttered the leaves of her notebook and found an order from Towne to a local florist. "He says here, 'Anything but orchids—she doesn't like them.'"

"But I've been sending her orchids every week."

"Perhaps she didn't want to tell you——"

"And you think I should have something else for the wedding bouquet?"

"I think she might like it better." There was a faint flush on her cheek.

"What would you suggest?"

"I can't be sure what Miss Towne would like."

"What would you like?" intently.

She considered it seriously—her slender fingers clasped on her book. "I think," she told him, finally, "that if I were going to marry a man I should want what he wanted."

He laughed and leaned forward. "Good heavens, are there any women like that left in the world?"

Her flush deepened, she rose and went towards the door. "Perhaps I shouldn't have said anything."

His voice changed. "Indeed, I am glad you did." He had risen and now held the door open for her. "We men are stupid creatures. I should never have found it out for myself."

She went away, and he sat there thinking about her. Her impersonal manner had always been perfect, and he had found her little flush charming.

It was because of Lucy Logan, therefore, that Edith had white violets instead of orchids in her wedding bouquet. And it was because, too, of Lucy Logan, that other things happened. Three of Edith's bridesmaids were house-guests. Their names were Rosalind, Helen and Margaret. They had, of course, last names, but these have nothing to do with the story. They had been Edith's classmates at college, and she had been somewhat democratic in her selection of them.

"They are perfect dears, Uncle Fred. I'll have three cave-dwellers to balance them. Socially, I suppose, it will be a case of sheep and goats, but the goats are—darling."

They were, however, the six of them, what Delafield called a bunch of beauties. Their bridesmaid gowns were exquisite—but unobtrusive. The color scheme was blue and silver—and the flowers, forget-me-nots and sweet peas. "It's a bit old-fashioned," Edith said, "but I hate sensational effects."

Neither the sheep nor the goats agreed with her. Their ideas were different—the goats holding out for something impressionistic, the sheep for ceremonial splendor.

There was to be a wedding breakfast at the house. Things were therefore given over early to the decorators and caterers, and coffee and rolls were served in everybody's room. Belated wedding presents kept coming, and Edith and her bridal attendants might be seen at all times on the stairs or in the hall in silken morning coats and delicious caps.

When the wedding bouquet arrived Edith sought out her uncle in his study on the second floor.

"Look at this," she said; "how in the world did it happen that he sent white violets? Did you tell him, Uncle Fred?"

"No."

"Sure?"

"Cross my heart."

They had had their joke about Del's orchids. "If he knew how I hated them," Edith would say, and Uncle Fred would answer, "Why don't you tell him?"

But she had never told, because after all it didn't much matter, and if Delafield felt that orchids were the proper thing, why muddle up his mind with her preferences?

"Anyhow," she said now, "I am glad my wedding bouquet is different." As she stood there, lovely in her sheer draperies, the fragrant mass of flowers in her arms, her eyes looked at him over the top, wistfully. "Uncle Fred," she asked, unexpectedly, "do you love me?"

"Of course——"

"Please don't say it that way——" Her voice caught.

"How shall I say it?"

"As if you—cared."

He stood up and put his hands on her shoulders. "My dear child," he said, "I do."

"You've been no end good to me," she said, and dropped the bouquet on a chair and clung to him, sobbing.

He held her in his arms and soothed her. "Being a bride is a bit nerve-racking."

She nodded. "And I mustn't let my eyes get red."

She kissed him shyly on the cheek. They had never indulged much in kisses. He felt if she had always been as sweetly feminine, he should have been sorry to have her marry.

He did not see her again until she was in her wedding gown, composed and smiling.

"Has Del called you up?" he asked her.

"No, why should he?"

He laughed. "Oh, well, you'll have plenty to say to each other afterward." But the thought intruded that with such a bride a man might show himself, on this day of days, ardent and eager.

Rosalind and Helen and Margaret, shimmering, opalescent, their young eyes radiant under their wide hats, joined the other bridesmaids in the great limousine which was to take them to the church. Cousin Annabel went with other cousins. Edith and her uncle were alone in their car. Frederick's man, Briggs, who had been the family coachman in the days of horses, drove them.

Washington was shining under the winter sun as they whirled through the streets to the old church. "Happy is the bride the sun shines on," said Frederick, feeling rather foolish. It was somewhat difficult to talk naturally to this smiling beauty in her bridal white. She seemed miles removed from the aggressive maiden with whom he had fought and made up and fought again.

The wedding party was assembled in one of the side rooms. Belated guests trickled in a thin stream towards the great doors that opened and shut to admit them to the main auditorium. A group of servants, laden with wraps, stood at the foot of the stairs. As soon as the procession started they would go up into the gallery to view the ceremony.

In the small room was almost overpowering fragrance. The bridesmaids, in the filtered light, were a blur of rose and blue and white. There was much laughter, the sound of the organ through the thick walls.

Then the ushers came in.

"Where's Del?"

The bridegroom was, it seemed, delayed. They waited.

"Shall we telephone, Mr. Towne?" someone asked at last.

Frederick nodded. He and his niece stood apart from the rest. Edith was smiling but had little to say. She seemed separated from the others by the fact of the approaching mystery.

The laughter had ceased; above the whispers came the tremulous echo of the organ.

The usher who had gone to the telephone returned and drew Towne aside.

"There's something queer about it. I can't get Del or Bob. They may be on the way. But the clerk seemed reticent."

"I'll go to the 'phone myself," said Frederick. "Where is it?"

But he was saved the effort, for someone, watching at the door, said, "Here they come," and the room seemed to sigh with relief as Bob Sterling entered.

No one was with him, and he wore a worried frown.

"May I speak to you, Mr. Towne?" he asked.

Edith was standing by the window looking out at the old churchyard. The uneasiness which had infected the others had not touched her. Slender and white she stood waiting. In a few minutes Del would walk up the aisle with her and they

would be married. In her mind that program was as fixed as the stars.

And now her uncle approached and said something. "Edith, Del isn't coming——"

"Is he ill?"

"I wish to Heaven he were dead."

"What do you mean, Uncle Fred?"

"I'll tell you—presently. But we must get away from this——"

His glance took in the changed scene. A blight had swept over those high young heads. Two of the bridesmaids were crying. The ushers had withdrawn into a huddled group. The servants were staring—uncertain what to do.

Somebody got Briggs and the big car to the door.

Shut into it, Towne told Edith:

"He's backed out of it. He left—this." He had a note in his hand. "It was written to Bob Sterling. Bob was with him at breakfast time, and when he came back, this was on Del's dresser."

She read it, her blue eyes hot:

"I can't go through with it, Bob. I know it's a rotten trick, but time will prove that I am right. And Edith will thank me.

"Del."

She crushed it in her hand. "Where has he gone?"

"South, probably, on his yacht."

"Wasn't there any word for me?"

"No."

"Is there any other—woman?"

"It looks like it. Bob is utterly at sea. So is everybody else."

All of her but her eyes seemed frozen. The great bouquet lay at her feet where she had dropped it. Her hands were clenched.

Towne laid his hand on hers. "My dear—it's dreadful."

"Don't——"

"Don't what?"

"Be sorry."

"But he's a cur——"

"It doesn't do any good to call him names, Uncle Fred."

"I think you must look upon it as a great escape, Edith."

"Escape from what?"

"Unhappiness."

"Do you think I can ever escape from the thought of this?" The strong sweep of her arm seemed to indicate her bridal finery.

He sat in unhappy silence, and suddenly she laughed. "I might have known when he kept sending me orchids. When a man loves a woman he knows the things she likes."

It was then that Towne made his mistake. "You ought to thank your lucky stars——"

She blazed out at him, "Uncle Fred, if you say anything more like that,—it's utterly idiotic. But

you won't face *facts*. Your generation never does. I'm not in the least thankful. I'm simply furious."

There was an hysterical note in her voice, but he was unconscious of the tension. She was not taking it in the least as he wished she might. She should have wept on his shoulder. Melted to tears he might have soothed her. But there were no tears in those blue eyes.

She trod on her flowers as she left the car. Looking straight ahead of her she ascended the steps. Within everything was in readiness for the wedding festivities. The stairway was terraced with hydrangeas, pink and white and blue. In the drawing-room were rose garlands with floating ribbons. And there was a vista of the dining-room—with the caterer's men already at their posts.

Except for these men, a maid or two—and a detective to keep his eye on things, the house was empty. Everybody had gone to the wedding, and presently everybody would come back. The house would be stripped, the flowers would fade, the caterers would carry away the wasted food.

Edith stopped at the foot of the stairs. "How did they announce it at the church?"

"That it had been postponed. It was the only thing to do at the moment. Of course there will be newspaper men. We'll have to make up a story——"

"We'll do nothing of the kind. Tell them the truth, Uncle Fred. That I'm not—wanted. That

I was kept—waiting—at the church. Like the heroine in a movie."

She stood on the steps above him, looking down. She was as white as her dress.

"I don't want to see anybody. I don't mind losing Del. He doesn't count. He isn't worth it. But can you imagine that any man—*any* man, Uncle Fred, could have kept *me*—waiting?"

CHAPTER V
THE UGLY DUCKLING

The thing that Frederick Towne got out of his niece's flight was this. "She wouldn't let anybody sympathize with her. Simply locked the door of her room, and in the morning she was gone. It has added immeasurably to the gossip."

His listeners had, however, weighed him in the balance of understanding and sympathy, and had found him wanting. The youth in them sided with Edith. But none of this showed in their manner. They were polite and hospitable to the last. Frederick, ushered out into the storm by Baldy, still saw Jane like a bird, warm in her nest.

"You see," Baldy said to his sister, when he came back, "how he messed things up."

Jane nodded. "He doesn't know——"

"*Unemotional*"—Baldy's voice seemed to call on all the gods to listen, "you should see her eyes——"

"Well, he's rather an old dear," said Jane, and having thus disposed airily of the great Frederick Towne, she went about the house setting things to right for the night.

"Merrymaid's out," she told her brother; "you'd better get her."

He opened the door and the storm seemed to whirl in upon him. He called the old cat and was presently aware, as he stood on the porch, that she danced about him in the dark. He chased her blindly, and at last got his hands on her. She was wet to the thighs, where she had waded in the drifts, but galvanized like a small electric motor by the intense chill of the night.

The wind shrieked and seemed to shake the world. Before Baldy entered the house he turned and faced the night—"*Edith*" was his voiceless cry, "*Edith—Edith——*"

By morning the violence of the storm had spent itself. But it was still bitterly cold. The snow was blue beneath the leaden sky. The chickens, denied their accustomed promenade, ate and drank and went to sleep again in the strange dusk. Merrymaid and the kitten having poked their noses into the frigid atmosphere withdrew to the snug haven of a basket beneath the kitchen stove. Sophy sent word that her rheumatism was worse, and that she could not come over. Jane, surveying the accumulated piles of dishes, felt a sense of unusual depression. While Frederick Towne had talked last night she had caught a glimpse of his world—the great house—six servants—gay girls in the glamour of good clothes, young men who matched the girls, money to meet every emergency—a world in which nobody had to wash dishes—or make soup out of Sunday's roast.

She was cheered a bit, however, by the announcement that her brother had decided to stay home from the office.

"I'll have a try at that magazine cover——"

Her spirits rose. "Wouldn't it be utterly perfect if you got the prize——?"

"Not much chance. The thing I need is a good model——"

"And I won't do?" with some wistfulness.

They had talked of it before. Baldy refused to see possibilities in Jane. "Since you bobbed your hair, you're too modern——" She was, rather, medieval, with her straight-cut frocks and her straight-cut locks. But she was a figure so familiar that she failed to appeal to his imagination.

"Editors like 'em modern, don't they?"

But his thoughts had winged themselves to that other woman whom his fancy painted in a thousand poses.

"If Edith Towne were here—I'd put her on a marble bench beside a sapphire sea."

"I'll bet you couldn't get an editor in the world to look at it. Sapphire seas and classic ladies are a million years behind the times——"

"They are never behind the times——"

Jane shrugged, and changed the subject. "Darling—if you'll put your mind to mundane things for a moment. To-morrow is Thanksgiving Day, the Follettes are to dine with us, and we haven't any turkey."

"Why haven't we?"

"You were to get it when you went to town, and now you're not going——"

"I am *not*—not for all the turkeys in the world. We can have roast chickens. That's simple enough, Janey."

"It may seem simple to you. But who's going to cut off their heads?"

"Sophy," said Baldy. Having killed Germans in France he refused further slaughter.

"Sophy has the rheumatism——"

"Oh, well, we can feast our souls——" Young Baldwin's mood was one of exaltation.

Jane leaned back in her chair and looked at him. "Your perfectly poetic solution may satisfy you, but it won't feed the Follettes."

With some irritation, therefore, he promised, if all else failed, to himself decapitate the fowls. "But your mind, Jane, never soars above food——"

Jane, with her chin in her hands, considered this. "A woman," she said, "who keeps house for a poet—must anchor herself to—something. Perhaps I'm like a captive balloon—if you cut the cable, I'll shoot straight up to the skies——"

She liked that thought of herself, and smiled over it, after Baldy had left her. She wondered if the cable would ever be cut. If the captive balloon would ever soar.

So she went about her simple tasks, putting the

bone on to boil for soup, preparing the vegetables for it—wondering what she would have for dessert—with all his scorn of domestic details, Baldy was apt to be fastidious about his sweets—and coming finally to her sweeping and dusting in the front part of the house.

The telephone rang and she answered it. Evans was at the other end of the wire.

"Mother wants to speak to you."

Mrs. Follette asked if she might change her plans for Thanksgiving. "Will you and your brother dine with us, instead of our coming to you? Our New York cousins find that they have the day free, unexpectedly. They had been asked to a house party in Virginia, but their hostess has had to postpone it on account of illness."

"Is it going to be very grand? I haven't a thing to wear."

"Don't be foolish, Jane. You always look like a lady."

"Thank you, Mrs. Follette." Jane hoped that she didn't look as some ladies look. But there were, of course, others. It was well for her at the moment, that Mrs. Follette could not see her eyes.

"And I thought," went on the unconscious matron, "that if you were not too busy, you might go with Evans to the grove and get some greens. I'd like the house to look attractive. Is the snow too deep?"

"Not a bit. When will he come?"

"You'd better arrange with him. Here he is."

Evans' voice was the only unchanged thing about him. The sound of it at long distance always brought the old days back to Jane.

"After lunch?" he asked.

"Give me time to dress."

"Three?"

"Yes."

When luncheon was over, Jane went up-stairs to get into out-of-door clothes. At the foot of the stairs she had a glimpse of herself in the hall mirror. She wore a one-piece lilac cotton frock—with a small square apron, and an infinitesimal bib. It was a nice-looking little frock, but she had had it for a million years. That was the way with all her clothes. The suit she was going to put on had been dyed. It had been white in its first incarnation. It was now brown. There was no telling its chromatic future.

She heard steps on the porch, and turned to open the door for Evans.

But it was not Evans. Briggs, Frederick Towne's chauffeur, stood there with a box in his arms. "Mr. Towne's compliments," he said, "and shall I set it in the hall?"

"Oh, yes, thank you." Her surprise brought the quick color to her cheeks. She watched him go back down the terrace, and enter the car, then she opened the box.

Beneath clouds of white tissue paper she came

upon a long, low basket, heaped with grapes and tangerines, peaches and pomegranates. Tucked in between the fruits were shelled nuts in fluted paper cases, gleaming sweets in small glass jars, candied pineapples and cherries, bunches of fat raisins, stuffed dates and prunes.

Jane talked to the empty air. "How dear of him——"

The white tissue paper fell in drifts about her as she lifted the basket from the box.

There was a little note tied to the handle. Towne's personal paper was thick and white. Jane was aware of its expensiveness and it thrilled her. His script was heavy and black—the note had, unquestionably, an air.

"Dear Miss Barnes:

"I can't tell you how much I enjoyed your hospitality last night—and you were good to listen to me with so much sympathy. I am hoping that you'll let me come again and talk about Edith. May I? And here's a bit of color for your Thanksgiving feast.

"Gratefully always,
"Frederick Towne."

Jane stood staring down at the friendly words. It didn't seem within reason that Frederick Towne meant that he wanted to come—to see her. And she really hadn't listened with sympathy. But—oh, of course, he could come. And it was

heavenly to have a thing like this happen on a day like this.

As she straightened up with the basket in her hands, she saw herself again in the long mirror—a slender figure in green—bobbed black hair—

golden and purple fruits. She gasped and gazed again. There was Baldy's picture ready to his hand—November! Against a background of gray—that glowing figure—Baldy could idealize her—make the wind blow her skirts a bit—give her a fluttering ribbon or two, a glorified loveliness.

She sought him in his studio. "I've got something to show you, darling-dear."

He was moody. "Don't interrupt me, Jane."

She rumpled up his hair, which he hated. "Mr. Towne sent us some fruit, Baldy, and this." She held out the note to him.

He read it. "He doesn't say a word about me."

"No, he doesn't," her eyes were dancing; "Baldy, it's your little sister, Jane."

"You didn't do a thing but sit there and knit——"

"Perhaps he liked to see me—knitting——"

Baldy passed this over in puzzled silence.

"Where's the fruit?"

"In the house."

He rose. "I'll go in with you——" He felt out of sorts, discouraged. The morning had been spent in sketching vague outlines—a sweep of fair hair under a blue hat—detached feet in shoes with

shining buckles—a bag that hung in the air without hands. At intervals he had stood up and looked out at the blank snow and the dull sky. The room was warm enough, but he shivered. He suffered vicariously for Edith Towne. He had hoped that she might telephone. He had stayed home really for that.

His studio was in the garage and was heated by a little round stove. Jane said the garage reminded her of the Boffins' parlor—a dead line was drawn between art and utility. Baldy's rug and old couch and paints and brushes flung a challenge as it were to the little Ford, the lawn mower, the garden hose and the gasoline cans.

"I have spent three hours doing nothing," he said, as he shut the door behind him; "not much encouragement in that."

"I have a model for you."

"Where?"

"I'll show you."

He followed her in, full of curiosity.

She showed him the fruit, then picked up the basket. "Look in the mirror, not at me," she commanded.

Reflected there in the clear glass, so still that she seemed fixed in paint, Baldy really gave for the first time an artist's eye to the possibilities of his little sister. In the midst of all that crashing color——!

"Gosh," he cried, "you're good-looking!"

His air of utter astonishment was too much for Jane. She set the basket on the steps, and laughed until she cried.

"I don't see anything funny," he told her.

"Well, you wouldn't, darling."

She wiped her eyes with her little handkerchief, and sat up. "I am just dropping a tear for the ugly duckling."

"Have I made you feel like that?"

"Sometimes."

Their lighted-up eyes met, and suddenly he leaned down and touched her cheek—a swift caress. "You're a little bit of all right, Janey," which was great praise from Baldy.

CHAPTER VI
"STAY IN THE FIELD, OH, WARRIOR!"

Mrs. Follette had been born in Maryland with a tradition of aristocratic blood. It was this tradition which had upheld her through years of poverty after the Civil War. A close scanning of the family tree might have disclosed ancestors who had worked with their hands. But these, Mrs. Follette's family had chosen to ignore in favor of one grandfather who had held Colonial office, and who had since been magnified into a personage.

On such slight foundation, Mrs. Follette had erected high towers of social importance. As a wife of a government clerk, her income was limited, but she lived on a farm, back of Sherwood Park, which she had inherited from her father. The farm was called Castle Manor, which dignified it in the eyes of the county. Mrs. Follette's friends were among the old families who had occupied the land for many generations. She would have nothing to do with the people of Sherwood Park. She held that all suburbs are negligible socially. People came to them from anywhere and went from them to be swallowed up in obscurity. There was

no stability. She made an exception, only, of the Baldwin Barneses. There was good Maryland blood back of them, and more than that, a Virginia Governor. To be sure they did not care for these things; old Baldwin's democracy had been almost appalling. But they were, none the less, worth while.

Mr. Follette, during his lifetime, had walked a mile each morning to take the train at Sherwood Park, and had walked back a mile each night, until at last he had tired of two peripatetic miles a day, and of eight hours at his desk, and of eternally putting on his dinner coat when there was no one to see, and like old Baldwin Barnes, he had laid him down with a will.

At his death all income stopped, and Mrs. Follette had found herself on a somewhat lonely peak of exclusiveness. She could not afford to go with her richer neighbors, and she refused to consider Sherwood seriously. Now and then, however, she accepted invitations from old friends, and in return offered such simple hospitality as she could afford without self-consciousness. She might be a snob, but she was, to those whom she permitted to cross her threshold, an incomparable hostess. She gave what she had without apology.

She had, too, a sort of admirable courage. Her ambitions had been wrapped up in her son. What her father might have been, Evans was to be. They had scrimped and saved that he might go to

college and study law. Then, at that first dreadful cry from across the seas, he had gone. There had been long months of fighting. He had left her in the flower of his youth, a wonder-lad, with none to match him among his friends. He had come back crushed and broken. He, whose career lay so close to his heart—could do now no sustained work. Mentally and physically he must rest. He might be years in getting back. He would never get back to gay and gallant boyhood. That was gone forever.

Yet if Mrs. Follette's heart had failed her at times, she had never shown it. She was making the farm pay for itself. She supplied the people of Sherwood Park and surrounding estates with milk. But she never was in any sense—a milkwoman. It was, rather, as if in selling her milk she distributed favors. It was on this income that she subsisted, she and her son.

It was because of Mrs. Follette's social complexes that Jane had been forced to limit her invitations for the Thanksgiving dinner. She would have preferred more people to liven things up for Evans and Baldy, but Mrs. Follette's prejudices had to be considered.

Evans, democratic, like his father, laughed at his mother's assumptions. But he rarely in these days set himself against her. It involved always a contest, and he was tired of fighting.

That was why he had asked Jane to help him

in the stand he had taken against the New York trip. He felt that he could never hold out against his mother's arguments.

"She'd keep eternally at it, and I'd have to give in," he told himself with the irritability which was so new to him and so surprising. As a boy he had been good-tempered even in moments of disagreement with his mother.

Going down to luncheon, he hoped the subject would not come up. The afternoon was before him, and Jane. He wanted no cloud to mar it.

On the steps he passed Mary, his mother's maid, making the house immaculate for the guests of to-morrow. She was singing an old song, linking herself musically with the black men of generations back. Mary was over sixty, and her voice was thin and piping. Yet there was, after all, a sort of fierce power in that thin and piping voice.

"Stay in the fiel',
Stay in the fiel', oh, wah-yah—
Stay in the fiel'
Till the wah is ended."

Again Evans felt that sense of unaccountable irritation. He wished that Mary wouldn't sing....

Later as he and Jane swung along together in the clear cold Jane said:

"I've such a lot to tell you———"

She told it in her whimsical way—Baldy's adventure,

Frederick Towne's visit, the basket of fruit.

"Baldy is simply mad about Edith Towne. He hasn't been able to talk of anything else. Of course, he'll have to get over it but he isn't looking ahead."

"Why should he get over it?"

Her chin went up. "He's a clerk in the departments, and she a—plutocrat———"

"Perhaps she won't look at it like that."

"Oh, but she has *men* at her feet. And Baldy's a boy. Evans, if I had lovely dresses 'n' everything, I'd have men at my feet."

"Why should you want them at your feet?"

"Every woman does. We want to grind 'em under our heels," she stamped in the snow to show him; "but Baldy and I are a pair of Cinderellas, minus—godmothers———"

She was in a gay mood. She was wrapped in her old orange cape, and the sun, breaking the bank of sullen clouds in the west, seemed to turn her lithe young body into flame.

"Don't you *love* a day like this, Evans?" She pressed forward up the hill with all her strength. Evans followed, panting. At the top they sat down for a moment on an old log—which faced the long aisles of snow between thin black trees. The vista was clear-cut and almost artificial in its restraint of color and its wide bare spaces.

Evans' little dog, Rusty, ran back and forth—following this trail and that. Finally in pursuit of

a rabbit, he was led far afield. They heard him barking madly in the distance. It was the only sound in the stillness.

"Jane," Evans said, "do you remember the last time we were here?"

"Yes." The light went out of her eyes.

"As I look back it was heaven, Jane. I'd give anything on God's earth if I was where I was then."

All the blood was drained from her face. "Evans, you wouldn't," passionately, "you wouldn't give up those three years in France———"

He sat very still. Then he said tensely, "No, I wouldn't, even though it has made me lose you—Jane———"

"You mustn't say such things——"

"I must. Don't I know? You were such an unawakened little thing, my dear. But I could have—waked you. And I can't wake you now. That's my tragedy. You'll never wake up—for me——"

"Don't——"

"Well, it's true. Why not say it? I've come back a—scarecrow, the shadow of a man. And you're just where I left you—only lovelier—more of a woman—more to be worshipped—Jane——"

As he caught her hand up in his, she had a sudden flashing vision of him as he had been when he last sat with her in the grove—the swing of his strong figure, his bare head borrowing gold from

the sun—the touch of assurance which had been so compelling.

"I never knew that you cared——"

"I knew it, but not as I did after your wonderful letters to me over there. I felt, if I ever came back, I'd move heaven and earth." He stopped. "But I came back—different. And I haven't any right to say these things to you. I'm not going to say them—Jane. It might spoil our—friendship."

"Nothing can spoil our friendship, Evans——"

He laid his hand on hers. "Then you are mine—until somebody comes along and claims you?"

"There isn't anybody else," she turned her fingers up to meet his, "so don't worry, old dear," she smiled at him but her lashes were wet. Her hand was warm in his and she let it stay there, and after a while she said, "I have sometimes thought that if it would make you happy, I might——"

"Might—love me?"

"Yes."

He shook his head. "I didn't say it for that. I just had to have the truth between us. And I don't want—pity. If—if I ever get back—I'll make you love me, Jane." There was a hint of his old masterfulness—and she was thrilled by it.

She withdrew her hand and stood up. "Then I'll—pray—that you—get back——"

"Do you mean it, Janey?"

"I mean it, Evans."

"Then pray good and hard, my dear, for I'm going to do it."

They smiled at each other, but it was a sacred moment.

The things they did after that were rendered unimportant by the haze of enchantment which hung over Evans' revelation. No man can tell a woman that he loves her, no woman can listen, without a throbbing sense of the magnitude of the thing which has happened. From such beginnings is written the history of humanity.

Deep in a hollow where the wind had swept up the snow, and left the ground bare they found crowfoot in an emerald carpet—there were holly branches dripping red berries like blood on the white drifts. They filled their arms, and at last they were ready to go.

Evans whistled for Rusty but the little dog did not come. "He'll find us; he knows every inch of the way."

But Rusty did not find them, and they were on the ridge when that first awful cry came to them.

Jane clutched Evans. "What is it—oh, what *is* it?"

He swallowed twice before he could speak. "It's—Rusty—one of those steel traps"—he was panting now—his forehead wet—"the negroes put them around for rabbits——" Again that frenzied cry broke the stillness. "They're hellish things——"

Jane began to run in the direction of the sound. "Come on, Evans—oh, come quick——"

He stumbled after her. At last he caught at her dress and held her. "If he's hurt I can't stand it."

It was dreadful to see him. Jane felt as if clutched by a nightmare. "Stay here, and don't worry. I'll get him out——"

It was a cruel thing to face. There was blood and that little trembling body. The cry reduced now to an agonized whimpering. How she opened the trap she never knew, but she did open it, and made a bandage from her blouse which she tore from her shoulders regardless of the cold. And after what seemed to be ages, she staggered back to Evans with her dreadful burden wrapped in her cape. "We've got to get him to a veterinary. Run down to the road and see if there's a car in sight."

There was a car, and when Evans stopped it, two men came charging up the bank. Jane gave the dog into the arms of one of them. "You'll have to go with them, Evans," she said and wrapped herself more closely in her cape. "There are several doctors at Rockville. You'd better ask the station-master about the veterinary."

After they had gone, she stood there on the ridge and watched the car out of sight. She felt stunned and hysterical. It had been awful to see Rusty, but the most awful thing was that vision of Evans

stumbling through the snow. A broken body is for tears—a broken spirit is beyond tears.

She shuddered and pressed her hands against her eyes. Then she went down the hill and across the road in the darkening twilight. She crept into the house. Baldy must not see her; there was blood on her cape and her clothes were torn, and Baldy would ask questions, and he would call Evans a—coward....

It was late when Evans came to Castle Manor with his dog in his arms. Rusty was comfortable and he had wagged a grateful tail. The pain had gone out of his eyes and the veterinary had said that in a few days the wound would heal. There were no vital parts affected—and he would give some medicine which would prevent further suffering.

Mrs. Follette was out, and old Mary was in the kitchen, singing. She stopped her song as Evans came through. He asked her to help him and she brought a square, deep basket and made Rusty a bed.

"You-all jes' put him heah by the fiah, and I'll look atter him."

Evans shook his head. "I want him in my room. I'll take care of him in the night."

He carried the dog up-stairs with him, knelt beside him, drew hard deep breaths as the little fellow licked his hand.

"What kind of a man am I?" Evans said sharply in the silence. "God, what kind of a man?"

Through the still house came old Mary's thin and piping song:

"Stay in the fiel',
Stay in the fiel', oh, wah-yah—
Stay in the fiel'
Till the wah is ended."

Evans got up and shut the door....

CHAPTER VII
A FAMISHED PILGRIM

Jane was waked usually by the hoarse crow of an audacious little rooster, who sent his challenge to the rising sun.

But on Thanksgiving morning, she found herself sitting up in bed in the deep darkness—slim and white and shivering—oppressed by some phantom of the night.

She came to it gradually. The strange events of yesterday. Evans. Her own share in his future.

Her room was icy. She climbed out of bed, and closed the windows, lighted the lamp on her little table, wrapped herself in a warm robe, and sat up among her pillows, to think the thing out.

The lamp had a yellow shade, and shone like a full moon among the shadows. Jane, just beyond the circle of light, was a spectral figure with her black hair and the faint blue of her gown.

Her own share in Evans' future? Had she really linked her life with his? She had promised to pray that he might get back—she had pledged youth, hope and constancy to his cause. And she had promised before she had seen that stumbling figure in the snow!

In the matters of romance, Jane's thoughts had always ventured. She had dreamed of a gallant lover, a composite hero, one who should combine the reckless courage of a Robin Hood with the high moralities of a Galahad. With such a lover one might gallop through life to a piping tune. Or if the Galahad predominated in her hero, to an inspiring processional!

And here was Evans, gray and gaunt, shaken by tremors, fitting himself into the background of her future. And she didn't want him there. Oh, not as he had been out there in the snow!

Yet she was sorry for him with a sympathy that wrung her heart. She couldn't hurt him. She wouldn't. Was there no way out of it?

Her hands went up to her face. She had a simple and childlike faith. "Oh, God," she prayed, "make us all—happy——"

Her cheeks were wet as she lay back on her pillows. And a certain serenity followed her little prayer. Things would work together in some way for good.... She would let it rest at that.

When at last the rooster crowed, Jane cast off the covers and went to the windows, drawing back the curtains. There was a faint whiteness in the eastern sky—amethyst and pearl, aquamarine, the day had dawned!

Well, after all, wasn't every day a new world? And this day of all days. One must think about the thankful things!

She discussed that with Baldy at the breakfast table.

Baldy scoffed. "I'm not a hypocrite. It has been a rotten year."

"Well, money isn't everything, and we have each other."

"Money is a lot. And just because we haven't all been killed off is no special reason why we should thank the Lord."

"Baldy, I want to thank him for the little things. Our little house, and warmth and light, and you, coming home at night——"

"My dear child, we don't own the house, and I'm really not much when I get here."

"That isn't true, Baldy. And aren't you thankful that you have me?"

There was a quaver in her voice, and he was not hard-hearted. Neither was he in a mood for sentiment.

"What's the matter, old dear? Want me to throw bouquets at you?"

"Yes, I do. I'm low in my mind this morning."

He saw that she meant it. "Anything happened, Janey?" he asked in a different tone.

"Oh, nothing to talk about. But—I wish I had a shoulder to weep on, Baldy."

"Weep on mine."

She shook her head. "No. You'd be about as comforting as a wooden Indian."

"I like that," hotly.

"Your intentions are good. But your mind isn't on me. It's on Edith Towne."

"What makes you think that?"

"Oh, you've one ear cocked towards the telephone——"

He flushed. "Well, who wouldn't? I want to hear from her."

He wanted to hear so much that he did not go to church lest he miss her call. But Jane went, and sat in the Barnes' pew, and was thankful, as she had said, for love and warmth and light.

Throughout the sermon, she stared at the stained glass window which was just above the Follette pew. It was a memorial to two lads who had lost their lives in France. The window showed the young heroes as shining knights—and that was the way people thought about them. They had been, really, rather commonplace fellows. But death had transfigured them. They would remain always in the eyes of this world as young and splendid.

And there beneath them sat this morning a man who had, too, been young and splendid. But who was wrapped in no shining armor of illusion. He had come back a hero, but had been among them long enough to lose his halo. It was manifestly unfair. Jane resolved that she would keep in her heart always that vision of Evans as a shining knight. Whoever else forgot, she would not forget.

Evans, with his mother in the pew, looked straight ahead of him. He seemed worn and weary

—a dark shadow set against the brightness of those comrades on the glowing glass.

After church, he waited in the aisle for Jane. "I'll walk down with you. Mother is going to ride with Dr. Hallam."

They walked a little way in silence, then he said, "Rusty is comfortable this morning."

"Your mother told me over the telephone."

He limped along at her side. "Jane, I didn't sleep last night—thinking about it. It is a thing I can't understand. A dreadful thing."

"I understand. You love Rusty. It was because you love him so much——"

"But to let a woman do it. Jane, do you remember—years ago? That mad dog?"

She did remember. Evans had killed it in the road to save a child. It had been a horrible experience, but not for a moment had he hesitated.

"I wasn't afraid then, Janey."

"This was different. You couldn't see the thing you loved hurt. It wasn't fear. It was affection."

"Oh, don't gloss it over. I know what you felt. I saw it in your eyes."

"Saw what?"

"Contempt."

She turned on him. "You didn't. Perhaps, just at first. I didn't understand...." She fought for self-control, but in spite of it, the tears rolled down her cheeks.

"Don't, Janey, don't." He was in an agony of remorse. "I've made you cry."

She blinked away the tears. "It wasn't contempt, Evans."

"Well, it should have been. Why not? No man who calls himself a man would have let you do it."

They had come to the path under the pines, and were alone in that still world. Jane tucked her hand in the crook of Evans' arm. "Dear boy, stop thinking about it."

"I shall never stop."

"I want you to promise me that you'll try. Evans, you know we are going to fight it out together...."

His eyes did not meet hers. "Do you think I'd let you? Well, you think wrong." He began to walk rapidly, so that it was hard to keep pace with him. "I'm not worth it."

And now quite as suddenly as she had cried, she laughed, and the laugh had a break in it. "You're worth everything that America has to give you." She told him of the things she had thought of in church. "You are as much of a hero as any of them."

He shook his head. "All that hero stuff is dead and gone, my dear. We idealize the dead, but not the living."

It was true and she knew it. But she did not want to admit it. "Evans," she said, and laid her

cheek for a moment against the rough sleeve of his coat, "don't make me unhappy. Let me help."

"You don't know what you are asking. You'd grow tired of it. Any woman would."

"Why look ahead? Can't we live for each day?"

She had lighted a flame of hope in him. "If I might——" eagerly.

"Why not? Begin right now. What are you thankful for, Evans?"

"Not much," uneasily.

"Well, I'll tell you three things. Books and your mother and me. Say that over—out loud."

He tried to enter into her mood. "Books and my mother and Jane."

She caught at another thought. "It almost rhymes with Stevenson's 'books and food and summer rain,' doesn't it?"

"Yes. What a man he was—cheerful in the face of death. Jane, I believe I could face death more cheerfully than life——"

"Don't say such things"—they had come to the little house on the terrace, "don't say such things. Don't think them."

"As a man thinks—— Do you believe it?"

"I believe some of it."

"We'll talk about it to-night. No, I can't come in. Dinner is at seven." He lingered a moment longer. "Do you know what a darling you are, Jane?"

She stood watching him as he limped away.

Once he turned and waved. She waved back and her eyes were blurred with tears.

In Jane's next letter to Judy she told about the dinner.

"I didn't know what to wear. But Baldy insisted on my old white. In his present mid-Victorian mood he would like me in 'book-muslin,' if things were made of it. It is a wispy rag of chiffon, and I was hard up for slippers, so Baldy painted a pair of gray suede with silver paint, and I made a flat band of silver leaves for my hair.

"The effect wasn't bad, even Baldy admitted it, and Evans quoted Shelley—something about 'an orbed maiden with white fire laden.' Evans and Baldy are having a perfect orgy of Keats and Shelley. They soar over our heads. They hate realism and pessimism—they say it is a canker at the heart of civilization. That all healthy nations are idealistic and optimistic. It is only when countries are senile that they grow cynical and sour. You should hear them.

"We had a delicious dinner. It seems to me, Judy, that my mind dwells a great deal on things to eat. But, after all, why shouldn't I? Housekeeping is my job.

"Mrs. Follette doesn't attempt to do anything that she can't do well, and it was all so simple and satisfying. In the center of the table was some of the fruit that Mr. Towne sent in a silver epergne, and there were four Sheffield candlesticks with white candles.

"Mrs. Follette carved the turkey. Evans can't do things like that—she wore her perennial black lace and pearls, and in spite of everything, Judy, I

can't help liking her, though she is such a beggar on horseback. They haven't a cent, except what she makes from the milk, but she looks absolutely the lady of the manor.

"The cousins are very fashionable. One of them, Muriel Follette, knows Edith Towne intimately. She told us all about the wedding, and how people are blaming Edith for running away and are feeling terribly sorry for Mr. Towne. Of course they didn't know that Baldy and I had ever laid eyes on either of them. But you should have seen Baldy's eyes, when Muriel said things about Edith. I was scared stiff for fear he'd say something. You know how his temper flares.

"Well, Muriel said some catty things. That everybody is sure that Delafield Simms is in love with someone else, and that they are saying Edith might have known it if she hadn't always looked upon herself as the center of the universe. And they feel that if her heart is broken, the decent thing would be to mourn in the bosom of her family. Of course I'm not quoting her exact words, but you'll get the idea.

"And Baldy thinks his queen can do no wrong, and was almost *bursting*. Judy, he walks in a dream. I don't know what good it is going to do him to feel like that. He will have to always worship at a distance like Dante. Or was it Abelard? I always get those *grande passions* mixed.

"Anyhow, there you have it. Edith Towne rode in Baldy's Ford, and he has hitched that little wagon to a star!

"Well, after dinner, we set the victrola going and Baldy had to dance with Muriel. She dances extremely well, and I know he enjoyed it, though

he wouldn't admit it. And Muriel enjoyed it. There's no denying that Baldy has a way with him.

"After they had danced a while everybody played bridge, except Evans and me. You know how I hate it, and it makes Evans nervous. So we went in the library and talked. Evans is dreadfully discouraged about himself. I wish that you were here and that we could talk it over. But it is hard to do it at long distance. There ought to be some way to help him. Sometimes it seems that I can't stand it when I remember what he used to be."

Evans had carried Jane off to the library high-handedly. "I want you," was all the reason he vouchsafed as they came into the shabby room with its leaping flames in the fireplace, its book-lined walls, its imposing portrait above the mantel.

The portrait showed Evans' grandfather, and beneath it was a photograph of Evans himself. The likeness between the two men was striking—there was the same square set of the shoulders, the same bright, waved hair, the same air of youth and high spirits. The grandfather in the portrait wore a blue uniform, the grandson was in khaki, but they were, without a question, two of a kind.

"You belong here, Jane," said Evans, "on one side of the fireplace, with me on the other. That's the way I always see you when I shut my eyes."

"You see me now with your eyes wide open——"

"Yes. Jane, I told Mother this afternoon that I wouldn't go to New York. So that's settled, without your saying anything."

"How does she feel about it?"

"Oh, she still thinks that I should go. But I'll stay here," he moved his head restlessly. "I want to be where you are, Jane. And now, my dear, we're going to talk things out. You know that yesterday you made a sort of— promise. That you'd pray for me to get back—and that if I got back—well, you'd give me a chance. Jane, I want your prayers, but not your promise."

"Why not?"

"I am not fit to think of any woman. When I am—well—if I ever am—you can do as you think best. But you mustn't be bound."

She sat silent, looking into the fire.

"You know that I'm right, don't you, dear?"

"Yes, I do, Evans. I thought of it, too, last night. And it seems like this to me. If we can just be friends—without bothering with—anything else—it will be easier, won't it?"

"I can't tell you how gladly I'd bother, as you call it. But it wouldn't be fair. You are young, and you have a right to happiness. I'd be a shadow on your—future——"

"Please don't——"

He dropped on the rug at her feet. "Well, we'll leave it at that. We're friends, forever," he reached up and took her hands in his, "forever?"

"Always, Evans——"

"For better, for worse—for richer, for poorer?"

"Of course——"

They stared into the fire, and then he said softly, "Well, that's enough for me, my dear, that's enough for me——" and after a while he began to speak in broken sentences. "'Ah, silver shrine, here will I take my rest.... After so many hours of toil and quest.... A famished pilgrim....' That's Keats, my dear. Jane, do you know that you are food and drink?"

"Am I?" unsteadily.

"Yes, dear little thing, if I had you always by my fire I could fight the world."

When Jane and Baldy reached home that night, Baldy stamped up and down the house, saying things about Muriel Follette. "A girl like that to criticise."

"She danced well," said Jane, who had taken off the silver wreath, and had kicked off the silver slippers, and was curled up in a big chair as comfortable as a white cat.

"What right had she to say things?"

"People are saying them."

"Did she have to repeat them?"

"Darling Baldy, she didn't know."

"Know what?"

"How you felt about it."

He stopped and stood in front of her. "How do you know what I feel?"

"Oh, well, you seem to have made yourself Miss Towne's champion."

"I've done nothing of the kind, Jane. But I have a human interest in a fellow creature."

"Well," said Jane, "I have a human interest, too."

"Aren't you ever serious, Janey?"

"It's better to laugh than to cry." There was a little catch in her voice. Baldy wound the clock, and she watched him.

"What time is it?"

"Twelve-thirty."

She yawned. "I'm going to bed."

The telephone rang, and Baldy was off like a shot. Jane uncurled herself from her chair and lent a listening ear. It was a moment of exciting interest. Edith Towne was at the other end of the wire!

Jane knew it by Baldy's singing voice. He didn't talk like that to commonplace folk who called him up. She was devoured with curiosity.

He came in, at last, literally walking on air. And just as Jane had felt that his voice sang, so she felt now that his feet danced.

"Janey, it was Edith Towne."

"What did she say?"

"Just saw my advertisement. Paper delayed——"

"Where is she?"

"Beyond Alexandria. But we're not to give it away."

"Not even to Mr. Towne?"

"No. She's asked me to bring her bag, and some other things."

He threw himself into a chair opposite Jane, one leg over the arm of it. He was a careless and picturesque figure. Even Jane was aware of his youth and good looks.

Edith had, as it seemed, asked him to have Towne send the ring back to Delafield—to have her wedding presents sent back, to have a bag packed with her belongings.

"I am going to take it to her on my car——"

"And you a perfect stranger. I think it's utterly mad, Baldy."

"Why mad? And she doesn't feel that I'm a perfect stranger."

"Oh!"

"And it is because I am a perfectly disinterested person."

"You're not disinterested."

"What makes you say that?"

"Oh, you know, Baldy. You're terribly smitten."

For a moment his eyes blazed, then he swaggered. "If I am, what then? I'd rather worship a woman like that for the rest of my life than marry anybody I've ever seen——"

"You don't know a thing about her except that she has lovely eyes."

She had risen, and as she stood in front of him there was again that effect of two young cockerels on the edge of an encounter. Then they were saved by their sense of humor. "Oh, go to bed," young Baldwin told her; "you're jealous, Janey."

She started up the stairs but before she had reached the landing he called after her. "Jane, what have you on hand for to-morrow?"

She leaned over the rail and looked down at him. "Friday? Feed the chickens. Feed the cats. Help Sophy clean the silver. Drink tea at four with Mrs. Allison, and three other young things of eighty."

"Well, look here. I don't want to face Towne. He'll say things about Edith—and insist on her coming back—she says he will, and that's why she won't call him up. And you've got more diplomacy than I have. You might make it all seem—reasonable. Will you do it, Jane?"

"Do you mean that you want me to call on him at his office?"

"Yes. Go in with me in the morning."

"Baldy, are you shirking? Or do you really think me as wonderful as your words seem to imply?"

"Oh, if you're going to put it like that."

She smiled down at him. "Let's leave it then that I am—wonderful. But suppose Mr. Towne

doesn't fall for your plan? Perhaps he won't let her have the bag or a check-book or money or—anything——"

Jane saw then a sudden and passionate change in her brother. "If he doesn't let her have it, I will. I may be poor but I'll beg or borrow rather than have her brought back to face those—cats—until she wants to come."

CHAPTER VIII
JANE AS DEPUTY

Frederick Towne never arrived in his office until ten o'clock. So Jane was ahead of him. She sat in a luxurious outer room, waiting.

To the right was a great open space—with desks boxed in by glass partitions. The wall paper was green, so that the people at the desks had the effect of fish in an aquarium. There was the constant staccato tap of typewriters, and now and then a girl got up, swam as it were, out of one of the glass boxes and into another.

The girls were most of them well dressed. Much better dressed than Jane who had on a cheap gray suit and a soft little hat of the same color. One of the girls, fair-haired and slender, was in the nearest glass box. She wore a black serge frock and a string of ivory beads. She looked to Jane much more distinguished than any of the others.

When Frederick came in he saw Jane at once, and held out his hand smiling. "You've heard from Edith?"

"Yes. Last night. Too late to let you know."

"Good. We'll go into my room." He led the way, and Jane was at once aware of the effect of his cordial manner upon the fish who had been

swimming in and out of the aquarium. Between the time of Frederick's entrance and the moment when he closed the door upon them, they seemed to hang suspended. She supposed that after that they swam again.

If the outer room had resembled an aquarium, Frederick's was like a forest—there was a plant or two and more green paper—the shine of old mahogany—and in one of the shadowy corners a bronze elephant.

Jane was thrilled by a sense of things happening. Outwardly calm, she was inwardly stirred by excitement.

She sat in a big leather chair which nearly swallowed her up, and stated her errand.

"Baldy thought I'd better come, he's so busy, and anyhow he thinks I have more tact." She tilted her chin at him and smiled.

"And you thought it needed tact."

"Well, don't you, Mr. Towne? We really haven't a thing to do with it, and I'm sure you think so. Only now we're in it, we want to do the best we can."

"I see. Since Edith has chosen you and your brother as ambassadors, you've got to use diplomacy."

"She didn't choose me, she chose Baldy."

"But why can't she deal directly with me?"

"She ran away from you. And she isn't ready to come back."

"She ought to come back."

"She doesn't think so. And she's afraid you'll insist."

"What does she want me to do?"

"Send her the bag with the money and the check-book, and let Baldy take out a lot of things. She gave him a list; there's everything from toilet water to talcum."

"Suppose I refuse to send them?"

"You can, of course. But you won't, will you?"

"No, I suppose not. I shan't coerce her. But it's rather a strange thing for her to be willing to trust all this to your brother. She has seen him only once."

"Well," said Jane, with some spirit, "you've seen Baldy only once, and wouldn't you trust him?"

She flung the challenge at him, and quite surprisingly he found himself saying, "Yes, I would."

"Well," said Jane, "of course."

He leaned back in his chair and looked at her. Again he was aware of quickened emotions. She revived half-forgotten ardors. Gave him back his youth. She used none of the cut and dried methods of sophistication. She was fearless, absolutely alive, and in spite of her cheap gray suit, altogether lovely.

So it was with an air of almost romantic challenge that he said, "What would you advise?"

"I'd let her alone, like little Bo-Peep. She'll come home before you know it, Mr. Towne."

"I wish that I could think it—however, it's a great comfort to know that she's safe. I shall give it out that she is visiting friends, and that I've heard from her. And now, about the things she wants. It seems absolutely silly to send them."

"I don't think it's silly."

"Why not?"

"Oh, clothes make such a lot of difference to a woman. I can absolutely change my feelings by changing my frock."

"What kind of feelings do you have when you wear gray?"

"Cool and comfortable ones—do you know the delightful things that are gray? Pussy-willows, and sea-gulls, and rainy days—and oh, a lot of things"—she surveyed him thoughtfully, "and old Sheffield, and—well, I can't think of everything." She rose. "I'll leave the list with you and you can telephone Baldy when to come for them."

"Don't go. I want to talk to you."

"But you're busy."

"Not unless I want to be."

"But I am. I have to go to market——"

"Briggs can take you over. I'll call up the garage."

"Briggs! Can you imagine Briggs driving through the streets of Washington with a pound of sausage and a three-rib roast?"

"Do you mean that you are going to take your parcels back with you?"

"Yes. There aren't any deliveries in Sherwood."

He hesitated for a moment, then touched her shoulder lightly with his forefinger. "Look here. Let Briggs take you to market, then come back here, and we'll run up to the house, get the things for lunch at Chevy Chase, and put you down, sausages, bags and all, at your own door in Sherwood."

"Really?" She was all shining radiance.

"Really. You'll do it then? Sit down a moment while I call up Briggs."

He called the garage and turned again to Jane. "I'll dictate some important letters, and be ready for you when you get back."

Jane, being shown out finally by the elegant Frederick, was again aware of the interest displayed by the fish in the aquarium. She was also aware that the girl in black serge with the white beads had risen, and that Towne was saying, "When I come back you can take my letters, Miss Logan."

He went all the way down to the first floor of the big building, and Jane and her cheap gray suit were once more under observation, this time by people on the sidewalk, as Briggs and Towne got her into the car. She rode away in great state and elegance. She was not quite sure whether she was really Jane Barnes. It seemed much more likely that she was Cinderella in a coach made out of a pumpkin, and that Briggs had been metamorphosed

from a rat. She leaned against the luxury of the fawn-colored cushions, and overlooked the outside world of pedestrians. Until to-day she had been one of them, but now she rode above them—the limousine was like some stately galleon breasting the tides of traffic. Jane's imagination carried her far. Even when she came to the market the enchantment persisted, especially when Briggs proved to be perfectly human and helpful instead of the automaton she had thought him. "If you don't mind my going in with you, Miss," he said, "I'd like it."

So Jane went through the fine old market, with its long aisles brilliant with the bounty of field and garden, river, and bay and sea. There were red meats and red tomatoes and red apples, oranges that were yellow, and pumpkins a deeper orange. There were shrimps that were pink, and red-snappers a deeper rose. There was the gold of butter and the gold of honey—the green of spinach, the green of olives and the green of pickles in bowls of brine, there was the brown of potatoes overflowing in burlap bags, and the brown of bread baked to crustiness—the brown of the plumage of dead ducks—the white of onions and the white of roses.

Jane bought modestly and Briggs carried her parcels. He even made a suggestion as to the cut of the steak. His father, it seemed, had been a butcher.

They drove back then for Frederick. Briggs

went up for him, and returned to say that Mr. Towne would be down in a moment.

Frederick was, as a matter of fact, finishing a letter to Delafield Simms:

"I am assuming that you will get your mail at the Poinciana, but I shall also send a copy to your New York office. Edith has asked me to return the ring to you. I shall hold it until I learn where it may be delivered into your hands.

"As for myself, I can only say this—that my first impulse was to kill you. But perhaps I am too civilized to believe that your death would make things better. You must understand, of course, that you've put yourself beyond the pale of decent people."

Lucy's pencil wavered—a flush stained her throat and cheeks—then she wrote steadily, as Frederick's voice continued:

"You will find yourself blackballed by several of the clubs. Whatever your motive, the world sees no excuse."

He stopped. "Will you read that over again, Miss Logan?"

So Lucy read it—still with that hot flush on her cheeks, and when she had finished Frederick said, "You can lock the ring in the safe until I give you further instructions."

A clerk came in to say that the car was waiting, and presently Frederick Towne went away and

Lucy was left alone in the great room, which was not to her a forest of adventure, as it had seemed to Jane, but a great prison where she tugged at her chains.

She thought of Delafield Simms sailing fast to southern waters. Of those purple seas—the blazing stars in the splendid nights. Delafield had told her of them. They had often talked together.

She turned the ring around on her finger, studying the carved figure. The woman with the butterfly wings was exquisite—but she did not know her name. She slipped the ring on the third finger of her left hand. Its diamonds blazed.

She locked it presently in the safe—then came back and read the letter which Towne had signed. She sealed it and stamped the envelope. Then she wrote a letter of her own. She made a little ring of her hair, and fastened it to the page. Beneath it she wrote, "Lucy to Del—forever." She kissed the words, held the crackling sheet against her heart. Her eyes were shining. The great room was no longer a prison. She saw beyond captivity to the open sea.

CHAPTER IX
THE SCARECROW

Mrs. Allison and the three old ladies with whom Jane was to drink tea, were neighbors. Mrs. Allison lived alone, and the other three lived in the homes of their several sons and daughters. They played cards every Friday afternoon, and Jane always came over when Mrs. Allison entertained and helped her with the refreshments. They were very simple and pleasant old ladies with a nice sense of their own dignity. They resented deeply the fact of Mrs. Follette's social condescensions. The lady of the manor spoke to them when she met them on the street or in church, but she never invited them to her house. She was, in effect, the chatelaine, while they were merely Smith and Brown and Robinson!

Well, at any rate, they had Jane. Some of the other young people scorned these elderly tea-parties, and if they came, were apt to show it in their manner. But Jane was never scornful. She always had the time of her life, and the old ladies felt particularly joyous and juvenile when she was one of them.

But this afternoon Jane was late. Tea was always

served promptly at four. And it happened that there were popovers. So, of course, they couldn't wait.

"I telephoned to Sophy," said Mrs. Allison, "and Jane has gone to town. I suppose something has kept her. Anyhow we'll start in."

So the old ladies ate the popovers and drank hot sweet chocolate, and found them not as delectable as when Jane was there to share them.

Things were, indeed, a bit dull. They discussed Mrs. Follette, whose faults furnished a perpetual topic. Mrs. Allison told them that the young Baldwins had dined at Castle Manor on Thanksgiving. And that there had been other guests.

"How can she afford it," was the unanimous opinion, "with that poor boy on her hands?"

"He's hanging around now, waiting for Jane's train," said Mrs. Allison, bringing in hot supplies from the kitchen. "He met the noon train, too."

The old ladies knew that Evans was in love with Jane. He showed it, unmistakably. But they hoped that Jane wouldn't look at him. He was dear and good, and had been wonderful once upon a time. But that time had passed, and it was impossible to consider Mrs. Follette as Jane's mother-in-law!

"He's sitting up there on the terrace," Mrs. Allison further informed them. "Do you think I'd better ask him to come over?"

They thought she might, but her hospitable purpose

was never fulfilled, for as she stepped out on the porch, a long, low limousine stopped in front of the house, and out of it came Jane in all the glory of a great bunch of orchids, and with a man by her side, whose elegance measured up to the limousine and the lovely flowers.

They came up the path and Jane said, "Mrs. Allison, may I present Mr. Towne, and will you give him a cup of tea?"

"Indeed, I will," Mrs. Allison seemed to rise on wings of gratification, "only it is chocolate and not tea."

And Frederick said that he adored chocolate, and presently Mrs. Allison's little living-room was all in a pleasant flutter; and over on Jane's terrace, Evans Follette sat, a lonely sentinel, and pondered on the limousine, and the elegance of Jane's escort.

Once old Sophy called to him, "You'll ketch your death, Mr. Evans."

He shook his head and smiled at her. A man who had lived through a winter in the trenches thought nothing of this. Physical cold was easy to endure. The cold that clutched at his heart was the thing that frightened him.

The early night came on. There were lights now in Mrs. Allison's house, and within was warmth and laughter. The old ladies, excited and eager, told each other in flashing asides that Mr. Towne was the *great* Frederick Towne. The one whose name was so often in the papers, and his niece,

Edith, had been deserted at the altar. "You know, my dear, the one who ran away."

When Jane said that she must be getting home, they pressed around her, sniffing her flowers, saying pleasant things of her prettiness—hinting of Towne's absorption in her.

She laughed and sparkled. It was a joyous experience. Mr. Towne had a way of making her feel important. And the adulation of the old ladies added to her elation.

As Frederick and Jane walked across the street towards the little house on the terrace, a gaunt figure rose from the top step and greeted them.

"Evans," Jane scolded, "you need a guardian. Don't you know that you shouldn't sit out in such weather as this?"

"I'm not cold."

She presented him to Frederick. "Won't you come in, Mr. Towne?"

But he would not. He would call her up. Jane stood on the porch and watched him go down the steps. He waved to her when he reached his car.

"Oh, Evans," she said, "I've had such a day."

They went into the house together. Jane lighted the lamp. "Can't you dine with us?"

"I hoped you might ask me. Mother is staying with a sick friend. If I go home, I shall sup on bread and milk."

"Sophy's chops will be much better." She held her flowers up to him. "Isn't the fragrance heavenly?"

"Towne gave them to you?"

She nodded. "Oh, I've been very grand and gorgeous—lunch at the Chevy Chase club—a long drive afterward——" she broke off. "Evans, you look half-frozen. Sit here by the fire and get warm."

"I met both trains."

"*Evans*—why will you do such things?"

"I wanted to see you."

"But you can see me any time——"

"I cannot. Not when you are lunching with fashionable gentlemen with gold-lined pocket-books." He held out his hands to the blaze. "Do you like him?"

"Mr. Towne? Yes, and I like the things he does for me. I had to pinch myself to be sure it was true."

"If what was true?"

"That I was really playing around with the great Frederick Towne."

"You talk as if he were conferring a favor."

She had her coat off now and her hat. She came and sat down in the chair opposite him. "Evans," she said, "you're jealous." She was still vivid with the excitement of the afternoon, lighted up by it, her skin warmed into color by the swift flowing blood beneath.

"Well, I am jealous," he tried to smile at her, then went on with a touch of bitterness, "Do you know what I thought about as I sat watching the lights at Mrs. Allison's? Well, as I came over to-day I passed a snowy field—and there was a scarecrow in the midst of it, fluttering his rags, a lonely thing, an ugly thing. Well, we're two of a kind, Jane, that scarecrow and I."

Her shocked glance stopped him. "Evans, you don't know what you are saying."

He went on recklessly. "Well, after all, Jane, the thing is this. It's a man's looks and his money that count. I'm the same man inside of me that I was when I went away. You know that. You might have loved me. The thing that is left you don't love. Yet I am the same man——"

As he flung the words at her, her eyes met his steadily. "No," she said, "you are not the same man."

"Why not?"

"The man of yesterday did not think—dark thoughts——"

The light had gone out of her as if he had blown it with a breath. "Jane," he said, unsteadily, "I am sorry——"

She melted at once and began to scold him, almost with tenderness. "What made you *look* at the scarecrow? Why didn't you turn your back on him, or if you *had* to look, why didn't you wave and say, 'Cheer up, old chap, summer's coming, and

you'll be on the job again'? To me there's something debonair in a scarecrow in summer—he dances in the breeze and seems to fling defiance to the crows."

He fell in with her mood. "But his defiance is all bluff."

"How do you know? If he keeps away a crow, and adds an ear of corn to a farmer's store—hasn't he fulfilled his destiny?"

"Oh, if you want to put it that way. I suppose you are hinting that I can keep away a crow or two——"

"I'm not hinting, I am telling it straight out."

They heard Baldy's step in the hall. Jane, rising, gave Evans' head a pat as she passed him. "You are thinking about yourself too much, old dear; stop it."

Baldy, ramping in, demanded a detailed account of Jane's adventure.

"And I took Briggs to market," she told him gleefully, midway of her recital; "you should have seen him. He carried my parcels—and offered advice——"

Baldy had no ears for Briggs' attractions. "Did you get the things Miss Towne wanted?"

"We did. We went to the house and I waited in the car while Mr. Towne had the bags packed. He wanted me to go in but I wouldn't. We brought her bags out with us."

"Who's we?"

"Mr. Towne and I, myself," she added the spectacular details.

"Do you mean that you've been playing around with him all day?"

"Not all day, Baldy. Part of it."

"I'm not sure that I like it."

"Why not?"

"A man like that. He might fill your head with ideas."

"I hope my head is filled with ideas, Baldy."

"You know what I mean."

"You mean that I might think he would fall in love with me. Well, I don't. But he likes to play and so do I. I hope he'll do it some more. And you and Evans are a pair of croakers. Here, I've been having the time of my life, and you're both trying to take the joy out of it."

They began to protest. She flung off their apologies. "Oh, let's eat dinner. Between the two of you you've spoiled my day."

But she was too light-hearted to hold resentment, and by the time the coffee came she was herself again. After dinner, Baldy telephoned Edith, and came back to set the victrola going to a most riotous tune and danced with Jane. It was an outlet for his emotions. *Edith ... Edith ... Edith ...* was the tune to which he danced.

Then he made Jane play his accompaniment and
sang the passionate lines of a poet much derided by the moderns:
"She is coming, my own, my sweet,
Were it ever so airy a tread,
My heart would hear her and beat,
Had it lain for a century dead,
Would start and tremble under her feet,
And blossom in purple and red."
The waves of lovely sound rose higher and higher, seemed to break over and engulf them:
"My heart would hear her and beat....
Would start and tremble under her feet,
And blossom in purple and red."

Evans, walking home an hour later, took the path which led beneath the pines. The old trees showed thin and black against the moon-bright sky. Beyond the pines was the field with the scarecrow. Evans might have avoided it by following the road, but he was drawn to it by a sort of sinister attraction, and by the memory of the things he had said to Jane.

Under the moon the scarecrow took on more than ever the semblance of a man. Lightly clad in straw hat and pajamas, it seemed to shiver and shake in the bleak and bitter night.

Evans leaned on a fence post and surveyed his fantastic prototype. The air was very still—no sound but the faint whistle of the wind.

Then out of the stillness—clear as a bell—Jane's husky voice. "*The man of yesterday did not think dark thoughts.*"

He seemed to answer her. "Why shouldn't I think them? My dreams are dead. And oh, my dear, what have you to do with dead dreams?"

He had thought he would be satisfied just to have her near him. But he knew now that he would not be satisfied. He had known it from the moment he had seen her with Towne. Always hereafter there would be the fear that she might be taken from him. And it was Frederick Towne who might take her. He had everything to offer. Any girl's head might be turned.

Towne's infatuation was evident. And Jane was exquisite—in mind and soul as well as body. It wasn't a thing for a man to miss.

He was chilled to the bone when at last he took leave of the ghostly figure in the straw hat. The old scarecrow seemed to lean towards him wistfully as he went away.... Oh, the thing was so human—he wanted to offer it shelter, a warm hearth.... He flung back at it as the best he could do, Jane's words, "Cheer up, old chap, summer's coming."

When he reached home, Evans went at once to the library. Rusty was in his basket by the fire. He lifted himself stiffly and whined. Evans knelt beside the basket, and held up a saucer of milk that the old dog might drink. Then he took a book

from the shelf and sat down to read. His mother had not returned. She had telephoned to him at Jane's that she might be late.

But he could not read. He sat with his book in his hand, and looked up at the portrait of his grandfather, and at the photograph of himself. After a while he rose and took the photograph from the shelf, observing it at close range.

What a gallant young chap he had been, and what a pair he and Jane would have made! There was no vanity in that—he would have matched his youth with hers in those days. Oh, the man in the picture was a fit mate for Jane!

The man who held the picture in his hand was a mate for—nobody!

With a sudden furious gesture, he flung it from him—the glass broke against the wall when it struck.

Rusty whined in his basket, his nose over the edge of it. His master stood as still as a statue in the center of the hearth.

When Mrs. Follette returned, her son met her at the door. If he was pale, she did not speak of it. "I am half-frozen, Evans; we came in an open car."

"Sit down by the fire, and I'll get you some hot milk."

"I wish you would. I must not risk a cold."

It was a fact that she could not. She was up early every morning, directing the men who worked

for her, and superintending the careful handling of the milk. Evans had offered, repeatedly, to help her, but she liked to do it herself. She was very competent, and she had built up her own business while her son was in the war. It seemed best to carry it on without him. She did not like to think of Evans as a milkman. A woman did not so easily lose caste—distinguished Englishwomen had gone into all kinds of occupations. The thing was to do it with an air. She had decided shrewdly that she must in some way differentiate her product from that of the ordinary dairyman, so she had called it Gold Seal milk, and each bottle was closed with a small gold seal bearing her family crest. Evans had laughed at her, but her shrewdness had been justified. She kept her cows in fine condition and sent her cards to doctors. The cards, too, bore the gold seal. And soon her reputation was established. Big cars stopped at her door, and people who came expecting to find a crude countrywoman were ushered into the old library with its portraits and an imposing background of books. There Mrs. Follette, in quiet black with white cuffs and collars, her gray hair high, received them. Her customers went away impressed and told others.

Outwardly calm on such occasions, Mrs. Follette was inwardly excited. She had a feeling that the situation smacked of Marie Antoinette at Little Trianon. She was glad she had thought of selling milk—it seemed to link her subtly with royalty.

She had a royal air now as she sat before the fire. She always dressed for dinner. Her shabby black gown showed a round of white neck. She wore a string of jet beads and her satin slippers were adorned with jet buckles. She had pretty feet—and she surveyed them complacently. Then her eyes traveled beyond them to something that lay in a far corner.

She went over to it and picked it up. It was the photograph of Evans which had always stood on the mantel. The broken glass fell from it with a tinkling sound. She had it in her hand when Evans came in.

"How in the world did it happen?"

He set the small tray carefully on the table. "I threw it."

"But—my dear boy, why?"

He stood looking at her. She saw his paleness. "Oh, well, for a moment I was a—fool."

She was not an imaginative woman. But she knew what he meant. And her chin quivered. She was no longer royal. She was the mother of a hurt child. "I hoped things might—grow easier——"

"They grow harder——"

He sat down on the rug at her feet as he had sat through the years of little boyhood. Her left hand with its old-fashioned diamond rings hung by her side. He took it in his. "Don't worry, Mumsie, I told you I was a—fool. And it was all over in a second——"

She knew it was not over, but she drank her milk. Then she drew his head against her knees, and told him about her visit and her sick friend. Nothing more was said of the picture, but all through her recital he clung to her hand.

CHAPTER X
BALDY AS AMBASSADOR

Baldy Barnes faring forth to find Edith Towne on Sunday morning was a figure as old as the ages—youth in quest of romance.

It was very cold and the clouds were heavy with wind. But neither cold nor clouds could damp his ardor—at his journey's end was a lady with eyes of burning blue.

People were going to church as he came into the city and bells were ringing, but presently he rode again in country silences. He crossed the long bridge into Virginia and followed the road to the south.

It was early and he met few cars. Yet had the way been packed with motors, he would have still been alone in that world of imagination where he saw Edith Towne and that first wonderful moment of meeting.

So he entered Alexandria, passing through the narrow streets that speak so eloquently of history. Beyond the town was another stretch of road parallel to the broad stream, and at last an ancient roadside inn, of red brick, with a garden at the back, barren now, but in summer a tangle of bloom, with an expanse of reeds and water plants, extending

out into the river, and a low spidery boat-landing, which showed black at this season above the ice.

For years the old inn had been deserted, until motor cars had brought back its vanished glories. Once more its wide doors were open. There was nothing pretentious about it. But Baldy knew its reputation for genuine hospitality.

He wondered how Edith had kept herself hidden in such a place. It was amazing that no one had discovered her. That some hint of her presence had not been given to the newspapers.

He found her in a quaint sitting-room up-stairs. "I think," she said to him, as he came in, "that you are very good-natured to take all this trouble for me——"

"It isn't any trouble." His assurance was gone. With her hat off she was doubly wonderful. He felt his youth and inexperience, yet words came to him, "And I didn't do it for you, I did it for myself."

She laughed. "Do you always say such nice things?"

"I shall always say them to you. And you mustn't mind. Really," Jane would have recognized returning confidence in that cock of the head, "I'm just a page—twanging a lyre."

They laughed together. He was great fun, she decided, different.

"You are wondering, I fancy, how I happened
to come here," she said, leaning back in her chair, her burnished hair
against its faded cushions. "Well, an old cook of Mother's, Martha Burns,
is the wife of the landlord. She will do anything for me. I have had all my
meals up-stairs. I might be a thousand miles away for all my world knows
of me."

"I was worried to death when I thought of you out in the storm."

"And all the while I was sitting with my feet on the fender, reading about
myself in the evening papers."

"And what you read was a-plenty," said Baldy, slangily. "Some of those
reporters deserve to be shot."

"Oh, they had to do it," indifferently, "and what they have said is
nothing to what my friends are saying. It's a choice morsel. Every girl who
ever wanted Del's millions is crowing over the way he treated me."

The look in his eyes disconcerted her. "Do you really think that?"

"Of course. We're a greedy bunch."

"I don't like to hear you say such things."

"Why not?"

"Because—you aren't greedy. You know it. It wasn't his millions you
were after."

"What was I after? I wish you'd tell me. I don't know."

"Well, I think you just followed the flock.

Other girls got married. So you would marry. You didn't know anything
about love—or you wouldn't have done it."

"How do you know I've never been in love?"

"Isn't it true?"

"I suppose it is. I don't know, really."

"You'll know some day. And you mustn't ever think of yourself as
mercenary. You're too wonderful for that—too—too fine——"

She realized in that moment that the boy was in earnest. That he was not
saying pretty things to her for the sake of saying them. He was saying them
all in sincerity. "It is nice of you to believe in me. But you don't know me.
I am like the little girl with the curl. I can be very, very good, but sometimes
I am 'horrid.'"

"You can't make me think it." He handed her a packet of letters. "Your
uncle sent these. There's one from Simms on top."

"I think I won't read it. I won't read any of them. It has been heavenly to be away from things. I feel like a disembodied spirit, looking on but having nothing to do with the world I have left."

They were smiling now. "I can believe that," Baldy said, "but I think you ought to read Simms' letter. You needn't tell me you haven't any curiosity."

"Well, I have," she broke the envelope. "More than that I am madly curious. I wouldn't confess it though to anyone—but you."

"They can cut me up in little pieces—before I break my silence."

Again they laughed together. Then she broke the seal of the letter. Read it through to herself, then read it a second time aloud.

"Now that it is all over, Edith, I want to tell you how it happened. I know you think it is a rotten thing I did. But it would have been worse if I had married you. I am in love with another woman, and I did not find it out until the day of our wedding.

"She isn't in the least to blame, and somehow I can't feel that I am quite the cad that everybody is calling me. Things are bigger sometimes than ourselves. Fate just took me that morning—and swept me away from you.

"It isn't her fault. She wouldn't go away with me, although I begged her to do it. And she was right of course.

"She is poor, but she isn't marrying me for my money. The world will say she is—but the world doesn't recognize the *real thing*. It has come to me, and if it ever comes to you, you're going to thank me for this—but now you'll hate me, and I'm sorry. You're a beautiful, wonderful woman—and I find no excuse for myself, except the one that it would have been a crime under the circumstances to tie us to each other.

"In spite of everything,

"Faithfully,

"Del."

There was a moment's silence, as she finished.

Then Edith said, "So that's that," and tore the letter into little shreds. Her blue eyes were like bits of steel.

"He's right," said Baldy. "I'd like to kill him for making you unhappy—but the thing was bigger than himself."

She shrugged her shoulders. "Of course if you are going to condone—dishonor——"

He was leaning forward hugging his knees. "I am not condoning anything. But—I know this—that some day if you ever fall in love, you'll forgive——"

"I am not likely to fall in love," coldly, "I'm too sensible——"

He studied her with his bright gray eyes. "Oh, no, you're not. You're not in the least—sensible. You think you are because the men you've met have been poor sticks who couldn't make you care——"

"I've met some of the most distinguished men in America—and a few of them have fallen in love with me——"

"Oh, I know. You've had strings of lovers—you're too tremendously lovely not to have. But they've all been afraid of you. No caveman stuff—or anything like that. Isn't that the truth?"

"I should hate a caveman."

"Of course, but you wouldn't be indifferent, and you'd end by caring———"

"I dislike brutal types—intensely——"

He sat with his chin in his hand, his shoulders hunched up like a faun or Pan at his pipes. "All cavemen aren't brutal types. Some day I'm going to paint a picture of a man carrying off a woman. And I'm going to make him a slender young god—and she shall be a rather substantial goddess—but she'll go with him—his spirit shall conquer her———"

She looked at him in surprise. "Then you paint?"

"I'll say I do. Terrible things—magazine covers. But in the back of my mind there are masterpieces——"

He was a whimsical youngster, she decided. But no end interesting. "I don't believe your things are terrible. And I shall want to see them——"

"You are going to see them. I have a studio in our garage. I sometimes wonder what happens at night when my little Ford is left alone with my fantasies. It must feel that it is fighting devils——"

He broke off to say, "I'm as garrulous as Jane. Please don't let me talk any more about myself."

"Is Jane your sister?"

"Yes. And now let's get down to realities. Your uncle wants you to come home."

"I'm not going. I know Uncle Fred. He'll make me feel like a returned prodigal. He'll kill the fatted calf, but I'll always know that there were husks——"

"And hogs," Baldy supplemented, dreamily. "Some people are like that."

"He's always been worshipped by women. And I didn't fall at his feet. That's why we didn't get on. He ruled his mother and his servants—and he couldn't rule me. And he'd run away to his affinities to be comforted, and they'd tell him what a cat I was——"

"Affinities?"

"Oh, I call them that, because there has always been a procession of them. Women he adores for the moment. But it never lasts, and they spoil him to death—and I won't spoil him. I like my own way, too, sometimes, and I fight for it. And I am the only person in the world who makes Uncle Frederick lose his temper. And he hates that. His manners are lovely as a rule, but he simply blows up when we get into an argument."

She was not a goddess—she was intensely human—a soul fighting to be free, and he wanted to help her fight.

"Look here," he said suddenly, "if I were you I'd go back."

"I will not."

"I think you ought. Face things out. Let your uncle understand that there are to be no postmortems. It is the only thing to do. You can't stay here forever."

"Did Uncle Fred make you his ambassador?" coldly.

"He did not. When I came, I felt that I would do anything to keep you away from home as long as

you liked. But I don't feel that way now. You'll just sit here and grow bitter about it—instead of thanking God on your knees."

He flung it at her, unexpectedly. There was a moment's intense silence. Then he said, "Oh, I hope you don't think I am preaching——"

"No—no——" and suddenly her head went down on her arm, that beautiful burnished head.

She was crying!

"I'm sorry," he told her, huskily.

And again there was silence.

She hunted for her handkerchief, and he handed her his. "You needn't be sorry," she said; "it seems—rather refreshing to have someone say things like that. Oh, I wonder if you know how hard we are—and cynical—the people of my set. And I don't believe any of us ever—thank God."

She wiped her eyes, found her own handkerchief, and handed his back to him. She did not know how he treasured it—afterward—a chalice for her tears. She found it many years later—shut away in a box with a sprig of heliotrope.

They talked for an hour after that. "There is no reason why you should hurry back," Baldy said, "but I'd let your uncle tell people where you are. Then the papers will drop it, don't you see?"

"I see. Of course I've been silly—but you can't think how I suffered."

She would not have admitted it to anyone else. But she met his sincerity with her own.

"I was going to have our lunch served up here," she said, "but I think I won't. The dining-room down-stairs is charming—and if anyone comes in that I know—I shan't care—as long as I'm going back."

The mammoth fireplace in the old dining-room had been restored to ancient uses. Martha and her husband had recognized its value as a background, so meat was roasted on the spit—a turkey to-day as it happened. The tables were lighted by high white candles—and there were old hunting prints on the walls.

The food was delicious, and having settled her problems, Edith showed herself delightfully gay and girlish. There was heliotrope in a Sheffield bowl on their table. "Martha grows old-fashioned flowers in pots," Edith said. She picked out a spray for him and he put it in his coat. "It's my favorite." She told him about Delafield's orchids. "Think of all those months," she said, "and he never knew the flowers I like."

There were other people in the room, but it was not until the end of the meal that anyone came whom Edith recognized.

"Eloise Harper—and she sees me," was her sudden remark. "Now watch me carry it off."

She stood up and waved to a party of four people, two men and two women, who stood in the door.

They saw her at once, and the effect of their coming was a stampede.

"Blessed child," said the girl who was in the lead, "have you eloped? And is this the man?"

"This is Mr. Barnes," said Edith, "who comes from my uncle. I am to go back. But I have had a corking adventure."

Only Baldy knew what was in her heart, and how hard it was to face them. But on the surface she was as sparkling as the rest of them. "I shall probably be in the papers again to-morrow morning. You know you won't be able to keep it, Eloise."

Eloise, red-haired and vivid in a cloak and turban of wood-brown, seemed to stand mentally on tiptoe. "I wouldn't miss the talk I am going to have with the reporters to-night."

One of the men of the party protested. "Don't be an idiot, Eloise."

"Well, I owe Edith something. Don't I, darling?"

"You do." There was a flame in back of Edith's eyes. "She liked Delafield before I did."

"Cat," said Eloise lightly. "I liked his yacht, but Benny's is bigger, isn't it, Benny?" She turned to the younger man of the party who had not spoken.

"I'll say it is," Benny agreed, cheerfully, "and it isn't just my yacht that she's after. She has a real little case on me."

The second woman, older than Eloise, tall and

fair-haired in smoke-gray with a sweep of dull blue wing across her hat, said, "Edith, you bad child, your uncle has been frightfully worried."

"Of course, you'd know, Adelaide. And it does him good to be worried. I am an antidote for the rest of you."

Everybody laughed except Baldy. He ran his fingers with a nervous gesture through his hair. He was like a young eagle with a ruffled crest.

Martha came up to arrange for a table. "Bring your coffee over and sit with us," Eloise said; "we want to hear all about it."

Edith shook her head. "I don't belong to your world yet. And I've had a heavenly time without you."

They went on laughing. Silence settled on the two they left behind. And out of that silence Edith asked, "You didn't like the things we said?"

"Hateful!"

"Do you always show what you feel like that?"

"Jane says I do."

"Well, if it had been anybody but Eloise Harper and Adelaide Laramore. Adelaide is Uncle Fred's latest."

She rose. "Let's go up-stairs. If I stay here I shall want to throw things at their heads. And I don't care to break Martha's dishes."

They stopped at the other table, however, for a light word or two, then went up to Edith's sitting-room on the second floor. When they were once more by the fire, she said, "And now what do you think of me? Nice temper?"

"I think," he said, promptly, "that they probably deserved it."

She laid her hand for a fleeting moment on his arm. "You are rather a darling to say that. I was really horrid."

When he was ready at last to go, she decided, "Tell Uncle Frederick to send Briggs out for me in the morning. I might as well have it over, now that Eloise is going to spread the news."

"I wish you'd go in with me—to-night."

"Oh, but I couldn't——"

"Why not?"

She weighed it—"And surprise Uncle Fred?"

"I think we'd better telephone, so he can kill the fatted calf."

"Yes. He doesn't like things sprung on him. Hurts his dignity—but he's rather an old dear, and I love him—do you ever quarrel with the people you love?"

"Jane and I fight. Great times."

"I have a feeling I shall like Jane."

"You will. She's the best ever. Not a beauty, but growing better-looking every day. Bobbed her hair—and I nearly took her head off. But she's rather a peach."

"I'll have you both down for dinner some day. I think we are going to be friends"—again that light touch on his arm.

He caught her hand in his. "I shall only ask that you let the page twang his lyre." Then with a deeper note, "Miss Towne, I can't tell you how much your friendship would mean."

"Would it? Oh, I am going to have some good times with you and your little sister, Jane. I am so tired of people like Eloise and Adelaide, and Benny and—Del...."

On this same afternoon little Lucy Logan was writing to Delafield Simms.

"It seems like a dream, lover, that you are to come for me in February, and that then we'll be married. And that all the rest of my life I am to belong to you.

"Del, it isn't because you are rich. Of course I shall adore the things you can do for me. I am not going to pretend that I shan't. But if you were poor, I'd work for you—live for you. Oh, Del, I do hope that you will believe it.

"The other day, Mr. Towne said in one of his letters that you had always been fickle, that there had been lots of girls, Eloise Harper before Edith. And I wanted to scream right out and say, 'It isn't true. He hasn't ever really cared before this.' But of course I couldn't. But I broke a pencil point, and as for Mr. Towne, who is he to say such things about you? I haven't taken his letters for the last three years for nothing. There's always somebody— the last one was Mrs. Laramore, and now he has his eye on a little Jane Barnes, whose brother found Miss Towne's bag and the ring. She's rather a darling, but I hope she won't think he is in earnest.

"And now, my dear and my darling, good-night. I wonder how I dare call you that. But I am always saying it to myself, and at night I ask God to keep you—safe."

Five days later, Delafield read Lucy's letter. He was on his yacht in southern waters. His man had been sent in for the mail.

When he had finished, Delafield lay back in his deck chair and thought about it. Queer thing for him to fall like that for little Lucy. He had not believed that it was in him to care in that way for a woman. But he did. The letter lay like a live warm thing under his hand. It seemed to beat with his heart as Lucy's heart had beat against his own on that last morning in Frederick Towne's office, while his bride waited.

CHAPTER XI
THE DIM LANTERN

Jane, in Baldy's absence, dined on Sunday with the Follettes, in the middle of the day. In the afternoon she and Evans went for a walk, and came home to tea in the library.

Stretched in a long leather chair, Evans read to Jane and his mother "The Eve of St. Agnes."

"How bitter cold it was!

The owl, for all his feathers, was a-cold:

The hare limp'd trembling through the frozen grass,

And silent were the flock in woolly fold."

Jane, curled up on the couch in her favorite attitude, listened to that incomparable description of stark winter weather, and was glad of the warmth and coziness. She was glad, too, of this pleasant company—Mrs. Follette was a great dear, with her duchess air, and her devotion to Evans. And Evans, reading in that thrilling and unchanged voice, was at his best.

As for Mrs. Follette, she was always glad to have Jane visit them. The child was so cheerful, and Evans needed cheer. Then, too, Jane was a delightful compromise between the girl of yesterday and the ultra-modern maiden who shocked Mrs.

Follette not only by her lack of reverence but by her lack of reticence.

Jane might have bobbed hair, but she did not have a bobbed-hair mind. The meaning of this conclusion was quite clear to Mrs. Follette, however obscure it might be to others. Girls who cut off their hair, as a rule, went farther—Jane stopped at her hair.

Then, too, Jane had what might be called old-fashioned domestic qualities. She kept her little house as spick and span as she kept herself. In winter everything was burnished and bright; in summer crisp curtains waved in the warm breeze; there were cool shadows within the clean, quiet rooms.

At the moment, Mrs. Follette was weighing seriously the fact of Jane as a wife for Evans. She was pretty as well as cheerful. Had good manners. Of course, in the old days, Evans would, inevitably, have looked higher. There had been plenty of rich girls eager to attract him. He had had unlimited invitations. Women had, in fact, quite run after him. Florence Preston had rather made a fool of herself. And Florence's father had millions.

But now——? Mrs. Follette knew how little Evans had at the moment to offer. She hated to admit it, but the truth was evident. Watching the two young people, she decided that should Evans care for Jane, she would erect no barriers. As for Jane, marriage with Evans would be, in a way, a

rise in the world. She would live at Castle Manor instead of at Sherwood Park.

The poem had reached a point where Mrs. Follette felt that she ought to protest. She was not quite sure that she approved of the situation it outlined. The verse of the moment, for example—Porphyro's plea to the maid, old Angela:

"To lead him in close secrecy,
Even to Madelaine's chamber and there hide
Him in a closet of such privacy,
That he might see her beauty unspy'd
And win, perhaps, that night, a peerless bride."
Stripped of all its fine words, it was an impossible situation.
Apparently, however, the young people were without self-consciousness....
"Out went the taper, as she hurried in:
Its little smoke in pallid moonshine died——"
Evans looked up. "Could there be anything lovelier than that last line?"
Jane's eyes had dreams in them. "Don't stop," she said.
He read on.... "She closed the door ..." his voice took now a deeper note.
"Rose-bloom fell on her hands, together prest,
And on her silver cross soft amethyst,
And on her hair a glory like a saint:
She seemed a splendid angel, newly drest,
Save wings for heaven; Porphyro grew faint:
She knelt so pure a thing, so free from mortal taint."
"Evans," said his mother, as he paused again, "that poem doesn't seem to me exactly proper."
He gave her a surprised glance. "Don't spoil it for us, Mumsie."
"Oh, well," Mrs. Follette shrugged her nice shoulders, "we won't argue. But when I was a girl we didn't read things like that."
"But this was written before you were a girl."
"What difference does that make?"
"But the richness and color. You see it, Jane, don't you?"
"Yes. Finish it, Evans."
And when he came to the end, she said, "If only life were like that."

"Like what?"

"High romance. Porphyro says negligently, 'For o'er the southern moors I have a home for thee.' But lovers of to-day have to think of rent and food and clothes. And hotel bills for the honeymoon."

"Oh, you women"—he sat up flaming—"are you conspiring to spoil my poem? Jane, it is the dreams of men and women which shape their lives."

As his eyes met hers something stirred within her like the flutter of a bird's wings lifted to the sun....

It was after five when Baldy telephoned triumphantly: "Jane, Edith Towne has agreed to go home to-night. And I'm to take her. I called up Mr. Towne and told him and he wants you to be there when we come. He'll send Briggs for you and we are all to have dinner together."

"But, Baldy, I don't know Edith Towne. Why doesn't he ask some of her own friends?"

"She doesn't want 'em. Hates them all, and anyhow he has asked you. Why worry?"

"I'll have to go home and dress."

"Well, you're to let him know at once where Briggs can get you. I told him you were at the Follettes'."

Jane went back and repeated the conversation to Evans and his mother. Mrs. Follette was much interested. The Townes were most important people. "How nice for you, Jane."

But Evans disagreed with her. "What makes you say that, Mother? It isn't nice. It will simply be upsetting."

"I don't see why you say that, Evans," Jane argued. "I am not easily upset."

"But with all that money. You can't keep up with them."

"Don't put ideas into Jane's head," his mother remonstrated; "a lady is always a lady."

But Jane sided now with Evans. "I see what he means, Mrs. Follette. I haven't the clothes. I haven't a thing to wear to-night."

"Oh, I wasn't thinking of your looks." Evans got up and stood on the hearth-rug. "But people like that! Jane, I wish you wouldn't go."

She looked up at him with her chin tilted. "I don't see how I can refuse."

"Of course she can't. Evans, don't be so unreasonable," Mrs. Follette interposed; "it will be a wonderful thing for Jane to know Edith."

"Will it be such a wonderful thing for her to know Frederick Towne?" He flung it at them.

Jane demanded, "Don't you want me to have any good times?"

He stared at her for a moment, and when he spoke it was in a different tone. "Yes, of course. I beg your pardon, Janey."

Mrs. Follette, having effaced herself for the moment from the conversation, decided that things between her son and little Jane Barnes might reach a climax at any moment. "I believe he's half in love with her," she told herself in some bewilderment.

As for Frederick Towne, she didn't consider him for a moment. Jane was a pretty child. But Frederick Towne could have his pick of women. There would be nothing serious in this friendship with Jane.

Jane called up Towne. "It was good of you to ask me," she said. "I am at the Follettes', but I'll go home and dress and Briggs can come for me there."

"Come as you are."

"You wouldn't say that if you could see me. I took a walk with Evans this afternoon and I show the effects of it."

"Evans? Oh, Casabianca?"

"What makes you call him that?"

"I thought of it when I saw him waiting for you at the top of the terrace. 'The boy stood on the burning deck——'" he laughed.

"I don't think that's funny at all," said Jane, frankly.

"Don't you? Well, I beg your pardon. I'll beg it again when I get you here. Briggs will reach Sherwood at about seven. I would drive out myself, but I've an awful cold, and the doctor tells me I must stay in. And Cousin Annabel is sick in bed with a cold, so you must take pity on me and keep me company...."

Jane hung up the receiver. It would, she decided, be an exciting adventure. But she was not sure that she liked Frederick Towne....

Evans walked home with her. The air was warmer than it had been for days, and faint mists had risen. The mist thickened finally to a fog which rolled over them as if blown from the high seas. Yet the sea was miles away, and the fog was born in the rivers and streams, and in the melting snows.

They found it somewhat difficult to keep to the road. They were almost smothered in the thick

gray masses. Their voices had a muffled sound. Evans' hand was on Jane's arm so that they might keep together.

"Jane," he said, "I made a fool of myself about Towne. But honestly— I was afraid——"

"Of what?"

"That he might fall in love with you——"

"He's not thinking of me, Evans, and besides he's too old——"

"Do you really feel that way about it, Jane?"

"Of course—silly."

He could not see her face—but the words in her laughing lovely voice gave him a sense of reassurance.

"Janey," he said, "if I could only have you like this always. Shut away from the world."

"But I don't want to be shut away. I should feel—caged——"

"Not if you cared."

There was in his tone the huskiness of intense feeling. She was moved by it. "Oh, I know what you mean. But love won't come to me like that—shut in. I shall want freedom, and sunshine. I'll be a gull over the sea—a ship in full sail—a gypsy on the road—but I'll never be a ghost in a fog."

His hand dropped from her arm. "Perhaps you'll be a princess in a castle. Towne can make you that."

"Why do you keep harping on Mr. Towne? I don't like it."

"Because—oh, I think everybody wants you——"

And now it was she who caught at his arm in the mist, and leaned on it. "I'm not the least in love with Frederick Towne. And I shall never marry a man I don't love, Evans."

When they came to the little house they found old Sophy nodding in the kitchen. She always stayed with Jane when Baldy was away. So Evans said "Good-night" and started back.

He found the path between the pines, walked a few steps and stumbled. He sat down on the log that had tripped him. He had no wish to go on. His depression was intense. Night was before him and darkness. Loneliness. And Jane would be with Frederick Towne.

He had for Jane a feeling of hopeless adoration. She would never be his. For how could he try to keep her? "I'll be a gull over the sea—a ship in full sail—a gypsy on the road—never a ghost in a fog."

And he was just a ghost in a fog! Oh, what was the use of ever "climbing up the climbing wave"? One must have something of hope to live on. A dream or two—ahead.

How long he sat there he did not know. And all at once he was aware of a pale blur against the prevailing gloom. And then he heard Jane's voice calling, "Evans? Evans?"

He answered and she came up to him. "Your mother telephoned—that you had not come home—and she was worried."

She was holding the lantern up to the length of her arm. In her orange cloak she shone through the veil of mist, luminous.

"My dear," she said, gently, "why are you sitting here?"

"Because there isn't any use in going on."

She lowered the lantern so that it shone on his face. What she saw there frightened her. "Are you feeling this way because of me?" she asked in a shaking voice.

"Because of everything."

"Evans, I won't go to the Townes if you want me to stay."

He looked up at her as she bent above him with the lantern. She seemed to shine within and without, like some celestial visitor.

"Would you stay, Jane, if I wanted it?"

"Yes."

He stood up. "I don't want it. Not really. I'm not quite such a selfish pig," his smile was ghastly.

She was silent for a moment, then she said, "I'm going home with you, Evans. Wait until I tell Sophy to send Briggs after me."

He tried to protest, but she was firm. "I'll be back in a minute."

She returned presently, the lantern in one hand

and her slipper bag in the other. "I put on heavier shoes. I should ruin my slippers."

As they trod the path together, the light of the lantern shone in round spots of gold, now in front of them, now behind them. The fog pressed close, but the path was clear.

"Evans," said Jane, "I want you to promise me something."

"Anything, except—not to love you."

"It has nothing to do with love of me, but it has something to do with love of God."

He knew how hard it was for her to say that. Jane did not speak easily of such things.

She went on with some hesitation. Her voice, muffled by the fog, had a muted note of music.

"Evans, you mustn't let what I do make you or break you. Whether I love you or not, you must go on. You—you couldn't hold me if you weren't strong enough, even if I was your wife. And there is strength in you, if you'll only believe it. Oh, you must believe it, Evans. And you mustn't make me feel responsible. I can't stand it. To feel all the time that I am hurting—you."

She was sobbing. A little incoherent.

"And you *are* captain of your soul, Evans. You. Not anyone else. I can't be. I can be a help, and oh, I will help all I can. You know that. But—I love you like a big brother—not in any other way. If anything should happen to you, it would

be dreadful for me, just as it would be dreadful if anything happened to Baldy."

"Janey, my dear, don't," for she was clinging to his arm, crying as if her heart would break.

"But I do care for you so much, Evans. I was frantic when your mother telephoned. I wasn't quite dressed and I made Sophy get the lantern, and then I ran down the path, and looked for you."

He stopped and laid his hand on her shoulder. Her weakness, her broken words had roused in him a sudden protective tenderness.

"My little girl," he said, "don't. God helping me, I'm going to get back. And you are going to light my way. Jane, do you know when I saw you coming towards me with that dim lantern it seemed symbolic. Hope held out to me—seen through a fog, faintly. But a light, nevertheless."

"Oh, Evans, if I could love you, I would, you know that."

"I know. You'd tie up the broken wings of every bird. You'd give crutches to the lame, and food to the hungry. And that's the way you feel about me."

He had let her go now, and they stood apart, shrouded in ghostly white.

"God helping me," he said again, "I'll get back. That's a promise, Janey, and here's my hand upon it."

She gave him her hand. "God helping us both," she said.

He lifted her hand and kissed it. Then, in silence, they walked on, until they reached the house....

The Towne car was waiting, and Mrs. Follette in a flurry welcomed them. "I don't see why you didn't ride over with him."

"He hadn't come, and we preferred to walk."

"What was the matter with you, Evans?"

"Nothing much, Mother. I'm sorry you were fussed." He gave her no further explanation.

Jane put on her slippers and went off in the great car. And then Evans said, "I'm going over to Hallam's."

"Aren't you well, my dear?"

"I want to talk to him." He saw her anxious look, and bent and kissed her. "Don't worry, Mumsie, I'm all right."

Dr. Hallam's old estate adjoined the Follette farm. The doctor was a nerve specialist, and went every morning to Washington, coming back at night to the quiet of his charming home. He was unmarried and was looked after by men-servants. He had been much interested in Evans' case, and had in fact had charge of it.

The doctor was by the library fire, smoking a cigar and reading a brown book. He welcomed Evans heartily. "I was wondering when you would turn up again." He showed the title of his book, "Boswell. There was a man. As great as

the man he wrote about, and we are just beginning to find it out."

"Rare edition?" Evans sat down.

"Yes. Got it at Lowdermilk's yesterday."

"We've oodles of old books on our shelves. Ought to sell them, I suppose."

"I wouldn't sell one of mine." Hallam was emphatic. "I'd rather murder a baby."

Evans flamed suddenly. "I'd sell mine, if I could get the things I want."

"I don't want anything as much as I want my books."

"I do. I want life as I used to live it."

The doctor sat up and looked at him. "You mean before the war?"

"Yes."

"Good."

"I'm tired of being half a man. If there's any way out of it, I want you to tell me."

The doctor's eyes were bright with interest. He knew the first symptoms of recovery in such cases. The neurasthenic quality of Evans' trouble had robbed him of initiative. His waking-up was a promising sign.

"The thing to do, of course, is to get to work. Why don't you open an office?"

"A fat chance I'd have of getting clients."

"I think they'd come."

The doctor smoked for a time in silence, then he said, "Decide on something hard to do, and do

it. Do it if you feel you are going to die in the attempt."

There was something inspiring to Evans in the idea. Hard things. That was it. He poured out the story of the past few days. The awful scene with Rusty. To-night in the fog under the pines. "Wanted more than anything to drop myself in the river."

He was walking the floor, back and forth, limping to one edge of the rug, then limping to the other. "Then Jane came. Little Jane Barnes. You know her, and she told me—where to get off—said I was—captain of my soul———" He stopped in front of the doctor, and smiled whimsically. "Are any of us captains of our souls, doctor?"

"I'll be darned if I know." The doctor was intensely serious. "Will power has a lot to do with things. The trouble is when your will won't work———"

"Mine seems to be working on one cylinder." Again Evans was pacing the rug. "But that idea of an office appeals to me. It will take a bit of money, though. And it is rather a problem to know where to get it."

"Sell some of the old books. I'll buy them."

Light leaped into Evans' eyes. "It would be one way, wouldn't it? Mother would rather hate it. But what's a library against a life?" He seemed to fling the question to a listening universe.

The doctor laughed. "She'll be sensible if you put it up to her. And you must frivol a bit. Play around with the girls."

"I don't want any girls except Jane."

"Little Jane Barnes. Well, she'll do."

"I'll say she will."

The doctor, watching him as he walked back and forth, said, "The thing to do is to map out a normal day. Make it pretty close to the program you followed before the war. You haven't happened to keep a diary, have you?"

"Yes. It's a clumsy record. Mother started me when I was a kid."

"That's what we want. Read it every night, and do some of the things the next day that you did then. You will find you can stick closer than you think. And it will give you a working plan."

Evans sat down and discussed the idea. It was late when he rose to leave.

"It will be slow," was Hallam's final admonition, "but I believe you can do it. And when things go wrong, just honk and I'll lend you some gas," his big laugh boomed out, as they stood in the door together. "Nasty night."

"I have a lantern." Evans picked it up from the porch.

When Evans reached home his mother called from up-stairs, "I thought you were never coming."

"Hallam and I had a lot to talk about."

He came running up, and entering her room found her propped up on her pillows.

Mrs. Follette in bed lost nothing of her dignity. Her gray hair at night was braided and wound into a coronet above her serene forehead. She wore something knitted in white and black about her shoulders. There was a prayer-book on her bedside table—and pineapple posts to her bed. She had inherited her religion and her furniture from her ancestors, and she kept them both in order.

"Mother," said Evans, and stood looking down at her, "Hallam wants me to sell some of the old books and use the money to open an office."

"What kind of office?"

"Law. In town."

"But are you well enough, Evans?"

"He says that I am. He says that I must think that I am well, Mother."

"But——"

"Dearest, don't spoil it with doubts. It's my life, Mother."

There was a look on his face which she had not seen since his return. Uplifted, eager. A light in his eyes, like the light which had shone in the eyes of a boy.

She found it difficult to speak. "My dear, the books are yours. Do as you think best."

He leaned over and kissed her, lifting her a bit. There was energy as well as affection in the quick

caress. She drew herself away laughing, breathless. "How strong you are."

"Am I? Well, I think I am. And I am going to conquer the world, Mumsie."

His exaltation lasted during the reading of the diary. It was a fat little book, and the pages were written close in his fine firm script. He found things between the leaves—a four-leaved clover Jane had sent him when he made the football team. A rose, colorless and dry. Florence Preston had given it to him.

He dropped the rose in the waste-basket. How could he ever have thought of Florence? Love wasn't a thing of blue eyes and pale gold hair. It was a thing of fire and flame and fighting.

Fighting! That was it. With your back to the wall—and winning!

For some day he meant to win Jane. Did she think she could be in the world and not be his? And if she loved strength she should have it. He bent his head in his hands—his hands clasped tensely. There was a prayer in his heart. His whole being ached with the agony of his effort.

"Oh, God, let me fight and win. Bring me back to the full measure of a man."

Again he opened the book. Bits of printed verse dropped out of it. Jane had sent him this, "*One who never turned his back, but marched breast-forward.*"

Well, he had turned his back. That day in the snow. The thought gripped him. Made him white and sick. He stood up, praying again in an agony of mind, "Bring me back."

He opened the book and read of Jane, and of himself as he had once been. He skipped the record of his college days, except where he found such reference as this: "Little Jane is growing up. She met me at the station and held out her hand to me. I used always to kiss her, but this time I didn't dare. She was different somehow, but some day I'll kiss her."

And this: "Jane is rather a darling. But I am beginning to believe that I like 'em fair." That was when he had a terrible crush on Florence Preston, whose coloring was blue and gold. But it hadn't lasted, and he had come back to Jane with a sense of refreshment.

He found at last the pages given over to those first days after he had been admitted to the Washington bar, and had hung out his shingle.

"Sat at my desk all the morning. Great bluff. One client received with great effect of busy-ness. Had lunch with a lot of fellows—pancakes and sausages—ate an armful. Tea with three débutantes at the Shoreham—peaches. Dance at the Oakleys' in Georgetown. Corking time. One deadly moment when the butler took my overcoat. Poor people ought not to dance where there are butlers."

Remembering that incident, he leaned back in his chair and laughed. The Oakleys had all the money in the world, and a background of aristocracy. Evans' overcoat was rusty and shiny at the elbows. The butler, a recent importation from London, had been imposing in knee-breeches and many buttons. His manner had been perfect, but Evans had been aware of the servant's scorn of rustiness and shininess. Then his own good sense had come to the rescue, and he had gone in and had danced with as light heels as the rest of them.

He found more than one reference to his poverty. "I shall have to stop eating, or I can't wear my evening clothes. And I can't afford new ones. Jane says she hates to have me lose weight—that I look big and beautiful now like Michelangelo's David at the Corcoran. I don't know whether she is in earnest. One never knows. Her eyes never tell."

And again: "If I had money enough, I'd ask Jane to marry me. But I can't pay for Huyler's and matinée tickets. And anyhow, I'm sure she wouldn't have me. Not right off the bat. We're made for each other all right. And some day, if she doesn't know it, I'll make her."

There were spring days with Jane. "Gee, but it's good to be alive. Jane and I walked down to the glen this morning. Picked wild flowers, dogtooth violets, hepatica, anemones; and we sang—with nobody to hear us. I let out my voice—in

the Toreador's song, and Jane sat there and looked and listened, and said when I had finished, 'It's like the opera, Evans.' I believe she meant it, and she didn't want me to stop.... I felt pretty fine to have her there, liking it.... Oh, she's a darling. I wanted to tell her, but I didn't."

Autumn came: "Jane and I went to-day to gather fox grapes. Mother is making jelly and so is Jane. The vines were a great tangle. Shut in among them we seemed a thousand miles away from the world. Jane made herself a wreath of grape leaves, and looked like a nymph of the woods. I told her so and she gazed at me with those great gray eyes of hers and said, 'Evans, when the gods were young they must have lived like this—with grapes for their food, and the birds to sing for them, and the little wild things of the wood for company. It would be heavenly, wouldn't it?' She's a queer kid. Life with her wouldn't be humdrum. She's so intensely herself."

"We talked a bit about the war. I told her I should go if France needed me. I am not going to wait until this country gets into it. We owe a debt to France...."

He stopped there, and closed the book. He did not care to read farther. Oh, his debt to France had been paid. And after that day with Jane among the tangled vines things had moved faster—and faster.

He didn't want to think of it....

a sparkling array of modern things, diamonds in platinum—long pendants of jade and jet—opals dripping like liquid fire along slender chains.

She hung over them.

"Which do you like best?" he asked.

"The pearls?"

He was doubtful. "Not the white ones. These——" he picked up a pair of sapphires set in seed pearls—rather barbaric things that hung down for an inch or more. "They'll suit your style. Have you ever worn earrings?"

"No."

"Try them."

He helped her to adjust them—and his hand touched her smooth warm cheek. He was conscious of her closeness, but gave no sign.

There was a little mirror above the mantel. "Look at yourself," he said.

She tilted her head so that the jewels shook. The blue lights of the stones made her skin incandescent.

Frederick surveyed her critically. "You ought

to have a more sophisticated gown. Silver brocade with a wisp of a train."

"It changes me, doesn't it? I am not sure that I like them."

"I do. Edith has always wanted those earrings. But I won't let her have them. I am saving them for—my wife."

"You ought to have wives to wear them—like Solomon."

"Do you mean that you are recommending it?"

"Of course not. Only one woman couldn't ever wear them all, could she?"

"She might." Again he was pleased by her lack of self-consciousness. What a joy she was after Adelaide.

As if the name had brought her, a voice spoke from the door. "I wouldn't let Waldron announce me, Ricky; may I come in?"

She stopped as she saw Jane. "Oh, you're not alone?"

"This is Miss Barnes, Adelaide. I think you met her brother to-day at luncheon. Edith telephoned that you and Eloise had found her."

"That's what I came about, to warn you. Eloise has the reporters on her trail. She'll be over in a minute. But the harm will be done, I am afraid, before you can stop her."

"Oh, I'm resigned. Edith's coming back to-night. Miss Barnes' brother is bringing her."

"Really?" Adelaide Laramore was appraising

Jane. A shabby child. From the threshold she had had a moment of jealousy. But the moment was past. Frederick was extremely fastidious. He adored beauty and this Barnes child was not beautiful.

What Mrs. Laramore failed to see was that Jane's beauty was of a very special kind. It was not standardized. It was not marcelled and cold-creamed, and rouged and powdered. But it had to do with lighted-up eyes, with youth and a free spirit. And it was these things in her which had attracted Frederick.

Jane was unfastening the earrings. "Aren't they heavenly, Mrs. Laramore?"

"The sapphires?" Mrs. Laramore sat down on the couch. Her evening wrap slipped back, showing her white neck. Her fair hair was swept up from her forehead. She had a long face, with pink cheeks and pencilled eyebrows. She was like a portrait on porcelain, and she knew it, and emphasized the effect. "The sapphires? Yes. They're the choice of the lot."

She went on to speak of Eloise. "She is simply hopeless. She has told the most hectic tales and all the papers have sent men out to the Inn."

"Well, they escaped. They started early and have been hung up at Alexandria."

"Eloise and Benny and the Captain dined with me. She was still telephoning when I left. I told her that I did not sanction it, and that I should come straight over and tell you. But she laughed and said she didn't care. That she thought it was great fun and that you were a good sport."

"I shan't see her," shortly; "she ought to know better. Setting reporters on Edith like a pack of wolves."

"I told her how you would feel," Adelaide reiterated.

"I should see her if I were you, Mr. Towne," said a crisp, young voice.

Adelaide turned with a gasp. With her slippered feet crossed in front of her, Jane looked like a child. For the first time Mrs. Laramore got a good view of those candid gray eyes. They had a queer effect on her. Eyes like that were most uncommon. Fearless. The girl was not afraid of Frederick. She was not afraid of anyone.

"Why should I see her?" Frederick demanded.

"Won't it just add to her sense of melodrama if you don't? And why should you care? Your niece is coming home. And that's the end of it."

"You mean," Frederick demanded, "that I am to carry it off with an air?"

Jane nodded. "Make comedy of it instead of tragedy."

Adelaide slipping out of her wrap was revealed as elegant and distinguished in silver and black.

"May I have a cigarette, Ricky, to settle my nerves? Eloise is tremendously upsetting." Adelaide was plaintive.

Jane watched her with lively curiosity. The women she knew did not smoke. Baldy's flappers did, but they were abnormal and of a new generation. Mrs. Laramore was old enough to be Jane's mother, and Jane had a feeling ... that mothers ... shouldn't smoke....

But none the less, Adelaide Laramore and her exotic ways were amusing. She had a brittle and artificial look, like the Manchu lady in the Museum, or something in wax.

Jane was brought back from her meditation by the riotous entrance of Eloise and the two men.

"I knew Adelaide was telling tales."

"I told you I was coming, Eloise."

Eloise stared at Jane when Frederick presented her. "You look like your brother. Twins?"

"No." Jane decided that she liked Miss Harper better than she did Mrs. Laramore—which wasn't saying—much....

"The reporters are on their way to Alexandria—full cry." Eloise all in emerald green, with her red hair in a classic coiffure, was like some radiant witch, exultant of evil. "You mustn't scold me, Frederick. It was terribly exciting to tell them, and I adore excitement."

"They aren't there."

"Where are they?"

Frederick chanted composedly, "We three know ... but we will never tell...."

"Adelaide will, when I get her alone."

"I will not."

"Then Miss Barnes will. Do you know how young you look, Miss Barnes? I feel as if you'd tell me anything for a stick of candy."

They roared at that. And Jane said, "Nobody ever made me do anything I didn't want to do."

And now Benny and the Captain looked at her, and looked again. What a voice the child had, and eyes!

Eloise, on the couch, hugged her knees and surveyed her gold slippers. "They are putting my picture in the paper and Adelaide's. They saw one on my desk——"

Mrs. Laramore cried out, "Benny, why did you let her do it?" and there was a great uproar—in which Eloise could be heard saying:

"And they are going to have a picture of the Inn, and one of your brother if they can get it, Miss Barnes."

Jane began to feel uncomfortable. She was, she told herself, as much out of place as a pussy-cat in a Zoo. These women and these men reminded her somehow of the great sleek animals who snarled at each other in the Rock Creek cages. Frederick did not snarl. But she had a feeling he might if Eloise kept at him much longer.

It was in the midst of the hubbub that Edith entered. She walked in among them as composedly as she had faced them at the Inn.

"Hello," she said, "you sound like a jazz band."

She went straight up to Frederick and kissed him. "I suppose Eloise is shouting the news to the world." She tucked her hand in his arm. "There are more than a million reporters outside. Mr. Barnes is keeping them at bay."

"Where did they find you?"

"Heard of us, I suppose, at the Alexandria hotel. We didn't realize it until we reached here, and then they piled out and began to ask questions."

Frederick lifted her hand from his arm. "I'll go and send them away."

Eloise jumped up. "I'll go with you."

And then Frederick snarled, "Stay here."

But neither of them went, for Baldy entered, head cocked, eyes alight— Jane knew the signs.

"They've gone," he said. "I told you I'd get rid of them, Miss Towne."

He nodded to them all. Absolutely at his ease, lifted above them all by the exaltation of his mood. Finer, Jane told herself, than any of them—his beautiful youth against their world-weariness.

Edith was smiling at Jane. "I knew you at once. You are like your brother."

They were alike. A striking pair as they stood together. "It is because of Mr. Barnes and his sister that we got in touch with Edith," Frederick explained. He had regained his genial manner.

"Oh, really." Adelaide knew that she and her friends ought to go at once. Edith looked tired, and Eloise at moments like this was impossible.

But she hated to leave anyone else in the field. "Can't I give you a lift?" she asked Jane, sweetly, "you and your brother."

But it was Frederick who answered. "Miss Barnes lives at Sherwood Park. Briggs will take her out."

So Adelaide went away, and Eloise and the two men, and Edith turned to her uncle and said, "I'm sorry."

Her face was white and her eyes were shining, and all of a sudden she reached up her arms and put them about his neck and sobbed as if her heart would break.

And then, and not until then, little Jane knew that Edith was not like one of the animals at the Zoo.

CHAPTER XIII
JANE POURS TEA

In Jane's next letter to Judy she told her how the evening with the Townes had ended.

"Edith insisted that I should stay all night. She's a perfect darling, so absolutely and utterly exquisite, and yet so human. She and her uncle simply can't look at things from the same angle. And they are both to blame. Anything sets them off,—you should have seen them—like people in a play.

"I slept in the spare room—and well, I lay awake half the night looking at it, and admiring myself in one of Edith's nighties! I never saw such underthings, Judy! For a princess! Her room is all rose and silver and ivory, and the room I slept in is in pale yellow—with a canopy to my bed of gold brocade.

"Edith and I had breakfast together. Everything brought up on a tray and set in her little sitting-room, and we wore lace caps and breakfast coats, and looked—superlative! Edith is the most beautiful person—like one of the Viking women—with her hair in thick fair braids. I told her that, and she laughed. 'What a pair of poets you are,' she said, 'you and your brother.'

"It was good to hear her laugh. She cried dreadfully the night before. Coming back was

hard for her—and then Mr. Towne got on her nerves. They both wanted me to stay, and Baldy stayed, too, and I know his head bumped the clouds. And this morning on his way to the office, he bought a bunch of heliotrope for Edith and sent it up to her.

"The trouble with Edith is that her life hasn't been *real*, Judy. Not in the way that your life and mine and Baldy's is real. She has never had any work to do, and nothing has ever depended upon her. Think of it. There's no reason why she can't stay in bed all day if she wants to. And she can gratify any mood of the moment. The consequence is that half the time she is bored stiff. She says that was the reason she became engaged to Delafield Simms. Anything for a change.

"It looks as if she and I were going to be frightfully friendly. She told me that she wants me for a friend. That Eloise Harper and her kind are horrible to her after the things that have happened.

"To-morrow afternoon she and her uncle are coming out here to tea, and I'm going to have the Follettes over. Mrs. Follette will love it. But Evans won't. He doesn't like Mr. Towne.

"And now, my dearest-dear, I am worried about that hint in your last letter that you are not well. Take care of yourself, and remember I have only one precious sister, and the kiddies have only one mother. We need you in our young lives, and you mustn't work too hard."

When she had written the last line, Jane sat very still at her desk. She was thinking of Evans. She hadn't seen him for three days. Not since the Sunday night she had gone to the Townes. That

night in the fog had impressed her strangely. She had felt for Evans something that had nothing to do with admiration for him nor respect nor charm. His weakness had drawn her to him, as a mother might be drawn to a child. His struggle was, she felt, something which she must share. Not as his wife! No.... That kind of love was different. If only he would let her be his little sister, Jane.

He had not even called her up. When she had invited him and his mother to tea with the Townes, Mrs. Follette had answered, and had accepted for both of them. Evans, she said, was in Washington, and would be out on the late train.

When he arrived ahead of the others on the afternoon of her tea, Jane said, "Where have you been? Do you know it has been four days since we've seen each other?"

"Weren't you glad to get rid of me? I've thought of you every minute." He dropped into a seat beside her.

She was gazing at him with lively curiosity. "How nice you look."

"New suit. Like it?"

"Yes. And you act as if somebody had left you a million dollars."

"Wish he had. I bought this outfit with a first edition 'Alice in Wonderland,'" he laughed and explained. "I've been getting rid of some of our rare books. I feel plutocratic in consequence.

Five hundred dollars, if you please, for that old Hogarth, with the scathing Ruskin inscription. And I'm going to open an office, Jane."

"In Washington?"

"On Connecticut Avenue. Same building, same room, where I started."

"Evans, how splendid!"

"Yes. You did it, Jane."

"I? How?"

"The night of the fog. I never realized before what a walking-stick I've been—leaning on you. Henceforth you're the Lady of the Lantern. It won't be so fatiguing."

He was smiling at her, and she smiled back. Yet quite strangely and inconsistently, she felt as if in changing his attitude towards her, he had robbed her of some privilege. "I didn't mind being a walking-stick."

"Well, I minded. After this I'll walk alone. And I'm going to work hard, and play around a bit. Will you have tea with me to-morrow, Jane? At the Willard? To celebrate my first tottering steps."

She agreed, eagerly. "It will be like old times."

"Minus a lot, old lady."

That was the way he had talked to her years ago. The plaintive note was gone.

"Take the three-thirty train and I'll meet you. I'll pay for the taxi with what's left of 'Alice.'"

"Don't be too extravagant."

"Nothing is too good for you, Jane. I can't say it as I want to say it, but you'll never know what you seemed to me on Sunday as you came through the mist."

His voice shook a little, but he recovered himself in a moment. "Here come the Townes." He rose as Edith entered with young Baldwin.

After that Evans followed Baldy's lead as a dispenser of hospitality. The two of them passed cups, passed thin bread and butter, passed little cakes, passed lemon and cream and sugar, flung conversational balls as light as feathers into the air, were, as Baldy would have expressed it, "the life of the party."

"Something must have gone to Casabianca's head," Frederick Towne remarked to Jane. "Have you ever seen him like this?"

"Years ago. He was tremendously attractive."

"Do you find him attractive now?" with a touch of annoyance.

"I find him—wonderful"—her tone was defiant—"and I've known him all my life."

"If you had known me all your life would you call me wonderful?"

She looked at him from behind her battlements of silver. "How do I know? People have to prove themselves."

Dr. Hallam had driven Mrs. Follette over. He rarely did social stunts, but he liked Jane. And

he had been interested enough in Evans to want to glimpse him in his new rôle.

Strolling up to the tea-table, he was aware at once of a situation which might make for comedy, or indeed for tragedy. It was evident that Towne was much attracted to little Jane Barnes. If Jane reciprocated, what of young Follette?

Hallam knew Towne, and himself a bachelor of quite another type, without vanity where women were concerned, he had a feeling of contempt for a man whose reputation was linked with a long line of much-talked about ladies. And now little Jane was the reigning queen. He didn't like the idea of her youth, and Towne's late forties.

"I saw Mrs. Laramore yesterday," he said, abruptly, "lovely as ever——"

"Yes, of course." Towne wished that Hallam wouldn't talk about Adelaide. He wished that all of the others would go away and leave him alone with Jane.

"Mrs. Laramore," said Jane unexpectedly, "makes me think of the lady of Shallott. I don't know why. But I do. I have really never seen such a beautiful woman. But she doesn't seem real. I have a feeling that if anything hit her, she'd break like china."

They laughed at her, and Edith said, "Adelaide will never break. She'll melt. She's as soft as wax." Then pigeonholing Mrs. Laramore for more vital matters. "Uncle Fred, I am going out to Baldy's studio; he's painting Jane."

Frederick was at once interested. "Her portrait?"

"No. A sketch for a magazine competition," Baldy explained.

"May I see it?"

Baldy, yearning for solitude and Edith, gave reluctant consent. "Come on, everybody."

So everybody, including Dr. Hallam and Mrs. Follette, made their way to the garage.

Edith and young Baldwin arrived first. "And this is where you work," she said, softly.

"Yes. Look here, will you sit here so that I can feast my eyes on you? I've dreamed of you in that chair—in classic costume. Do you know that you were made for a goddess?"

"I know that you are a romantic boy."

Yet as she sat in the garden seat which he had transformed into a throne for her by throwing a rug over it and setting it up above the others on a small platform, she sighed a little.

Here in this small room he spent his spare moments. He looked out through that small square window on the rains and snow, and the young green of the spring—and he tried to paint his dreams, yet was held back because he was chained to the galley of a Government job. And if he was not chained, what might he not do? If someone waved a wand and set him free? And if the someone who

waved a wand loved him? Inspired him? Might he not give to the world some day a masterpiece? Well, why not? She found herself thrilling with the thought. To be a torch and light the way!

"How old are you?" she asked him.

"Twenty-five."

"I don't believe it. I'm twenty-two, and I feel a thousand years older than you."

"You will always be—ageless."

She laughed. "How old is Jane?"

"Twenty. Yet people take us for twins."

"She doesn't look it and neither do you."

The others came in and Edith went back to her thoughts. He wasn't too young. She was glad of that....

The sketch of Jane was on an easel. There she stood, a slender figure in her lilac frock—bobbed black hair, lighted-up eyes—the lifted basket with its burden of gold and purple and green!

Towne stood back and looked at it. Jane at his side said, "That's some of the fruit you sent."

"Really?" Frederick had no eyes for anything but Jane, in her lilac frock. Jove, but the boy had caught the spirit of her!

He turned to Baldy. "It is most unusual. And I want it."

"Sorry," said Baldy, crisply. "I am sending it off to-morrow."

"How much is the prize?"

"Two thousand dollars."

"I will write a check for that amount if you will let me have this."

"I am afraid I can't, Mr. Towne."

"Why not?"

"Well, I feel this way about it. It isn't worth two thousand dollars. But if I win the prize it may be worth that to the magazine—the advertising and all that."

"Isn't that splitting hairs?"

"Perhaps, but it's the way I feel."

"But if you don't win the prize you won't have anything."

"No."

"And you'll be out two thousand dollars." The lion in the Zoo was snarling.

And above him, breathing an upper air, was this young eagle. "I'll be glad to give the sketch to you if it comes back," said Baldy, coolly, "but I rather think it will stick."

It was, in a way, a dreadful moment for Towne. There was young Baldwin sitting on the edge of the table, swinging a leg, debonair, defiant. And Edith laughing in her sleeve. Frederick knew that she was laughing. He was as red as a turkey cock.

It was Jane who saved him from apoplexy. She was really inordinately proud of Baldy, but she knew the dangers of his mood. And she had her duties as hostess.

"Baldy wants to see himself on the news stands,"
she said, soothingly; "don't deprive him of that pleasure, Mr. Towne."

"Nothing of the kind, Jane," exclaimed her brother.

"Baldy, I won't quarrel with you before people. We must reserve that pleasure until we are alone."

"I'm not quarrelling."

Jane held up a protesting hand. "Oh, let's run away from him, Mr. Towne. When he begins like that, there's no end to it."

She carried Frederick back to the house, and Evans, looking after them, said vindictively to Hallam, "Old Midas got his that time."

Dr. Hallam chuckled. "You don't hate him, do you? Evans, don't let him have Jane. He isn't worth it."

"Neither am I," said Evans. "But I would know better how to make her happy."

Back once more in the bright little living-room, Towne said to Jane, "May I have another cup of tea?"

"It's cold."

"I don't care. I like to see you pour it with your lovely hands."

She spread her hands out on the shining mahogany of the tea-table. "Are they lovely? Nobody ever told me."

His hand went over hers. "The loveliest in the world."

She sat there in a moment's breathless silence.

Then she drew her hands away. Touched a little bell. "I'll have Sophy bring us some hot water."

Sophy came and went. Jane poured hot tea with flushed cheeks.

He took the cup when she handed it to him. "Dear child, you're not offended?"

"I'm not a child, Mr. Towne." Her lashes were lowered, her cheeks flushed.

He put his cup down and leaned towards her. "You are more than a child to me—a beloved woman. Jane, you needn't be afraid of me.... I want you for my wife!"

Her astonished eyes met his. "But we haven't known each other a week."

"I couldn't love you more if I had known you a thousand years."

"Mr. Towne—please." He was very close to her.

"Kiss me, Jane."

She held her slender figure away from him. "You must not."

"I must."

"No, really.... Please," she was breathing quickly. "Please." She was on her feet, the tea-table between them.

He saw his mistake. "Forgive me."

Her candid eyes met his. "Mr. Towne, would you have acted like this ... with Edith's friends?"

Edith's friends! The child's innocence! Adelaide's kisses went for a song. Eloise frankly offered

hers. Edith was saved by only some inner grace.

"Jane, they are not worth your little finger. I put you above all. On a pedestal. Honestly. And I want you to marry me."

"But I don't love you."

"I'll make you. I have everything to give you."

Had he? What of Robin Hood and Galahad? What of youth and youth's audacity, high resolves, flaming dreams?

She felt something of this subconsciously. But she would not have been a feminine creature had she not felt the flattery of his pursuit.

"Jane, I'll make life a fairy tale. We'll travel everywhere. Sail strange seas. Wouldn't you love it—all those countries you have never seen—and just the two of us? And all the places you have read about? And when we come home I'll build you a house—wherever you say—with a great garden."

He was eloquent, and the things he promised were woven into the woof of all her girlish imaginings.

"I ought not to listen," she said, tremulously.

But he knew that she had listened. He was wise enough to leave it—there.

He rose as he heard the others coming back. "Will you ride with me to-morrow afternoon? Don't be afraid of me. I'll promise to be good."

"Sorry. I'm to have tea in town with Evans."

"Can't you break the engagement?"

"I don't break engagements." The cock of her head was like Baldy's.

"Oh, you don't. Some day you'll be breaking them for me." But he liked her independence. It promised much that would be stimulating. And he would always be the Conqueror. He liked to think that he would be—the Conqueror.

So he went away secure in the thought of Jane's final surrender. There was everything in it for her, and the child must see it. Her hesitation was natural. She couldn't, of course, come at the first crook of his finger. But she would come.

CHAPTER XIV
A TELEGRAM

"Janey——!"

"Yes, Baldy." Jane sat up in bed, dreams still in her eyes. She had been late in getting to sleep. There had been so much to think of—Frederick Towne's proposal—the startling change in Evans——

"It's a telegram. Open the door, dear."

She caught up her dressing-gown and wrapped it around her. "A telegram?" She was with him now in the hall. "Baldy, is it Judy?"

"Yes. She's ill. Asks if you can come on and look after the kiddies."

"Of course." She swayed a little. "Hold on to me a minute, Baldy. It takes my breath away."

"You mustn't be scared, old girl."

"I'll be all right in ... a minute...."

His arms were tight about her. "It seems as if I should go, too, Janey."

"But you can't. I'll get things ready and ride in with you in the morning. I'll pack my trunk if you'll bring it down from the attic. I can sleep on the train to-morrow."

And when he had brought it she made him go back to bed. The house was very still. Merrymaid,

waked by the unusual excitement, came up-stairs and sat, round-eyed, by Jane, watching her fold her scant wardrobe and purring a song of consolation. Jane found time now and then to stop and smooth the sleek head, and once she picked Merrymaid up in her arms, and the tears dripped on the old cat's fur.

Philomel sang very early the next morning. It was Baldy who made the coffee, and who telephoned Sophy and the Follettes. Mrs. Follette insisted that Baldy should stay at Castle Manor in Jane's absence. "It will do Evans good, and we'd love to have him."

So that was settled. And Evans came over while the young people were breakfasting.

"Don't worry about anything," he said. "Baldy and I will look after the chickens—and take the little cats over to Castle Manor. I'll wrap them all in cotton wool rather than have anything happen to them. So don't worry."

The thing she worried about was Judy. "She told me in one of her letters that she wasn't well."

Baldy went to bring his car around, and Evans stood with his hand on the back of Jane's chair, looking down at her. "You'll write to me, Jane?"

"Oh, of course."

He shifted his hand from the chair back to her shoulder. "Dear little girl, if my blundering prayers will help you any—you'll have them."

She turned in her chair and looked up at him.

She could not speak. Their eyes met, and once more Jane had that breathless sense of fluttering wings within her that lifted to the sun.

Then Baldy was back, and the bags were ready, and there was just that last hand-clasp. "God bless you, Jane...."

Frederick Towne was at the train. He had been dismayed at the news of Jane's departure. "Do you mean that you are going to stay indefinitely?" he had asked over the wire.

"I shall stay as long as Judy needs me."

Frederick had flowers for her, books and a big box of sweets. People in the Pullman stared at Jane in the midst of all her magnificence. They stared too, at Towne, and at Briggs, who rushed in at the last moment with more books from Brentano.

Edith and Baldy were on the platform. Edith had come down with Towne. So Frederick, alone with Jane, said, "I want you to think of the things we talked about yesterday——"

"Please, not now. Oh, I'm afraid——"

"Of me? You mustn't be."

"Not of you—of everything—Life."

He took her hand and held it. "Is there anything else I can do for you? Everything I have is—yours, you know—if you want it."

He had to leave her then, with a final close clasp of the hand. She saw him presently standing beside Baldy on the station platform—the center of the eyes of everybody—the great Frederick Towne!

As the city slipped away and she leaned her head against the cushions and looked out at the flying fields—it seemed a stupendous thing that a man like Towne should have laid his fortune at her feet. Yet she had no sense of exhilaration. She liked the things he had to offer—yearned for them—but she did not want him at her side.

In her sorrow her heart turned to the boy who had stumbled over the words, "If my blundering prayers will help you——"

She found herself sobbing—the first tears she had shed since the arrival of the telegram.

When she reached Chicago, her brother-in-law, Bob Heming, met her. "Judy's holding her own," he said, as he kissed her. "It was no end good of you to come, Janey."

"Have you a nurse?"

"Two. Day nurse and night nurse. And a maid. Judy is nearly frantic about the expense. It isn't good for her, either, to worry. That's half the trouble. I tried to make her get help, but she wouldn't. But I blame myself that I didn't insist."

"Don't blame yourself, Bob. Judy wouldn't. She told me she could get along. And when Judy decides a thing, no one can change her."

"Well, times have been hard. And business bad. And Judy knew it. She's such a good sport."

They were in a taxi, so when tears came into

Heming's eyes, he made no effort to conceal them.

"I'm just about all in. You can't understand how much it means to me to have you here."

"And now that I am here," said Jane, with a gallantry born of his need of her, "things are going to be better."

The apartment was simply furnished and bore the stamp of Judy's good taste. A friend had taken the children out to ride, so the rooms were very quiet as Jane went through them.

Judy in bed was white and thin, and Jane wanted to weep over her, but she didn't. "You blessed old girl," she said, "you're going to get well right away."

"The doctor thinks I may have to have an operation. That's why I felt I must wire you." Judy was anxious. "I couldn't leave the babies with strangers. And it was so important that Bob should be at his work."

"Of course," said Jane; "do you think anything would have made me stay away?"

Judy gave a quick sigh of relief. How heavenly to have Janey! And what a dear she was with her air of conquering the world. Jane had always been like that—with that conquering air. It cheered one just to look at her.

The babies, arriving presently in a rollicking state of excitement over the advent of Auntie Jane, showed themselves delightful and adoring.

"Junior," said Jane, "are you glad I'm here?"

"Did you bring me anything?"

"Something—wonderful——"

"What?"

She opened her bag, and produced Towne's box of sweets. "May I give him a chocolate, Judy?"

"One little one, and just a taste for baby. Jane, where did you get that gorgeous box?"

"Frederick Towne."

"Really? My dear, your letters have been tremendously interesting. Haven't they, Bob?"

Her husband nodded. He was sitting by the bedside holding her hand. "Towne's a pretty big man."

In a moment of vaingloriousness, Jane wanted to say to them, "What do you think of your ugly duckling? Mr. Towne wants her to be his wife." But of course she didn't. Not before Bob. She'd tell Judy, later, of course.

The nurse came in then, and Jane went with Bob and the babies to the dining-room.

Junior over his bread and milk was frankly critical. "I didn't think you'd be so old. Mother said you'd play with me."

"I can play splendid games, Junior."

"Can you? What kind?"

"Well, there's one about a pussy-cat. And I'm the big cat and you're the little cat—and my name is Merrymaid."

"What is the little cat's name?"

"We'll have to find one. We can't just call him Kitty, can we?"

"Yes, we can. My name's Kitty, and your name is Merrymaid, and— what do we do, Aunt Janey?"

"We drink milk," promptly.

"An' what else?"

"We play with balls—I'll show you after dinner."

"I want you to show me now."

His father interposed. "Aunt Janey's tired. Wait till she's had her dinner."

Junior drank his milk thoughtfully. "I'm a kitty—and you're a cat. Why don't you drink milk, too, Aunt Janey?"

Jane smiled at Bob. "Do I have to answer all his questions?"

"Whether you do or not, he'll keep on asking."

But after dinner, Junior went to sleep in Jane's arms, having been regaled on a rapturous diet of "The Three Bears" and "The Little Red Hen."

"They're such beauties, Judy," said Jane, as she went back to her sister. "But they don't look like any of the Barnes."

"No, they're like Bob, with their white skins and fair hair. I wanted one of them to have our coloring. Do you know how particularly lovely you are getting to be, Janey?"

"Judy, I'm not."

"Yes, you are. And none of us thought it. And so Mr. Towne wants to marry you?"

"How do you know?"

"It is in your eyes, dear, and in the cock of your head. You and Baldy always look that way when something thrilling happens to you. You can't fool me."

"Well, I'm not in love with him. So that's that, Judy."

"But—it's a great opportunity, isn't it, Jane?"

"I suppose it is," slowly, "but I can't quite see it."

"Why not?"

"Well, he's too old for one thing."

"Only forty——? Rich men don't grow old. And he could give you everything—everything, Janey." Judy's voice rose a little. "Jane, you don't know what it means to want things for those you love and not be able to have them. Bob did very well until the slump in business. But since the babies came—I have worked until—well, until it seemed as if I couldn't stand it. Bob's such a darling. I wouldn't change *anything*. I'd marry him over again to-morrow. But I do know this, that Frederick Towne could make life lovely for you, and perhaps you won't get another chance to marry a man like that."

"Oh, don't—don't." It seemed dreadful to Jane to have Judy talk that way, as if life had in some way failed her. Life mustn't fail, and it wouldn't if one had courage. Judy was sick, and things didn't look straight.

"See here, old dear," Jane said, "go to sleep and stop thinking about how to make ends meet. That's my job, and I'll do it."

And Judy slipping away into refreshing slumber had that vision before her of Jane's young strength—of Jane's gay young voice like the sound of silver trumpets....

CHAPTER XV
EVANS PLAYS THE GAME

Life for Evans Follette after Jane went away became a sort of game in which he played, as he told himself grimly, a Jekyll and Hyde part. Two men warred constantly within him. There was that scarecrow self which nursed mysterious fears, a gaunt gray-haired self, The Man Who Had Come Back From the War. And there was that other, shadowy, elusive, The Boy Who Once Had Been. And it was the Boy who took on gradually shape and substance fighting for place with the dark giant who held desperately to his own.

Yet the Boy had weapons, faith and hope. The little diary became in a sense a sacred book. Within its pages was imprisoned something that beat with frantic wings to be free. Evans, shrinking from the program which he compelled himself to follow, was faced with things like this. "Gee, I wish the days were longer. I'd like to dance through forty-eight hours at a stretch. Jane is getting to be some little dancer. I taught her the new steps to-night. She's as graceful as a willow wand."

Well, a man with a limp couldn't dance. Or could he?

A Thomas Jefferson autograph went therefore to pay for twenty dancing lessons. Would the great Democrat turn in his grave? Yet what were ink scratches made by a dead hand as against all the meanings of love and life?

Evans bought a phonograph, and new records. He practised at all hours, to the great edification of old Mary, who washed dishes and scrubbed floors in syncopated ecstasies.

He took Baldy and Edith to tea at the big hotels, and danced with Edith. He apologized, but kept at it. "I'm out of practice."

Edith was sympathetic and interested. She invited the two boys to her home, where there was a music room with a magical floor. Sometimes the three of them were alone, and sometimes Towne came in and danced too, and Adelaide Laramore and Eloise Harper.

Towne danced extremely well. In spite of his avoirdupois he was light on his feet. He exercised constantly. He felt that if he lost his waist line all would be over. He could not, however, always control his appetite. Hence the sugar in his tea, and other indulgences.

Baldy wrote to Jane of their afternoon frivols.

"You should see us! Eloise Harper dancing with Evans, and old Towne and his Adelaide! And Edith and I! We're a pretty pair, if I do say it. We miss you, and always wish you were with us. Sometimes it seems almost heartless to do things

that you can't share. But it's doing a lot for Evans. Queer thing, the poor old chap goes at it as if his life depended upon it.

"We are invited to dine with the Townes on Christmas Eve. Some class, what? By we, I mean myself and the Follettes. Edith and Mrs. Follette see a lot of each other, and Mrs. Follette is tickled pink! You know how she loves that sort of thing—Society with a big S.

"There will be just our crowd and Mrs. Laramore for dinner, and after that a big costume ball.

"I shall go as a page in red. And Evans will be a monk and sing Christmas carols. Edith Towne is crazy about his voice. He sat down at the piano one day in the music room, and she heard him. Jane, his voice is wonderful—it always was, you know, but we haven't heard it lately. Poor old chap—he seems to be picking up. Edith says it makes her want to cry to see him, but she's helping all she can.

"Oh, she's a dear and a darling, Janey. And I don't know what I am going to do about it. I have nothing to offer her. But at least I can worship ... I shan't look beyond that....

"And now, little old thing, take care of yourself, and don't think we're playing around and forgetting you, for we're not. Even Merrymaid and the kit-cat look pensive when your name is mentioned. They share the library hearth with Rusty. The old fellow is on his feet now, not much the worse for his accident.

"Love to Judy and Bob, and the kiddies. And a kiss or two for my own Janey."

Jane, having read the letter, laid it down with a sense of utter forlornness. Evans and Eloise Harper! Towne and his Adelaide! A Christmas costume ball! Evans singing for Edith Towne!

Evans' own letters told her little. They were dear letters, giving her news of Sherwood, full of kindness and sympathy, full indeed of a certain spiritual strength—that helped her in the heavy days. But he had sketched very lightly his own activities.—He had perhaps hesitated to let her know that he could be happy without her.

But Evans was not happy. He did the things he had mapped out for himself, but he could not do them light-heartedly as the Boy had done. For how could he be light-hearted with Jane away? He had moments of loneliness so intense that they almost submerged him. He came therefore upon one entry in his diary with eagerness.

"Had a day with the Boy Scouts. Hiked up through Montgomery County. Caught some little shiners in the creek and cooked them. Grapes thick in the Glen. The boys were like small Bacchuses, and draped themselves in fruit and leaves. They are fine fellows. I have no patience with people who look upon boys as nothing but small animals. Why their dreams! And shy about them! Now and then they open their hearts to me— and I can see the fineness that's under the outer crust. They lie under the trees with me, and we talk as we follow the road."

Boys——! That was it! He'd get in touch with

them again. And he did. There were two, Sandy Stoddard and Arthur Lane, who came over and sat by the library fire with Rusty and the two cats, and popped corn, and wanted to hear about the war.

At first when they spoke of it, Evans would not talk—but a moment arrived when he found flaming words to show them how he felt about it.

"I know a lot of fellows," said Sandy Stoddard, "who say that America wouldn't have gone into it if she'd known a lot of things. And that most of the men who came back feel that they were just—fooled——"

"If they feel that way, they are fools themselves," said Evans, shortly.

"Well, they're all throwing bricks at us now," said Sandy. "France and Great Britain, and the rest of them. When you read the papers you feel as if America was pretty punk——"

"Sandy," said Evans, slowly, reaching for the right words because this boy must know the truth—"America is never punk. We're human, like the rest of the world. We're selfish like everybody else. But we're kind. And most of us still believe in God. I've gone through a lot," he was flushed with the sense of the intimacy of his confession; "you boys can't ever know what I've gone through unless you go through it some day yourselves. But every night I thank God on my knees that I was a part of a crusade that believed it was fighting for the right. Those of us who went in with that idea

came out of it with that idea. That's all I can say about it—and I'd do it again."

As he stood there on the hearth-rug, the boys gazed at him with awe in their eyes. They knew patriotic passion when they saw it, and here in this broken man was a dignity which seemed to make him a tower above them. They felt for the moment as if his head touched the stars.

"Don't misunderstand me," Evans continued; "war is hell. And most of us found horrors worse than any dreadful dream. But we learned one thing, that death isn't awful. It is kind and beneficent. And there's something beyond."

"Gee," said Sandy Stoddard, "I'm glad you said that."

But Arthur Lane did not speak. He saw Evans through a haze of hero-worship. He saw him, too, with a halo of martyrdom. The glass of the photograph on the mantel had been mended. There was the young soldier handsome and brave in his uniform. And here was his ghost—come back to say that it was all—worth while....

Association with these boys cleared up many things for Evans. They had ideals which must not be shattered. Not to their young eagerness must be brought the pessimism of a disordered mind—and tortured soul. They must have the truth. And the truth was this. That men who had laid down their lives to save others had seen an unforgetful vision. He wondered how many of his

comrades, even now, in the cynicism of after-war propaganda would sacrifice the memory of that high moment....

Besides the boys, Evans had another friend. He played a whimsical game with the scarecrow. He went often and leaned over the fence that shut in the frozen field. He hunted up new clothes and hung them on the shaking figure—an overcoat and a soft hat. It seemed a charitable thing to clothe him with warmth. In due time someone stole the overcoat, and Evans found the poor thing stripped. It gave him a sense of shock to find two crossed sticks where once had been the semblance of a man. But he tried again. This time with an old bathrobe and a disreputable cap. "It will keep you warm until spring, old chap...."

The scarecrow and his sartorial changes became a matter of much discussion among the negroes. Since Evans' visits were nocturnal, the whole thing had an effect of mystery until the bathrobe proclaimed its owner. "Mist' Evans done woh' dat e'vy day," old Mary told Mrs. Follette. "Whuffor he dress up dat ol' sca'crow in de fiel'?"

"What scarecrow?"

Old Mary explained, and that night Mrs. Follette said to her son, "The darkies are getting superstitions. Did you really do it?"

His somber eyes were lighted for a moment. "It's just a whim of mine, Mumsie. I had a sort of fellow feeling——"

"How queer!"

"Not as queer as you might think." He went back to his book. No one but Jane should know the truth.

And so he played the game. Working in his office, dancing with Edith and Baldy, chumming with the boys, dressing up the scarecrow. It seemed sometimes a desperate game—there were hours in which he wrestled with doubts. Could he ever get back? Could he? There were times when it seemed he could not. There were nights when he did not sleep. Hours that he spent on his knees....

So the December days sped, and it was just a week before Christmas that Evans read the following in his little book. "Dined with the Prestons. Told father's ham story.—Great hit. Potomac frozen over. Skated in the moonlight with Florence Preston.—Great stunt—home to hot chocolate."

Once more the Potomac was frozen over. Florence Preston was married. But he mustn't let the thing pass. The young boy Evans would have tingled with the thought of that frozen river.

It was after dinner, and Evans was in his room. He hunted up Baldy. "Look here, old chap, there's skating on the river. Can't we take Sandy and Arthur with us and have an hour or two of it? Your car will do the trick."

Baldy laid down his book. "I have no philanthropies on a night like this. Moonlight. I'll take you and the boys and then I'll go and get Edith Towne." He was on his feet. "I'll call her up now——"

The small boys were rapturous and riotous over the plan. When they reached the ice, and Evans' lame leg threatened to be a hindrance, the youngsters took him between them, and away they sailed in the miraculous world—three musketeers of good fellowship and fun.

Baldy having brought Edith, put on her skates, and they flew away like birds. She was all in warm white wool—with white furs, and Baldy wore a white sweater and cap. The silver of the night seemed to clothe them in shining armor.

Baldy said things to her that made her pulses beat. She found herself a little frightened.

"You're such a darling poet. But life isn't in the least what you think it."

"What do I think it?"

"Oh, all mountains and peaks and moonlight nights."

"Well, it can be——"

"Dear child, it can't. I have no illusions."

"You think you haven't."

It was late when at last they took off their skates and Edith invited them all to go home with her. "We'll have something hot. I'm as hungry as a dozen bears."

The boys giggled. "So am I," said Sandy Stoddard.

But Arthur said nothing. His eyes were occupied to the exclusion of his tongue. Edith looked to him like some angel straight from heaven. He had never seen anyone so particularly lovely.

So, packed in Baldy's Ford, they made the journey. The two small boys had an Arabian Nights' feeling as they were led through the great hall with its balconies, thence to the huge kitchen.

The servants had gone to bed, all except Waldron—who led the way, and offered his services.

"No, we'll do it ourselves, Waldron," Miss Towne told him. "Is Uncle Fred in?"

"No, Miss Towne."

"Well, if he comes, tell him where we are."

"Very good, Miss Towne," and Waldron backed out impressively, the round eyes of the little boys upon him.

Edith gave them the freedom of the amazing refrigerator, which was white as milk and as big as a house, and they brought forth with some hesitation viands which seemed as unreal as the rest of it—cold roast chickens with white frills on their legs, a plate of salad with patterns on top of it in red peppers and little green buttons which Evans said were capers— the remains of a glorified sort of Charlotte Russe—a castellated affair with candied fruits.

"Do they eat things like this every day?" Sandy asked Evans, with something like awe, "or am I dreamin'?"

Evans nodded. "Some feast, isn't it, old chap?" He was warmed by the radiance of the freckled boyish face.

Arthur Lane, always less talkative, had little to say. He was steeping himself in atmosphere. He had never been in a house like this. The kitchen with its panelled ceiling, its white enamel, its gleaming nickel, its firm, white painted furniture—its white and brown tiling. It was all as utterly fascinating as the things he read about in the fairy books.

"Now the kitchen," he said at last to Towne, "what's it so big for? Ain't there only three of them in the family?"

"Yes."

"Well, there are six of us at home, and you could put four of our kitchens into this. And that refrigerator—it's so big you could live in it. You know, Mr. Follette, it's bigger than our scout tents."

"Yes, it is," Evans smiled at him. "Well, when people have so much money, they think they need things."

"I'd like it." The boy was eager. "Wouldn't you?"

"I'm not sure."

"Gee—well, I am——" and young Arthur went over to thrash it out with Sandy.

Evans, left to himself, wondered. Did he want money? A great fortune? With Jane? The huge

silent house with all its servants? Jane, herself, trailing up the stairs in all the dazzling draperies imposed upon her by fashionable modistes? Jane, miles away from him at the end of that massive table in the great dining-room?

Were these his dreams? For Jane?

He knew they were not. When he thought of her, he thought of a little house. Of a living-room where a fire burned bright whose windows looked upon a little garden—crocuses and hyacinths in the spring, roses in June, snow in winter, with all the birds coming up for Jane to feed them. A library with books to the ceiling, and himself reading to Jane. A kitchen, a shining place, with a crisp maid to save Jane from drudgery. Two crisp maids, perhaps, some day, if there were kiddies.

He asked no more than that. Why, it was all the world for a man....

CHAPTER XVI
THE COSTUME BALL

So Christmas Eve came, and the costume ball at the Townes'. There were, as Baldy had told Jane, just six of them at dinner. Cousin Annabel was still in bed, and it was Adelaide Laramore who made the sixth. Edith had told Mrs. Follette frankly that she wished Adelaide had not been asked.

"But she fished for it. She always does. She flatters Uncle Fred and he falls for it."

Baldy brought Evans and Mrs. Follette in his little Ford. They found Mrs. Laramore and Frederick already in the drawing-room. Edith had not come down.

"She is always late," Frederick complained, "and she never apologizes."

Baldy, silken and slim, in his page's scarlet, stood in the hall and watched Edith descend the stairs. She seemed to emerge from the shadows of the upper balcony like a shaft of light. She was all in silvery green, her close-clinging robe girdled with pearls, her hair banded with mistletoe.

He met her half-way. "You shouldn't have worn it," he said at once.

"The mistletoe? Why not?"

"You will tempt all men to kiss you."

"Men must resist temptation."

"Well, queens command," he smiled at her, "and queens ask——"

She was doubtful of his meaning. "Do you think that I would ever ask for kisses?"

"You may. Some day."

Her blue eyes burned. "I think you don't quite know what you are saying."

"I do, dear lady. But we won't quarrel about it."

She switched to less dangerous topics. "I'm late for dinner. Is Uncle Fred roaring?"

"More or less. And Mrs. Laramore is purring."

They rather wickedly enjoyed their laugh at the expense of an older generation, and went in together to find Frederick icy with indignation.

Waldron announced dinner, and Frederick with Mrs. Follette on his arm preceded the others. Baldy and Edith came last.

"How many dances are you going to give me?"

"Not as many as I'd like. Being hostess, I shall have to divide myself among many."

"Cut yourself up into little stars as it were. Well, you know what Browning says of a star? 'Mine has opened its soul to me—therefore I love it'!"

His tone was light, but her heart missed a beat. There was something about this boy so utterly

engaging. He had set her on a pedestal, and he worshipped her. When she said that she was not worth worshipping, he told her, "You don't know——"

She was unusually silent during dinner. With Evans on one side of her and Baldy on the other she had little need to exert herself. Baldy was always adequate to any conversational tax, and Evans, in spite of his monk's habit, was not austere. He was, rather, like some attractive young friar drawn back for the moment to the world.

He showed himself a genial teller of tales—and capped each of Frederick's with one of his own. His mother was proud of him. She felt that life was taking on new aspects—this friendship with the Townes—her son's increasing strength and social ease—the lace gown which she wore and which had been bought with a Dickens' pamphlet. What more could she ask? She was serene and satisfied.

Adelaide, on the other side of Frederick Towne, was not serene and satisfied. She was looking particularly lovely with a star of diamonds in her hair and sheer draperies of rose and faintest green. "I am anything you wish to call me," she had said to Frederick when she came in—"an 'Evening Star' or 'In the Gloaming' or 'Afterglow.' Perhaps 'A Rose of Yesterday'——" she had put it rather pensively.

He had been gallant but uninspired. "You are too young to talk of yesterdays," he had said, but

his glance had held not the slightest hint of gallantry. She felt that she had, perhaps, been unwise to remind him of her age.

She was still more disturbed, when, towards the end of dinner, he rose and proposed a toast. "To little Jane Barnes, A Merry Christmas."

They all stood up. There was a second's silence. Evans drank as if he partook of a sacrament.

Then Edith said, "It seems almost heartless to be happy, doesn't it, when things are so hard for her?"

Adelaide interposed irrelevantly, "I should hate to spend Christmas in Chicago."

There was no response, so she turned to Frederick. "Couldn't Miss Barnes leave her sister for a few days?"

"No," he told her, "she couldn't."

She persisted, "I am sure you didn't want her to miss the ball."

"I did my best to get her here. Talked to her at long distance, but she couldn't see it."

"You are so good-hearted, Ricky."

Frederick could be cruel at moments, and her persistence was irritating. "Oh, look here, Adelaide, it wasn't entirely on her account. I want her here myself."

She sat motionless, her eyes on her plate. When she spoke again it was of other things. "Did you hear that Delafield is coming back?"

"Who told you?"

"Eloise Harper. Benny's sister saw Del at Miami. She is sure he is expecting to marry the other girl."

"Bad taste, I call it."

"Everybody is crazy to know who she is."

"Have they any idea?"

"No. Benny's sister said he talked quite frankly about getting married. But he wouldn't say a word about the woman."

"I hardly think he will find Edith heart-broken." Towne glanced across the table. Edith was not wearing the willow. No shadow marred her lovely countenance. Her eyes were clear and shining pools of sweet content.

Her uncle was proud of that high-held head. He and Edith might not always hit it off. But, by Jove, he was proud of her.

"No, she's not heart-broken," Adelaide's cool tone disturbed his reflections, "she is getting her heart mended."

"What do you mean?"

"They are an attractive pair, little Jane and her brother. And the boy has lost his head."

"Over Edith? Oh, well, she plays around with him; there's nothing serious in it."

"Don't be too sure. She's interested."

"What makes you insist on that?" irritably.

"I know the signs, dear man," the cat seemed to purr, but she had claws.

And it was Adelaide who was right. Edith had

come to the knowledge that night of what Baldy meant to her.

As she had entered the ballroom men had crowded around her. "Why," they demanded, "do you wear mistletoe, if you don't want to pay the forfeit?"

Backed up against one of the marble pillars, she held them off. "I do want to pay it, but not to any of you."

Her frankness diverted them. "Who is the lucky man?"

"He is here. But he doesn't know he is lucky."

They thought she was joking. But she was not. And on the other side of the marble pillar a page in scarlet listened, with joy and fear in his heart. "How fast we are going. How fast."

There was dancing until midnight, then the curtains at the end of the room were drawn back, and the tree was revealed. It towered to the ceiling, a glittering, gorgeous thing. It was weighted with gifts for everybody, fantastic toys most of them, expensive, meaningless.

Evans, standing back of the crowd, was aware of the emptiness of it all. Oh, what had there been throughout the evening to make men think of the Babe who had been born at Bethlehem?

The gifts of the Wise Men? Perhaps. Gold and frankincense and myrrh? One must not judge too narrowly. It was hard to keep simplicities in these opulent days.

Yet he was heavy-hearted, and when Eloise Harper charged up to him, dressed somewhat scantily as a dryad, and handed him a foolish monkey on a stick, she seemed to suggest a heathen saturnalia rather than anything Christian and civilized.

"A monkey for a monk," said Eloise. "Mr. Follette, your cassock is frightfully becoming. But you know you are a whited sepulchre."

"Am I?"

"Of course. I'll bet you never say your prayers."

She danced away, unconscious that her words had pierced him. What reason had she to think that any of this meant more to him than it did to her? Had he borne witness to the faith that was within him? And was it within him? And if not, why?

He stood there with his foolish monkey on his stick, while around him swirled a laughing, shrieking crowd. Why, the thing was a carnival, not a sacred celebration. Was there no way in which he might bear witness?

Edith had asked him to sing the old ballads, "Dame, get up and bake your pies," and "I saw three ships a-sailing." Evans was in no mood for the dame who baked her pies on Christmas day in the morning, or the pretty girls who whistled and sang—on Christmas day in the morning.

When all the gifts had been distributed the lights in the room were turned out. The only illumination
was the golden effulgence which encircled the tree.

In his monk's robe, within that circle of light, Evans seemed a mystical figure. He seemed, too, appropriately ascetic, with his gray hair, the weary lines of his old-young face.

But his voice was fresh and clear. And the song he sang hushed the great room into silence.

"O little town of Bethlehem,
How still we see thee lie,
Above thy deep and dreamless sleep,
The silent stars go by;
Yet in thy dark streets shineth,
The everlasting light,
The hopes and fears of all the years
Are met in thee to-night."

He sang as if he were alone in some vast arched space, beneath spires that reached towards Heaven, behind some grille that separated him from the world.

"For Christ is born of Mary,
And gathered all above,
While mortals sleep, the angels keep
Their watch of wondering love.
O, morning stars together
Proclaim the holy birth!
And praises sing to God the King
And peace to men on earth."

And now it seemed to him that he sang not to that crowd of upturned faces, not to those men and women in shining silks and satins, not to Jane who was far away, but to those others who pressed close—his comrades across the Great Divide!

So he had sung to them in the hospital, sitting up in his narrow bed— and most of the men who had listened were—gone.

"O, holy child of Bethlehem,
Descend to us, we pray,
Cast out our sin and enter in,
Be born in us to-day.
We hear the Christmas angels
The great glad tidings tell:
'Oh come to us, abide with us,
Our Lord Emmanuel.'"

As the last words rang out his audience seemed to wake with a sigh.

Then the lights went up. But the monk had vanished!

Evans left word with Baldy that he would go home on the trolley. "I am not quite up to the supper and all that. Will you look after Mother?"

"Of course. Say, Evans, that song was top notch. Edith wants you to sing another."

"Will you tell her I can't? I'm sorry. But the last time I sang that was for the fellows—in France. And it—got me———"

"It got me, too," Baldy confided; "made all this seem—silly."

So Evans left behind him all the youth and laughter and light-heartedness, and took the last trolley out to Castle Manor. He had a long walk after the ride, but the cold air was stimulating, the sky was full of stars and the night was very still. Oh, how good it was to be out in that still and star-lighted night!

When he reached Castle Manor he passed the barn on his way to the house. He opened the door and looked in. There was a lantern, faintly lit, and he could see the cows resting on their beds of straw—great dim creatures, smelling of milk and hay—calm-eyed, inscrutable.

He entered and sat down. He felt soothed and comforted by the tranquillity of the dumb beasts—the eloquent silence.

He was glad he had escaped from the clamor of the costume ball—from Eloise and her kind.

Yet the Man born at Bethlehem had not escaped. He had gone among the multitudes—speaking.

Well ... it couldn't be expected, could it, that men in these days would say to a girl like Eloise Harper, "For unto you is born this day in the city of David, a Saviour which is Christ the Lord"?

People didn't say such things in polite society ... and if they didn't, why not? And if they did, would the world listen?

CHAPTER XVII
NEWS FOR THE TOWN-CRIER

It was just before New Year's that Lucy Logan brought a letter for Frederick Towne to sign, and when he had finished she said, "Mr. Towne, I'm sorry, but I'm not going to work any more. So will you please accept my resignation?"

He showed his surprise. "What's the matter? Aren't we good enough for you?"

"It isn't that." She stopped and went on, "I'm going to be married, Mr. Towne."

"Married?" He was at once congratulatory. "That's a pleasant thing for you, and I mustn't spoil it by telling you how hard it is going to be to find someone to take your place."

"I think if you will have Miss Dale? She's really very good."

Frederick was curious. What kind of lover had won this quiet Lucy? Probably some clerk or salesman. "What about the man? Nice fellow, I hope——"

"Very nice, Mr. Towne," she flushed, and her manner seemed to forbid further questioning. She went away, and he gave orders to the cashier to see that she had an increase in the amount of her final check. "She will need some pretty things. And when we learn the date we can give her a present."

So on Saturday night Lucy left, and on the following Monday a card was brought up to Edith Towne.

She read it. "Lucy Logan? I don't believe I know her," she said to the maid.

"She says she is from Mr. Towne's office, and that it is important."

Now Josephine, the parlor maid, had a nice sense of the proprieties which she had learned from Waldron, who was not on duty in the front of the house in the morning. So she had given Lucy a chair in the great hall. Waldron had emphasized that business callers and social inferiors must never be ushered into the drawing-room. The grade below Lucy's was, indeed, sent around to a side door.

However, there Lucy sat—in a dark blue cape and a small blue hat, and she rose as Edith came up to her.

"Oh, let's go where we can be comfortable," Edith said, and led the way through the gray and white drawing-room beyond the peacock screen, to the glowing warmth of the fire.

They were a great contrast, these two women. Edith in a tea-gown of pale yellow was the last word in modishness. Lucy, in her modest blue, had no claims to distinction.

But Lucy was not ill at ease. "Miss Towne," she said, "I have resigned from your uncle's office. Did he tell you?"

"No. Uncle Fred rarely speaks about business."

With characteristic straightforwardness Lucy came at once to the point. "I have something I must talk over with you. I don't know whether I am doing the wise thing. But it is the only honest thing."

"I can't imagine what you can have to say."

"No you can't. It's this——" she hesitated, then spoke with an effort. "I am the girl Mr. Simms is in love with. He wants to come back and marry me."

Edith's fingers caught at the arm of the chair. "Do you mean that it was because of you—that he didn't marry me?"

"Yes. He used to come to the office when he was in Washington and dictate letters. And we got in the way of talking to each other. He seemed to enjoy it, and he wasn't like some men—who are just—silly. And I began to think about him a lot. But I didn't let him see it. And—he told me afterward, he was always thinking of me. And the morning of your wedding day he came down to the office—to say 'Good-bye.' He said he—just had to. And—well, he let it out that he loved me, and didn't want to marry you. But he said he would have to go on with it. And—and I told him he must not, Miss Towne."

Edith stared at her. "Do you mean that what he did was your fault?"

"Yes," Lucy's face was white, "if you want to put it that way. I told him he hadn't any right to marry you if he loved me." She hesitated, then lifted her eyes to Edith's with a glance of appeal. "Miss Towne, I wonder if you are big enough to believe that it was just because I cared so much—and not because of his money?"

It was a challenge. Edith had been ready to pour out her wrath on the head of this girl to whom she owed the humiliation of the past weeks, but there was about Lucy a certain sturdiness, a courage which was arresting.

"You think you love him?" she demanded.

"I know I do. And you don't. You never have. And he didn't love you. Why—if he should lose every cent to-morrow, and I had to tramp the road with him, I'd do it gladly. And you wouldn't. You wouldn't want him unless he could give you everything you have now, would you? Would you, Miss Towne?"

Edith's sense of justice dictated her answer. "No," she found herself unexpectedly admitting. "If I had to tramp the roads with him, I'd be bored to death."

"I think he knew that, Miss Towne. He told me that if he didn't marry you, your heart wouldn't be broken. That it would just hurt your pride."

Edith had a moment of hysterical mirth. How they had talked her over. Her lover—and her uncle's stenographer! What a tragedy it had been! And what a comedy!

She leaned forward a little, locking her fingers about her knees. "I wish you'd tell me all about it."

"I don't know just what to tell. Except that we've been writing to each other. I said that we must wait three months. It didn't seem fair to you to have him marry too soon."

Uncle Fred's stenographer sorry for her! "Go on," Edith said, tensely.

So Lucy told the simple story. And in telling it showed herself so naive, so steadfast, that Edith was aware of an increasing respect for the woman who had taken her place in the heart of her lover. She perceived that Lucy had come to this interview in no spirit of triumph. She had dreaded it, but had felt it her duty. "I thought it would be easier for you if you knew it before other people did."

Edith's forehead was knitted in a slight frown. "The whole thing has been most unpleasant," she said. "When are you going to marry him?"

"I told him on St. Valentine's day. It seemed—romantic."

Romance and Del! Edith had a sudden illumination. Why, this was what he had wanted, and she had given him none of it! She had laughed at him— been his good comrade. Little Lucy adored him—and had set St. Valentine's day for the wedding!

There was nothing small about Edith Towne. She knew fineness when she saw it, and she had a feeling of humility in the presence of little Lucy. "I think it was my fault as much as Del's," she stated. "I should never have said 'Yes.' People haven't any right to marry who feel as we did."

"Oh," Lucy said rapturously, "how dear of you to say that. Miss Towne, I always knew you were—big. But I didn't dream you were so beautiful." Tears wet her cheeks. "You're just—marvellous," she said, wiping them away.

"No, I'm not." Edith's eyes were on the fire. "Normally, I am rather proud and—hateful. If you had come a week ago——" Her voice fell away into silence as she still stared at the fire.

Lucy looked at her curiously. "A week ago?"

Edith nodded. "Do you like fairy tales? Well, once there was a princess. And a page came and sang—under her window." The fire purred and crackled. "And the princess—liked the song——"

"Oh," said Lucy, under her breath.

"Well, that's all," said Edith; "I don't know the end." She stretched herself lazily. Her loose sleeves, floating away from her bare arms, gave the effect of wings. Lucy, looking at her, wondered how it had ever happened that Delafield could have turned his eyes from that rare beauty to her own undistinguished prettiness.

She stood up. "I can't tell you how thankful I am that I came."

"You're not going to run away yet," Edith told her. "I want you to have lunch with me. Upstairs. You must tell me all your plans."

"I haven't many. And I really oughtn't to stay."

"Why not? I want you. Please don't say no."

So up they went, with the perturbed parlor maid speaking through the tube to the pantry. "Miss Towne wants luncheon for two, Mr. Waldron. In her room. Something nice, she says, and plenty of it."

Little Lucy had never seen such a room as the one to which Edith led her. The whole house was, indeed, a dream palace. Yet it was the atmosphere with which her lover would soon surround her. She had a feeling almost of panic. What would she do with a maid like Alice, who was helping Josephine set up the folding-table, spread the snowy cloth, bring in the hot silver dishes?

As if Edith divined her thought, she said when the maids had left, "Lucy, will you let me advise?"

"Of course, Miss Towne."

"Don't try to be—like the rest of us. Like Del's own crowd, I mean. He fell in love with you because you were different. He will want you to stay— different."

"But I shall have so much to learn."

Edith was impatient. "What must you learn?

Externals? Let them alone. Be yourself. You have dignity—and strength. It was the strength in you that won Del. You and he can have a life together that will mean a great deal, if you will make him go your way. But you must not go his——"

Lucy considered that. "You mean that the crowd he is with weakens him?"

"I mean just that. They're sophisticated beyond words. You're what they would call—provincial. Oh, be provincial, Lucy. Don't be afraid. But don't adopt their ways. You go to church, don't you? Say your prayers? Believe that God's in His world?"

Lucy's fair cheeks were flushed. "Why, of course I do."

"Well, we don't—not many of us," said Edith. "The thing you have got to do is to interest Del in something. Don't just go sailing away with him in his yacht. Buy a farm over in Virginia, and help him make a success of it."

"But he lives in New York."

"Of course he does. But he can live anywhere. He's so rich that he doesn't have to earn anything, and his office is just a fiction. You must make him work. Go in for a fad; blooded horses, cows, black Berkshires. Do you know what a black Berkshire is, Lucy?"

"No, I don't."

"Well, it's a kind of a pig. And that's the thing for you and Del. He really loves fine stock. And

you and he—think of it—riding over the country—planning your gardens—having a baby or two." Edith was going very fast.

"It sounds heavenly," said Lucy.

"Then make it Heaven. Oh, Lucy, Lucy, you lucky girl—you are going to marry the man you love. Live away from the world—share happiness and unhappiness——" She rose from the table restlessly, pushing back her chair, dropping her napkin on the floor. "Do you know how I envy you?"

She went to the window and stood looking out. "And here I sit, day after day, like a prisoner in a tower—and my page sings—that was the beginning of it—and it will be the end."

"No," Lucy was very serious, "you mustn't let it be the end. You—you must open the window, Miss Towne."

Edith came back to the table. "Open the window?" Her breath came fast. "Open the window. Oh, little Lucy, how wise you are...."

When Lucy had gone, Alice came in and dressed Edith's hair. She found her lady thoughtful. "Alice, what did they do with my wedding clothes?"

It was the first time she had mentioned them. Alice, sticking in hairpins, was filled with eager curiosity.

"We put them all in the second guest-suite," she said; "some of them we left packed in the trunks

just as they were, and some of them are hung on racks."

"Where is the wedding dress?"

"In a closet in a white linen bag."

"Well, finish my hair and we will go and look at it."

Alice stuck in the last pin. "The veil is over a satin roller. I did it myself, and put the cap part in a bonnet-box."

As they entered it, the second guest-suite was heavy with the scent of orange blooms. "How dreadful, Alice," Edith ejaculated. "Why didn't you throw the flowers away?"

"Miss Annabel wouldn't let me. She said you might not want things touched."

"Silly sentimentality." Edith was impatient.

The room was in all the gloom of drawn curtains. The dresses hung on racks, and, encased in white bags, gave a ghostly effect. "They are like rows of tombstones, Alice."

"Yes, Miss Towne," said Alice, dutifully.

The maid brought out the wedding dress and laid it on the bed.

Edith, surveying it, was stung by the memory of the emotions which had swayed her when she had last worn it. It had seemed to mock her. She had wanted to tear it into shreds. She had seen her own tense countenance in the mirror, as she had controlled herself before Alice. Then, when the maid had left, she had thrown herself on the

bed, and had writhed in an agony of humiliation.

And now all her anger was gone. She didn't hate Del. She didn't hate Lucy. She even thought of Uncle Fred with charity. And the wedding gown was, after all, a robe for a princess who married a king. Not a robe for a princess who loved a page. A tender smile softened her face.

"Alice," she said, suddenly, "wasn't there a little heliotrope dinner frock among my trousseau things?"

"Yes, Miss Towne. Informal." Alice hunted in the third row of tombstones until she found it.

"I want long sleeves put in it. Will you tell Hardinger, and have him send a hat to match?"

"Yes, Miss Towne."

The heliotrope frock had simple and lovely lines. It floated in sheer beauty from the maid's hands as she held it up. "There isn't a prettier one in the whole lot, Miss Edith."

"I like it," the fragrance of heliotrope was wafted from hidden sachets, "and as for the wedding gown," Edith eyed it thoughtfully, "pack it in a box with the veil and the rest of the things. I want Briggs to take it with the note to an address that I will give him."

"Oh, yes, Miss Towne." Alice was much interested in the address. She studied it when, later, she carried the box and the note down to Briggs.

Edith, having dispatched the box with a charming
note to Lucy Logan, had a feeling of ecstatic freedom. All the hurt and
humiliation of the bridal episode had departed. She didn't care what the
world thought of her. Her desertion by Del had been material for a day's
gossip—then other things had filled the papers, had been headlined and
emphasized. And what difference did it all make?

The things that mattered were those of which she had talked to Lucy.
An old house—mutual interests, all the rest of it. "I would tramp the road
with him," little Lucy had said. That was love—to count nothing hard but
the lack of it.

She was called to the telephone, and found Eloise Harper at the other
end. "Delafield is coming back," she said. "Benny has had a letter."

"Darling town-crier," said Edith, "you are late with your news."

"What do you mean by town-crier?"

"That's what we call you, dearest."

"Oh, do you?" dubiously. "Well, anyhow, Delafield is on his way back,
and he is going to be married as soon as he gets here."

"But he isn't. Not until February."

"How do you know?"

"The bride told me."

"Who?" incredulously.

"The bride."

Eloise gasped. "Edith, do you know who she is?"

"I do."

"Tell me."

"My dear, I can't. The whole world would know it."

"I swear I——"

"Don't swear, Eloise. You might perjure yourself," and Edith hung up
the receiver.

CHAPTER XVIII
AN INTERLUDE

The day after Christmas.

"Baldy, darling: The operation is over, and the doctor gives us hope. That is the best I can tell you. I haven't been allowed to see Judy, though they have let Bob have a peep at her, and she smiled.

"You can imagine that we have had little heart for good times. But the babies had a beautiful Christmas Day, with a tree—and stockings hung above the gas logs. How I longed for our own little wood fire, but the blessed darlings didn't know the difference. We couldn't spend much money, which was fortunate. The things that came from the east were so perfect. Yours, honey-boy, only you shouldn't have made the check so large. I shan't spend it unless it is very necessary. Mr. Towne sent flowers, loads of them—and perfectly marvellous chocolates in a box of gold lacquer—and Edith sent a string of carved ivory beads, and there was a blue Keats from Evans, and a ducky orange scarf from Mrs. Follette.

"I wish you could have seen the babies. Julia staggered around the tree on her uncertain little feet as if she were drunk, and then settled down to an adorable stuffed bunny, and Junior had eyes for nothing but the red automobile that the Townes ordered for him. I think it was dear of Edith and

her uncle. Junior is such a charming chap, with beautiful manners like his dad, but with a will of his own at times.

"I roasted a chicken for dinner, and—well, we got through it all. And now the babies are in bed, and Bob is at the hospital, and I am writing to you. But my heart is tight with fear.

"I mustn't think about Judy.

"Give my love to everybody. I have had Christmas letters from Evans and Edith and Mr. Towne. Baldy, Mr. Towne wants to marry me. I haven't told you before. It is rather like a dream and I'm not going to think about it. I don't love him, and so, of course, that settles it. But he says he can make me, and, Baldy, sometimes I wish that he could. It would be such a heavenly thing for the whole family. Of course that isn't the way to look at it, but I believe Judy wants it. She believes in love in a cottage, but she says that love in a palace might be equally satisfying, with fewer things to worry about.

"Somehow that doesn't fit in with the things I've dreamed. But dreams, of course, aren't everything....

"I had to tell you, dear old boy. Because we've never kept things from each other. And you've been so perfectly frank about Edith. Are things a bit blue in that direction? Your letter sounded like it.

"Be good to yourself, old dear, and love me more than ever."

Jane signed her name and stood up, stretching her arms above her head. It was late and she was very tired. A great storm was shaking the windows.

The wind from the lake beat against the walls with the boom of guns.

Jane pulled back the curtains—there was snow with the storm—it whirled in papery shreds on the shaft of light. All sounds in the street were muffled. She had a sense of suffocation—as if the storm pressed upon her— shutting her in.

She went into the next room and looked at the babies. Oh, what would they do if anything happened to Judy? What would Bob do? She dared not look ahead.

She walked the floor, a tense little figure, fighting against fear. The storm had become a whistling pandemonium. She gave a cry of relief when the door opened and her brother-in-law entered.

"I'm half-frozen, Janey. It was a fight to get through. The cars are stopped on all the surface lines."

"How is Judy?"

"Holding her own. And by the way, Janey, that friend of yours, Towne, sent another bunch of roses. Pretty fine, I call it. She's no end pleased."

"It's nice of him."

"Gee, I wish I had his money."

"Money isn't everything, Bobby."

"It means a lot at a time like this." His face wore a worried frown. Jane knew that Judy's hospital expenses were appalling, and bills were piling up.

"I work like a nigger," Bob said, ruefully, "and we've never been in debt before."

"When Judy is well, things will seem brighter, Bob." She laid her hand on his arm.

He looked up at her and there was fear in his eyes. "Jane, she must get well. I can't face losing her."

"We mustn't think of that. And now come on out in the kitchen and I'll make you some coffee." Jane was always practical. She knew that, warmed and fed, he would see things differently.

Yet in spite of her philosophy, Jane lay awake a long time that night. And later her dreams were of Judy—of Judy, and a gray and dreadful phantom which pursued....

The next day she went to the hospital and took Junior with her.

When he saw his mother in bed, Junior asked, "Do you like it, Mother-dear?"

"Like what, darling?"

"Sleeping in the daytime?"

"I don't always sleep." She looked at Jane. "Does little Julia miss me? I think about her in the night."

Jane knew what Judy's heart wanted. "She does miss you. I know it when she turns away from me. Perhaps I oughtn't to tell you. But I thought you'd rather know."

"I do want to know," said Judy, feverishly. "I

don't want them to forget. Jane, you mustn't ever let them—forget."

Jane felt as if she had been struck a stunning blow. She was, for a moment, in the midst of a dizzy universe, in which only one thing was clear. *Judy wasn't sure of getting well!*

Judy, with her brown eyes wistful, went on: "Junior, do you want Mother back in your own nice house?"

"Will you make cookies?"

"Yes, darling."

"Then I want you back. Aunt Janey made cookies, and she didn't know about the raisins."

"Mother knows how to give cookie-men raisin eyes. Mothers know a lot of things that aunties don't, darling."

"Well, I wish you'd come back." He stood by the side of the bed. "I'd like to sleep with you to-night. May I, Mother-dear?"

"Not to-night, darling. But you may when I come home."

But days passed and weeks, and Judy did not come home. And the first of February found her still in that narrow hospital bed. And it was in February that Frederick Towne wrote that he was coming to Chicago. "I shall have only a day, but I must see you."

Jane was not sure that she wanted him to come. He had been very good to them all, and he had not, in his letter, pressed for an answer

unduly. But she knew if he came, he would ask.

The next time she went to the hospital, she told Judy of his expected arrival. "To-morrow."

"Oh, Jane, how delightful."

"Is it? I'm not sure, Judy."

"It would be perfect if you'd accept him, Jane."

"But I'm not in love with him."

Judy, rather austere, with her black braids on each side of her white face, said, "Janey, do you know that not one girl in a thousand has a chance to marry a man like Frederick Towne?"

There was a breathless excitement about the invalid which warned Jane. "Now, darling, what real difference will it make if I don't marry him? There are other men in the world."

"Bob and I were talking about it," Judy's voice was almost painfully eager, "of how splendid it would be for—all of us."

For all of us. Judy and Bob and the babies! It was the first time that Jane had thought of her marriage with Towne as a way out for Judy and Bob....

From his hotel at the moment of arrival, Towne called Jane up. "Are you glad I'm here?"

"Of course."

"Don't say it that way."

"How shall I say it?"

"As if you meant it. Do you know what a frigid little thing you are? Your letters were like frosted cakes."

She laughed. "They were the best I could do."

"I don't believe it. But I am not going to talk of that now. When can I come and see you? And how much time have you to spare for me?"

"Not much. I can't leave the babies."

"Your sister's children. Can't you trust the maids?"

"Maids? Listen to the man! We haven't any."

"You don't mean to tell me that you are doing the housework."

"Yes, why not? I am strong and well, and the kiddies are adorable."

"We are going to change that. I'll bring a trained nurse up with me."

"Please don't be a tyrant."

"Tut-tut, little girl," she heard his big laugh over the telephone, "I'll bring the nurse and someone to help her, and a load of toys to keep the kiddies quiet. When I want a thing, Jane, I usually get it."

He and the nurse arrived together. A competent houseworker was to follow in a cab. Jane protested. "It seems dreadfully high-handed."

They were alone in the living-room. Miss Martin had, at once, carried the kiddies off to unpack the toys.

Frederick laughed. "Well, what are you going to do about it? You can't put me out."

"But I can refuse to go with you"—there was the crisp note in her voice which always stirred him.

"But you won't do that, Jane." He held out his hand to her, drew her a little towards him.

She released herself, flushing. "I am not quite sure what I ought to do."

"Why think of 'oughts'? We will just play a bit together, Jane. That's all. And you're such a tired little girl, aren't you?"

His sympathy was comforting. Everybody leaned on Jane. It was delightful to shift her burdens to this strong man who gave his commands like a king.

"Yes, I am tired. And if the babies will be all right——"

"Good. Now run in and see Miss Martin, and I think you'll be satisfied."

Jane found Junior rapturous over a Noah's Ark, with all the animals clothed in fur and hair, and the birds in feathers, and small Julia cuddled against the nurse's white breast, bright-eyed with interest over the Three Kittens.

"They'll be all right, Miss Barnes," Miss Martin said, smiling.

Jane sighed with relief. "It will seem good to play for a bit."

"You see how I get my way," Frederick said, as he helped her into the big hired limousine. "I always get it."

"It is rather heavenly at the moment," Jane admitted, "but you needn't think that it establishes a precedent."

"Wouldn't it be always—heavenly?"

"I'm not sure. You have the makings of a—Turk."

Yet she laughed as she said it, and he laughed, too. He was really very handsome, ruddy and bright and big—and with that air of gay deference. She liked to sit beside him, and listen to the things he had to tell her. It was peaceful after all the strenuous days.

She was aware that if she married Towne life would be always like this. A glorified existence. She would be like Curlylocks of the nursery rhyme....

"What are you smiling at?" Frederick demanded. His eyes as they met hers burned a bit. Jane was half-buried in a black fur robe—with only the white oval of her face and her little gray hat showing above it.

"Nursery rhymes." The smile deepened.

"Which one?"

"Curlylocks."

"I don't remember it. Oh, yes, by Jove, I do. She was the damsel who sat on a cushion and sewed a fine seam, and feasted on strawberries, sugar and cream?"

"Yes."

"Good. That's what I want to do for you. You know it?"

"Yes. But it might be—monotonous."

"What better thing could happen to you than to have someone take care of you?"

Jane sat up. "Oh, I want to *live*," she said, almost with fierceness. "I'd hate to think my husband was just a sort of—feather cushion."

"Is that the way you think of me?" His vanity was untouched. She didn't, of course, mean it.

"No. But love is life. I don't want to miss it."

"You won't miss it if you marry me. I swear it, Jane, I'll make you love me."

He was in dead earnest. And in spite of herself she was swayed by his attitude of conviction.

"Oh, we mustn't talk of it," she said, a bit breathlessly. "I'd rather not, please."

They lunched at a charming French restaurant, where Frederick had dared Jane to eat snails. She acquiesced rather unexpectedly. "I have always wanted to do it," she told him, "ever since I was a little girl and read Hans Andersen's story of the white snails who lived in a forest of burdocks, and whose claim to aristocracy was that their ancestors had been baked and served in a silver dish."

They had a table in a corner. He ordered the luncheon expertly.

"I can't tell you how much I am enjoying it," she said gratefully, as he once more gave her his attention.

"Do you really like it?"

"Immensely."

"Why not have it for the rest of your life?"

Her color deepened. "Sometimes I think it would be——" she hesitated.

"Heavenly," he finished the sentence for her. "Jane, you only have to say the word."

The waiter, with the first course, interrupted them. When he once more disappeared, Frederick persisted. "I'm going away to-morrow. Won't you give me my answer to-night? After lunch I'll take you home and you can rest a bit, and then I'll come for you and we'll dine together and see a play."

She tried to protest, but he pleaded. "This is my day. Don't spoil it, Jane."

It was nearly three o'clock when they left the table, and they had a long drive before them. Darkness had descended when they reached the house. It was still snowing.

Bob was up-stairs, walking around the little room like a man in a dream.

"I can't tell you," he confided to Jane after Frederick had left, "how queer I felt when I came in and found Miss Martin with the babies, and that stately old woman in the kitchen. And everything going like clockwork. Miss Martin explained, and—well, Towne just waves a wand, doesn't he, Janey, and makes things happen?"

"I don't know that I ought to let him do so much," Jane said.

"Oh, why not, Janey? Just take the good the gods provide...."

Before Frederick Towne reached his hotel he passed a shop whose windows were lighted against the early darkness. In one of the windows, flanked by slippers and stockings and a fan to match, was a French gown, all silver and faint blue, a shining wisp of a thing in lace and satin. Towne stopped the car, went in and bought the gown with its matching accessories. He carried the big box with him to his hotel. Resting a bit before dinner he permitted himself to dream of Jane in that gown, the pearls that he would give her against the white of her slender throat, the slim bareness of her arms, the swirl of a silver lace about her ankles—the swing of the boyish figure in its sheath of blue.

He permitted himself to think of her, too, in other gowns. His thoughts of her frocks were all definite. He had exquisite taste. If he married Jane, he would dress her so that people would look at her, and look again. Even in her poverty, she had learned to express herself in the things she wore. His money would make possible even more subtle expression.

So he thought of her in gray chiffon, black pearls in her ears—oh, to think of Jane in earrings!—with a touch of jade where the draperies swung loose—and with an oyster-white lining to the green cape which would cover the gown—a lynx collar up to her ears.

Or a tea-gown of tangerine lace—with bands of sable catching the open sleeves at the wrist—or in white—Jane's wedding dress must be heavy with pearls—she lent herself perfectly to medieval effects.

His mind came back to the blue and silver. It hung on the bed-post, shimmering in the light from his lamp. He wondered if he offered it to Jane, would she accept? He knew she wouldn't. Adelaide would have made no bones about it. There had been a lovely thing in black velvet he had given her, too, a wrap to match.

But Jane was different. She would shrug her shoulders and with that charming independence, decline his favors, tilting her chin, and challenging him with her lighted-up eyes.

Well, he liked her for it. Loved her for it. And some day she would wear the blue and silver frock. As he rose and put it back in the box, he seemed to shut Jane in with it. There hung about it the scent of roses. He knew of a rare perfume. He would order a vial of it for Jane. It merely hinted at fragrance.

The evening stretched ahead of him, full of radiant promise. He knew Jane's strength but he was ready for conquest.

His telephone rang. And Jane spoke to him.

"Mr. Towne," she said, "I can't dine with you. But can you come over later? Judy is desperately ill. I'll tell you more about it when I see you."

CHAPTER XIX
SURRENDER

Bob had cried when the news came from the hospital. It had been dreadful. Jane had never seen a man cry. They had been hard sobs, with broken apologies between. "I'm a fool to act like this...."

Jane had tried to say things, then had sat silent and uncomfortable while Bob fought for self-control.

Miss Martin had gone home before the message arrived. Bob was told that he could not see his wife. But the surgeon would be glad to talk to him, at eight.

"And I know what he'll say," Bob had said to Jane drearily, "that if I can get that specialist up from Hot Springs, he may be able to diagnose the trouble. But how am I going to get the money, Janey? It will cost a thousand dollars to rush him here and pay his fee. And my income has practically stopped. With all these labor troubles—there's no building. And Judy's nurses cost twelve dollars a day—and her room five. Oh, poor people haven't any right to be sick, Janey. There isn't any place for them."

Jane's face was pale and looked pinched.

"There's the check Baldy sent me for Christmas, fifty dollars."

"Dear girl, it wouldn't be a drop in the bucket."

"I know," thoughtfully. "Bob, do they think that if that specialist comes it will save Judy's life?"

"It might. It—it's the last chance, Janey."

Janey hugged her knees. "Can't you borrow the money?"

"I have borrowed up to the limit of my securities, and how can I ever pay?"

Her voice was grim. "We will manage to pay; the thing now is to save Judy."

"Yes," he tried, pitifully, to meet her courage. "If they'll get the specialist, we'll pay."

She had risen. "I'll call up Mr. Towne, and tell him I can't dine with him."

"But, Janey, there's no reason why you shouldn't keep your engagement."

She had turned on him with a touch of indignation. "Do you think I could have one happy moment with my mind on Judy?"

Bob had looked at her, and then looked away. "Have you thought that you might get the money from Towne?"

Her startled gaze had questioned him. "Get money from Mr. Towne?"

"Yes. Oh, why not, Janey? He'll do anything for you."

"But how could I pay him?"

There had been dead silence, then Bob said, "Well, he's in love with you, isn't he?"

"You mean that I can—marry him?"

"Yes. Why not? Judy says he's crazy about you. And, Jane, it's foolish to throw away such a chance. Not every girl has it."

"But, Bob, I'm not—in love with him."

"You'll learn to care—— He's a delightful chap, I'd say." Bob was eager. "Now look here, Janey, I'm talking to you like a Dutch uncle. It isn't as if I were advising you to do it for our sakes. It is for your own sake, too. Why, it would be great, old girl. Never another worry. Somebody always to look after you."

The wind outside was singing a wild song, a roaring, cynical song, it seemed to Jane. She wanted to say to Bob, "But I've always been happy in my little house with Baldy and Philomel, and the chickens and the cats." But of course Bob could say, "You're not happy now, and anyhow what are you going to do about Judy?"

Judy!

She had spoken at last with an effort. "I'll tell him to come over after dinner. We can ride for a bit."

"Why not stay here? I'll be at the hospital. And the storm is pretty bad."

She had looked out of the window. "There's no snow. Just the wind. And I feel—stifled."

It was then that she had called up Towne. "I can't dine with you.... Judy is desperately ill...."

The houseworker had prepared a delicious dinner, but Jane ate nothing. Bob's appetite, on the other hand, was good. He apologized for it. "I went without lunch, I was so worried."

Jane remembered her own lunch—how careless she had been for the moment, forgetting her heaviness of heart—served like a princess sheltered from every wind that blew!

And all the rest of her life might be like that! It wouldn't be so bad. She drank a cup of coffee, and then another. And Frederick had said that he could make her love him....

In the center of the table were some roses that Towne had given her. She stuck one of them in her girdle.

Bob finished his coffee, and stood up. "I must be going. Good luck to you, old girl...." His tone was almost cheerful. He walked around the table and touched his lips to her cheek.

When she was alone, she went in and looked at the babies. Junior had taken some of the animals to bed with him, and they trailed over the white cover—tiny tigers and elephants, lions and giraffes. Little Julia hugged her doll. How sweet she was, and such a baby!

And in the hospital Judy's arms ached to enfold that warm little body: Judy's heart beat with fear lest they should never enfold her again!

The bell rang. Jane, going to the door, found herself shaking with excitement.

Frederick came in and took both of her hands in his. "I'm terribly sorry about the sister. Is there anything I can do?"

She shook her head. She could hardly speak. "I thought if you wouldn't mind, we'd go for a ride. And we can talk."

"Good. Get your wraps." He released her hands, and she went into the other room. As she looked into the mirror she saw that her cheeks were crimson.

She brought out her coat and he held it for her. "Is this warm enough? You ought to have a fur coat."

"Oh, I shall be warm," she said.

As he preceded her down the stairs, Towne turned and looked up at her. "You are wearing my rose," he told her, ardently; "you are like a rose yourself."

She would not have been a woman if she had not liked his admiration. And he was strong and adoring and distinguished. She had a sense of almost happy excitement as he lifted her into the car.

"Where shall we drive?" he asked.

"Along the lake. I love it on a night like this."

The moon was sailing high in a rack of clouds. As they came to the lake the waves writhed like mad sea-monsters in gold and white and black.

"Jane," Frederick asked softly, "what made you wear—my rose?"

She sat very still beside him. "Mr. Towne," she said at last, "tell me how much—you love me."

He gave a start of surprise. Then he turned towards her and took her hand in his. "Let me tell you this! there never was a dearer woman. Everything that I have, all that I am, is yours if you will have it."

There was a fine dignity in his avowal. She liked him more than ever.

"Do you love me enough"—she hurried over the words, "to help me?"

"Yes." He drew her gently towards him. There was no struggle. She lay quietly against his arm, but he was aware that she trembled.

"Mr. Towne, Judy must have a great specialist right away. It's her only chance. If you will send for him to-night, make yourself responsible for—everything—I'll marry you whenever you say."

He stared down at her, unbelieving. "Do you mean it, Jane?"

"Yes. Oh, do you think I am dreadful?"

He laughed exultantly, caught her up to him. "Dreadful? You're the dearest—ever, Jane."

Yet as he felt her fluttering heart, he released her gently. Her eyes were full of tears. He touched her wet cheek. "Don't let me frighten you, my dear. But I am very happy."

She believed herself happy. He was really—irresistible.

A conqueror. Yet always with that touch of deference.

"Do you love me, Jane?"

"Not—yet."

"But you will. I'll make you love me."

With keen intuition, with his knowledge, too, of women, he asked for no further assurance. He leaned back against the cushions of the car, and holding her hand in his, made plans for their future. He would get the ring to-morrow. He would come again in a week. As soon as Judy was better, he and Jane would be married.

Then just before they reached home he asked for the rose. She gave it to him, all fading fragrance. He touched it to her lips then crushed it against his own.

"Must I be content with this?"

Her quick breath told her agitation. He drew her to him, gently. "Come, my sweet."

Oh, money, money. Jane learned that night the power of it!

Coming in with Frederick from that wild moonlighted world, flushed with excitement, hardly knowing this new Jane, she saw Bob transformed in a moment from haggard hopelessness to wild elation.

Frederick Towne had made a simple statement. "Jane has told me how serious things are, Heming. I want to help." Then he had asked for the surgeon's name; spoken at once of a change of rooms for Judy; increased attendance. There was much telephoning and telegraphing. An atmosphere of efficiency. Jane, looking on, was filled with admiration. How well he did things. And some day he would be her husband!

Towne was, indeed, at his best. Deeply in love with her, all his generous impulses were quickened for her service. When at last he had gone, she went to bed, and lay awake almost until morning. Doubts crowded upon her. Her cheeks burned as she thought of the bargain she had made. He would pay her sister's bills—and she would marry him. But it wasn't just that! He was so tender, so solicitous. Jane had not yet learned that one may be in love with being loved, which is not in the least the same as loving. Against the benefits which Towne bestowed upon her, she could set only her dreams of Galahad, of Robin Hood! Of romantic adventure! Her memories—of Evans Follette.

She sighed as she thought of him. He would be unhappy. Oh, darling old Evans! She cried a little into her pillow. She mustn't think of him. The thing was done. She was going to marry Frederick Towne!

CHAPTER XX
PAPER LACE

It was two days after Jane promised to marry Frederick Towne that Evans bought a Valentine for her.

The shops were full of valentines—many of them of paper lace—the fragile old-fashioned things that had become a new fashion. They had forget-me-nots on them and hearts with golden arrows, and fat pink cupids.

Evans found it hard to choose. He stood before them, smiling. And he could see Jane smile as she read the enchanting verse of the one he finally selected:

"Roses red, my dear,

And violets blue—

Honey's sweet, my dear,

And so are you."

As he walked up F Street to his office, his heart was light. It was one of the lovely days that hint of spring. Old Washingtonians know that such weather does not last—that March winds must blow, and storms must come. But they grasp the joy of the moment—masquerade in carnival spirit

—buy flowers from the men at the street corners—sweep into their favorite confectioner's to order cool drinks, the women seek their milliner's and come forth bonneted in spring beauty—the men drive to the links—and look things over.

Oh, what a world it is—this world of Washington when Winter welcomes, for the moment, Spring!

Evans wished that Jane were there to see. To let him buy flowers for her—ices. He wondered if the time would come when he might buy her a spring hat. Well, why not? If things went like this with him! He knew he was getting back. He could see it in the eyes of women. Where once there had been pity—was now coquettish challenge. He was having invitations. He accepted only a few, but they came increasingly.

And clients came. Not many, but enough to point the way to success. He had sold more of the old books. His mother's milk farm was becoming a fashionable fad.

Edith Towne had helped to bring Mrs. Follette's wares before her friends. At all hours of the day they drove out, Edith with them. "It is such an adorable place," she told Evans, "and your—mother! Isn't she absolutely herself? Selling milk with that empress air of hers. I simply love her."

Evans liked Edith Towne immensely. Even more than Baldy he divined her loneliness. "In
that great house there isn't a soul for real companionship. Towne's eaten up with egotism, and the cousin is an echo."

Edith asked herself out to dinner very often. "It is perfect with just the four of us," she told Mrs. Follette, and that lady, flattered almost to tears, said, "Telephone whenever you can come and take pot-luck."

Edith had planned to have dinner with them to-night. Evans took an early train to Sherwood. When he reached home Edith and his mother were on the porch and the Towne car stood before the gate.

"I've got to go back," Edith explained. "Uncle Fred came in from Chicago an hour or two ago and telephoned that he must see me."

"Baldy will be broken-hearted," Evans told her, smiling.

"I couldn't get him up. I tried, but they said he had left the office. I thought I'd bring him out with me." She kissed Mrs. Follette. "I'll come again soon, dear lady. And you must tell me when you are tired of me."

Evans went to the car with her, and came back to find his mother in an exalted mood. "Now if you could marry a girl like Edith Towne."

"*Edith*," he laughed lightly. "Mother, are you blind? She and Baldy are mad about each other."

"Of course she isn't serious. A boy like that."

"Isn't she? I'll say she is." Evans went charging
up the stairs to dress for dinner. "I'll be down presently."

"Baldy may be late; we won't wait for him," his mother called after him.

The dining-room at Castle Manor had a bare waxed floor, an old drop-leaf table of dark mahogany, deer's antlers over the mantel, and some candles in sconces.

Old Mary did her best to follow the rather formal service on which Mrs. Follette insisted. The food was simple, but well-cooked, and there was always a soup and a salad.

It was not until they reached the salad course that they heard the sound of Baldy's car. He burst in at the front door, as if he battered it down, stormed through the hall, and entered the dining-room like a whirlwind.

"Jane's going to be married," he cried, "and she's going to marry Frederick Towne!"

Evans half-rose from his chair. Everything turned black and he sat down. There was a loud roaring in his ears. It was like taking ether—with the darkness and the roaring.

When things cleared he found that neither his mother nor Baldy had noticed his agitation. His mother was asking quick questions. "Who told you? Does Edith know?"

Baldy threw himself in a chair. "Mr. Towne got back from Chicago this afternoon. Called me up and said he wanted me to come over at once to

his office. I went, and he gave me a letter from Jane. Said he thought it was better for him to bring it, and then he could explain."

He threw the note across the table to Mrs. Follette. "Will you read it? I'm all in. Drove like the dickens coming out. Towne wanted me to go home with him to dinner. Wanted to begin the brother-in-law business right away before I got my breath. But I left. Oh, the darned peacock!" Jane would have known Baldy's mood. The tempest-gray eyes, the chalk-white face.

"But don't you like it, Baldy?"

"Like it? Oh, read that note. Does it sound like Jane? I ask you, does it sound like *Jane*?"

It did not sound in the least like Jane. Not the Jane that Evans and Baldy knew.

"Baldy, dear. Mr. Towne will tell you all about it. I am going to marry him as soon as Judy is better. I know you will be surprised, but Mr. Towne is just wonderful, and it will be such a good thing for all of us. Mr. Towne will tell you how dreadfully ill Judy is. He wants to do everything for her, and that will be such a help to Bob.

"And so we will live happy ever after. Oh, you blessed boy, you know how I love you. Send a wire, and say that it is all right. Tell Evans and Mrs. Follette. They are my dearest friends and will always be."

She signed herself:

"Loving you more than ever,

"Jane."

Mrs. Follette looked up from the letter, took off her reading glasses, and said complacently, "I think it is very nice for her." The dear lady quite basked in the thought of her intimate friendship with the fiancée of Frederick Towne.

But the two men did not bask.

"*Nice, for Jane?*" they threw the sentences at her.

"Oh, can't you see why she has done it?" Baldy demanded. He caught up the note, pointing an accusing finger as he read certain phrases. "*It will be such a good thing for all of us ... he wants to do everything for her ... it will be such a help to Bob....*"

"Doesn't that show," Baldy demanded furiously, "she's doing it because Judy and Bob are hard up and Towne can help—I know Jane."

Evans knew her. Hadn't he said to her not long ago, "You'd tie up the broken wings of every wounded bird.... You'd give crutches to the lame, and food to the hungry...."

"I don't see why you should object," Mrs. Follette was saying; "it will be a fine thing for her. She will be Mrs. Frederick Towne!"

"I'd rather have her Jane Barnes for the rest of her life. Do you know Towne's reputation? Any woman can flatter him into a love affair. A fat Lothario." Baldy did not mince the words.

"But he hasn't married any of them," said Mrs. Follette triumphantly. She held to the ancient

and honorable theory that the woman a man marries need not worry about past love affairs since she had been paid the compliment of at least legal permanency.

"But Jane," Baldy said, brokenly, "you know her. She's a child, a darling child. With all her dreams———" He ran his fingers through his hair with the effect of a ruffled eagle.

Evans' lips were dry. "What did you say to Towne?"

"Oh, what *could* I say? That I was surprised, and all that. Something about hoping they'd be happy. Then I beat it and got here as fast as I could. I had to talk it over with you people or—burst." His eyes met Evans' and found there the sympathy he sought. "It's a rotten trick."

"Yes," said Evans, "rotten."

"I think," said Mrs. Follette, "that you must both see it is best." Yet her voice was troubled. Through her complacency had penetrated the thought of what Jane's engagement might mean to Evans. Yet, it might, on the other hand, be a blessing in disguise. There were other women, richer—who would help him in his career. And in time he would forget Jane.

Old Mary gave them their coffee. "Shall we walk for a bit, Baldy?" Evans said, when at last they rose.

The two men made their way towards the pine

grove. The twilight sky was a deep purple with a thin sickle of a moon and a breathless star.

And there in the little grove under the purple sky Evans said to Baldy, "I love her."

"I know. I wish to God you had her."

"Perhaps she has chosen wisely. Towne can make things—easy."

"But you should hear what Edith says about him. He's an old grouch around the house. And you know Janey? Like a bird—singing."

Like a bird singing!

"Baldy," Evans said, "I don't agree with you that it was—the money. That may have helped in her decision. But I think she cares——"

"For Towne—nonsense."

"It isn't nonsense. She knows nothing of love. She may have taken the shadow for the substance. And he can be very—charming." It wrung his heart to say it. But almost with clairvoyance he saw the truth.

When they returned to the house Baldy found a message from Edith. He was to call her up.

"Uncle Frederick has just told me," she said, "that Jane is to be my aunt. Isn't it joyful?"

"I'm not sure."

"Why not?"

"Oh, Towne's all right. But not for Jane."

"I see. But he's really in love with her, poor old duck. Talked about it all through dinner. He's going to try awfully hard to make her happy."

"Then you approve?"

He heard her gay laugh over the wire. "It will be nice—to have you—in the family. I'll be your niece-in-law."

"You'll be nothing of the kind."

"You can't help being—Uncle Baldy. Isn't that—delicious? And now, will you come in to-night and sit by my fire? Uncle Frederick is out."

"I've sat too often by your fire."

"Too often for your own peace of mind? I know that. And I'm glad of it." Again he heard a ripple of laughter.

"It isn't a thing to laugh at."

She hesitated, then said in a different tone, "I am not laughing. But I want you by my fire to-night."

It was late when Evans went up-stairs. He had spent the evening with his mother, discussing with her some matters where his legal knowledge helped. They did not speak of Jane. Their avoidance of the subject showed their preoccupation with it. But neither dared approach it.

On the bedside table in Evans' room lay the valentine he had bought for Jane. There it was, with its cupids and bleeding hearts—its forget-me-nots—and golden darts.

Of course he could not send it now. He couldn't ever send another valentine to Jane. She belonged to Towne.

It didn't seem credible. It was one of the things
—like war—that men refused to believe could ever happen. Yet it had happened.

After this Jane would be out of his life—utterly. It was all very well to talk of friendship. But he wouldn't be her friend. He didn't want to see her. He didn't want to hear her voice. He thought he should die when he had to meet her as Mrs. Frederick Towne.

But what was he going to do without her? What...?

He paced the room restlessly. Ahead of him had been always the hope that he might win her. And now, she was won, and not by him. It was—unthinkable.

His excitement increased. The valentine seemed to mock him as it lay there fragile in its loveliness.

"Roses red, my dear,

And violets blue,

Honey's sweet, my dear...."

He reached out his hand for it and tore it into shreds. Paper lace!... Paper lace!...

CHAPTER XXI
VOICES IN THE DARK

Arthur Lane and Sandy talked it over. "I wonder what has happened. He looks dreadful."

The two boys were on their way to Castle Manor. They wanted books. Evans' library was a treasure-house for youthful readers. It had all the old adventuring tales. And Evans had read everything. He would simply walk up to a shelf, lay his hand on a book, and say, "Here's one you'll like." And he was never wrong.

He had told them that the latch-string was always out for them. And they had learned to look for his welcome. Sometimes he asked them to stay, and 'phoned to their parents. And then they popped corn before the library fire, or made taffy in the kitchen. And sometimes Baldy Barnes was there and that wonderful Miss Towne. And Mrs. Follette. The boys didn't care in the least what the rest of Sherwood thought about Mrs. Follette. They liked her and when she made the taffy and stood over the boiling kettle with the big spoon in her hand, they thought her regal in spite of the humble nature of her occupation.

But of late, Evans Follette had met them with an effort. "Look for yourselves," he had said, when

they asked for books, and had sat staring into the fire. And he had not urged them to stay. His manner had been kind but inattentive. They were puzzled and a little hurt. "I feel sorta queer when he acts that way," Sandy was saying, "as if he didn't take any interest. I don't even know whether he wants us any more."

Arthur refused to believe his hero inhospitable. "It's just that he's got things on his mind."

They reached the house and rang the bell. Old Mary let them in. "He's in the library," she said, and they went towards it. The door was open and they entered. But the room was empty....

That morning Baldy had had a letter from Jane and had handed it to Evans. It was the first long letter since her engagement to Towne. Baldy had written to his sister, flamingly, demanding to know if she was really happy. And she had said:

"I shall be when Judy is better. That is all I can think of just now. Her life is hanging in the balance. We can never be thankful enough that we got the specialist when we did. He had found the trouble. The question now is whether she will have the strength for another operation. When she gets through with that! Well, then I'll talk to you, darling. I hardly know how I feel. The days are so whirling. Mr. Towne has been more than generous. If the little I can give him will repay him, then I must give it, dearest. And it won't be hard. He is so very good to me."

And now this letter had come after Towne's second visit:

"Baldy, dear, I am very happy. And I want you to set your mind at rest. I am not marrying Mr. Towne for what he has done for us all, but because I love him. Please believe it. You can't understand what he has been to me in these dark days. I have learned to know how kind he is—and how strong. I haven't a care in the world when he is here, and everything is so— marvellous. You should see my ring—a great sapphire, Baldy, in a square of diamonds. He is crazy to buy things for me, but I won't let him. I will take things for Judy but not for myself. You can see that, of course. I just go everywhere with him in my cheap little frocks, to the theatres and to all the great restaurants, and we have the most delectable things to eat. It is really great fun.

"Judy is so happy over the whole thing, that it is helping her to get well. She says she was half afraid to advise me, but she knew it was for my happiness. Bob simply walks on air. He says when business grows better, he will pay back every cent to Mr. Towne. And of course he must. But we haven't any of us been made to feel that we ought to be grateful. Mr. Towne says that he simply held out a friendly hand when we needed it, and that's all there is to it.

"Well, dearest dear, I wish I could hear Philomel sing o' mornings, and see Merrymaid and the kit-cat on the hearth, but best of all would be to have your own darling self on the other side of the table."

Since he had heard the news of Jane's approaching marriage, Evans had lived in a dream. The people about him had seemed shadow-shapes. He had walked and talked with them, remembering nothing afterward but his great weariness. He had eaten his meals at stated times, and had not known what he was eating. He had gone to his office, and behind closed doors had sat at his desk, staring.

Nothing mattered. All incentive was gone. He spoke of Jane to no one. Not even to his mother. He had a morbid horror of hearing her name. When he came across anything that reminded him of her, he suffered actual physical pain.

And now this letter! "You see what she says," Baldy had raged. "Of course she isn't in love with him. But she thinks she is. There's nothing more that I can do."

Evans had taken the letter to the library to read. He was alone, except for Rusty, who had limped after him and laid at his feet.

She loved—Towne. And that settled it. "I am marrying Mr. Towne because I love him." Nothing could be plainer than that. Baldy might protest. But the words were there.

As Evans sat gazing into the fire, he saw her as she had so often been in this old room—as a child, sprawled on the hearth-rug over some entrancing book from his shelves, swinging her feet on the edge of a table while he bragged of his athletic

prowess; leaning over war-maps, while he pointed out the fields of fighting; curled up in a corner on the couch while he read to her—*"Oh, silver shrine, here will I take my rest...."*

He could stand his thoughts no longer. Without hat or heavy coat, he stepped through one of the long windows and into the night.

As he walked on in the darkness, he had no knowledge of his destination. He swept on and on, pursued by dreadful thoughts.

On and on through the blackness.... No moon ... a wet wind blowing ... on and on....

He came to a bridge which crossed a culvert. No water flowed under it. But down the road which led through the Glen was another bridge, and beneath it a deep, still pool.

With the thought of that deep and quiet pool came momentary relief from the horrors which had hounded him. It would be easy. A second's struggle. Then everything over. Peace. No fears. No dread of the future....

It seemed a long time after, that, leaning against the buttress of the bridge, he heard, with increasing clearness, the sound of boys' voices in the dark.

He drew back among the shadows. It was Sandy and Arthur. Not three feet away from him—passing.

"Well, of course, Mr. Follette is just a man," Sandy was saying.

"Maybe he is," Arthur spoke earnestly, "but I don't know. There's something about him——"

He paused.

"Go on," Sandy urged.

"Well, something"—Arthur was struggling to express himself, "splendid. It shines like a light——"

Their brisk footsteps left the bridge, and were dulled by the dirt road beyond. Sandy's response was inaudible. A last murmur, and then silence.

Evans was swept by a wave of emotion; his heart, warm and alive, began to beat in the place where there had been frozen emptiness.

"Something splendid—that shines like a light!"

Years afterward he spoke of this moment to Jane. "I can't describe it. It was a miracle—their coming. As much of a miracle as that light which shone on Paul as he rode to Damascus. The change within me was absolute. I was born again. All the old fears slipped from me like a garment. I was saved, Jane, by those boys' voices in the dark."

The next day was Sunday. Evans called up Sandy and Arthur and invited them to supper. "Old Mary said you were here last night, and didn't find me. I've a book or two for you. Can you come and get them? And stay to supper. Miss Towne will be here and her uncle."

The boys could not know that they were asked

as a shield and buckler in the battle which Evans was fighting. It seemed to him that he could not meet Frederick Towne. Yet it had been, of course, the logical thing to ask him. Edith had invited herself, and Towne had, of course, much to tell about Jane.

Evans, therefore, with an outward effect of tranquillity, played the host. After supper, however, he took the boys with him to the library.

On the table lay a gray volume. He opened it and showed the Cruikshank illustrations.

"I've been reading this. It's great stuff."

"Oh, Pilgrim's Progress," said Sandy; "do you like it?"

"Yes." Evans leaned above the book where it lay open under the light. "Listen:

"'Then Apollyon, espying his opportunity, began to gather up close to Christian, and wrestling with him, gave him a dreadful fall: and with that, Christian's sword flew out of his hand. Then said Apollyon, *I am sure of thee now*: and with that, he had almost prest him to death, so that Christian began to despair of life. But as God would have it, while Apollyon was fetching of his last blow, thereby to make a full end of this good Man, Christian nimbly reached out his hand for his Sword, and caught it, saying, *Rejoice not against me, O mine Enemy! when I fall, I shall arise*: and with that, gave him a deadly thrust, which made him give back, as one that had received his mortal wound: Christian perceiving that, made at him again saying, *Nay, in all these things we are more than Conquerors, through him that loved us.* And with that, Apollyon spread forth his Dragon's wings, and sped him away, that Christian saw him no more.'"

Evans' ringing voice gave full value to the words. It seemed to Arthur, worshipping his hero, as if he flung a hurled defiance at some unseen foe—"*Rejoice not against me, O mine Enemy! when I fall, I shall arise!*"

Yet when he looked up from the book Evans' eyes were smiling.

"Would you like to take it home with you? It is a rare edition, but you know how to handle it. And I'd like to have you read it. Some day you may meet Apollyon. And may find it helpful. As I have."

Later as the boys walked home together, the precious volume under Arthur's arm, Sandy said, "He's more like himself, isn't he? More pep."

"I'll say he is," but Arthur was not satisfied. "I wish he'd told us what he meant when he talked about meeting Apollyon."

That night Evans found out for the first time something about his mother. "You look tired, dearest," he had said, when their guests were gone, and he and she had come into the great hall together.

"I am tired." She sat down on an old horsehair sofa. "I can't stand much excitement. It makes me feel like an old lady."

"You'll never grow old." He felt a deep tenderness for her in this moment of confessed weakness. She had always been so strong. Had refused to lean. She had, in fact, taken from him his son's prerogative of protectiveness.

He laid his hand on her shoulder. "You'd better see Hallam."

"I've seen him."

"What did he say?"

"My heart——"

He looked at her in alarm. "Mother! Why didn't you tell me?"

"What was the use? There's nothing to be worried about. Only he says I must not push myself."

"I am worried. Let me look after the men in the morning early. That will give you an extra nap."

"Oh, I won't do it, Evans. You have your work."

"It won't hurt me. And I am going to boss you around a bit." He stooped and kissed her. "You are too precious to lose, Mumsie."

She clung to him. "What would I do without you, my dear?"

He helped her up the stairs. And as she climbed slowly, his arm about her, he thought of that dark moment by the bridge.

If those young voices had not come to him in the night, this loving soul might have been stricken and made desolate; left alone in her time of greatest need.

CHAPTER XXII
AT THE OLD INN

Once more the Washington papers had headlines that spoke of Delafield Simms. He had married a stenographer in Frederick Towne's office. And it was Towne's niece that he had deserted at the altar.

And most remarkable of all, Edith Towne had been at the wedding. It was Eloise Harper who told the reporters.

"They were married at the old Inn below Alexandria this morning, by the local Methodist clergyman. Miss Logan is a Methodist—fancy. And Edith was bridesmaid."

But Eloise did not know that Lucy had worn the wedding dress and veil that Edith had given her and looked lovely in them. And that after the ceremony, Delafield had wrung Edith's hand and had said, "I shall never know how to thank you for what you have been to Lucy."

Edith's candid eyes had met his squarely. "You know you are not half good enough for her, Del," and he had said, humbly, "I'm not and that's the truth. But I am going to do my darndest to be what she thinks I am."

Martha and her husband had served a delicious breakfast in the big empty dining-room. Only Edith and Baldy were there besides the bride and groom. Lucy had very sensibly refused to have any fuss and feathers. "If it is quiet, people won't have so much to say about it."

Delafield's manner to Lucy was perfect. "What do you think she has made me do?" he asked Edith. "Buy a farm in Virginia. We are going to raise pigs—black Berkshires, because Lucy likes the slant of their ears and the curl of their tails. She has been reading books about them, and we are going to spend our honeymoon motoring around the country and buying stock."

Oh, bravo, bravo, little Lucy, not to risk boring this fashionable young husband with a conventional honeymoon! Edith wanted to clap her hands. But she made no sign, except to meet Lucy's quiet glance with a lift of the eyebrows.

Edith and Baldy lingered after the bride and groom had driven off in a great gray car—bound for the Virginia country place which Delafield had bought, and made ready for the occupancy in the twinkling of an eye.

"Gee, but you're superlative," Baldy told her as they walked in the garden.

"Am I?"

"Yes. And the way you carried it off."

"I didn't carry it off. It carried itself."

"Are you sure it didn't hurt?"

She smiled at him from beneath her big hat. "Not a bit."

The box hedges in the garden were showing a hint of new green. There was a plum tree blooming prematurely. The sun made brown shadows along the river's edge, and the wash of the waves from passing steamers went lip-lapping among the reeds and rushes.

The moment was ripe for romance. But Baldy almost feverishly kept the conversation away from serious things. They had talked seriously enough, God knew, the other night by Edith's fire. He had seen her lonely in the thought of her future.

"When Uncle Fred marries I won't stay here."

He had yearned to take her in his arms, to tell her that against his heart she should never again know loneliness. But he had not dared. What had he to offer? A boy's love. Against her gold.

He told himself with some bitterness that one fortune was enough in a family. Jane's engagement had changed things for her brother. The antagonism which Baldy had always felt for Frederick was intensified. The thought of Towne's money weighed heavily upon him. Jane had already placed herself under insuperable obligations. Even if she wished, she could not now shake herself free.

And Edith's money? He and Jane living on the Towne millions? He wouldn't have it.

So he talked of Jane. "She doesn't want her engagement announced until she gets back. I think she's right."

"I don't," Edith said lazily. "If I loved a man I'd want to shout it to the world."

They were sitting on a rustic bench under the blossoming plum tree. Edith's hands were clasped behind her head, and the winged sleeves of her gown fell back and showed her bare arms. Baldy wanted to unclasp those hands, crush them to his lips—but instead he stood up, looking over the river.

"Do you see the ducks out there? Wild ones at that. It's a sign of spring."

She rose and stood beside him. "And you can talk of—ducks—on a day like this?"

"Yes," he did not look at her, "ducks are—safe."

He heard her low laugh. "Silly boy."

He turned, his gray eyes filled with limpid light. "Perhaps I am. But I should be a fool if I told you how I love you. Worship you. You know it, of course. But nothing can come of it, even if I were presumptuous enough to think that you—care."

She swept out her hands in an appealing gesture. "Say it. I want to hear."

She was adorable. But he drew back a little. "We've gone too far and too fast. It is my fault, of course, for being a romantic fool."

"I'm afraid we're a pair of romantic fools, Baldy."

He turned and put his hands on her shoulders. "Edith, I—mustn't."

"Why not?"

"Not until I have something to offer you——"

"You have something to offer——"

"Oh, I know what you mean. But—I won't. Somehow this affair of Jane's with your uncle has made me see——"

"See what?"

"Oh, how the world would look at it. How *he'd* look at it."

"Uncle Frederick? He hasn't anything to do with it. I'm my own mistress."

"I know. But—— Oh, I can't analyze it, Edith. I love you—no end. More than—anything. But I won't ask you to marry me."

"Do you know how selfish you are?"

"I know how wise I am."

She made an impatient gesture. "You're not thinking of me in the least. You are thinking of your pride."

He caught her hand in his. "I *am* thinking of my pride. Do you suppose it is easy for me to let Jane—take money from him? To feel that there is no man in our family who can pay the bills? I am proud. And I'm glad of it. Edith—I want you to be glad that I won't take—alms."

Her wise eyes studied him for a moment. "You blessed boy. You blessed poet," she sighed, "I am proud of you, but my heart aches—for myself."

He caught her almost roughly in his arms and in a moment released her. "I'm right, dearest?"

"No, you're not right. If we married, we'd sail to Italy and have a villa by the sea. And you would paint masterpieces. Do you think my money counts beside your talent? Well, I don't."

"My dear, let me prove my talent first. As things are now, I couldn't pay our passage to the other side."

"You could. My money would be yours—your talent mine. A fair exchange."

He stuck obstinately to his point of view. "I won't tie you to any promise until I've proved myself."

"And we'll lose all these shining years."

"We won't lose a moment. I'm going to work for you."

He was, she perceived, on the heights. But she knew the weariness of the climb.

Coming out of the garden in the late afternoon, they were aware of other arrivals at the Inn.

"Adelaide and Uncle Fred, by all the gods," said Edith, as they peered into the dining-room from the dimness of the hall. "Oh, don't let them see us. Adelaide's such a bromide."

They crept out, found Baldy's car and sped towards the city. "I should say," Baldy proclaimed

sternly, "that for a man who is engaged, a thing like that is unspeakable."

"Oh, Uncle Fred and Adelaide," said Edith, easily; "she probably asked him. And she was plaintive. A plaintive woman always gets her way."

Adelaide had been plaintive. And she had hinted for the ride. "Why not an afternoon ride, Ricky? It would rest you."

"Sorry. But I'm tied up."

"I haven't seen you for ages, Ricky."

"I know, old girl. I've had a thousand things."

"I've—missed you."

It wasn't easy for Frederick to ignore that. Adelaide was an attractive woman.

"Oh, well. I can get away at four. We'll have tea at the old Inn."

"Heavenly. Ricky, I have a new blue hat."

"You could always wear blue." He decided that he might as well make things pleasant. There was a shock in store for her. Of course he'd have to tell her about Jane.

So Adelaide in the new blue hat—with a wrap that matched—with that porcelain white and pink of her complexion—with her soft voice, and appealing manner, had Frederick for three whole hours to herself.

She told him all the spicy gossip. Frederick, like most men, ostensibly scorned scandal, but lent a willing ear. What Eloise had said, what Benny had said, what all the world was saying about Del's marriage.

"And they were married here to-day. I didn't dream it until Eloise called me up just before lunch. Edith had told her."

"Edith was here?"

"Yes, and young Barnes."

She stopped there and poured the tea. She did it gracefully, but Frederick's thoughts swept back to Jane behind her battlements of silver.

"Four lumps, Ricky?"

"Um—yes."

"A penny for your thoughts."

"They're not worth a penny, Adelaide. Lots of lemon, please. And no cakes. I am trying to keep my lovely figure."

"Oh, why worry? I like big men."

"That's nice of you."

Martha's little sponge cakes were light as a feather. Adelaide broke one and ate daintily. Then she said, "How's little Jane Barnes?"

Frederick was immediately self-conscious. "She's still in Chicago."

"Sister better?"

"Much."

"When is she coming back?"

"Jane? As soon as Mrs. Heming can be brought home. In a few weeks, I hope."

Adelaide drank a cup of tea almost at a draught. She was aware of an impending disclosure. When

the blow came, she took it without the flicker of an eyelash.

"I am going to marry Jane Barnes, Adelaide. The engagement isn't to be announced until she returns to Washington. But I want my friends to know."

She put her elbows on the table, clasped her hands and rested her chin on them looking at him with steady eyes. "So that's the end of it, Ricky?"

"The end of what?"

"Our friendship."

"Why should it be?"

"Oh, do you think that your little Jane is going to let you philander?"

"I shan't want to philander. If that's the way you put it."

"So you think you're in—love with her."

"I know I am," the red came up in his cheeks, but he stuck to it manfully. "It's different from anything—ever that I've felt before."

"They all say that, don't they, every time?"

"Don't be so—cynical."

She shrugged her shoulders. "I'm not. Well, I shall miss you, Ricky, dear."

That was all, just that plaintive note. But Adelaide's plaintiveness was always effective.

So after tea they walked in the garden, and sat under the plum tree, and looked out upon the river—where the shadows were rose-red in the setting sun, and Adelaide said, "My life is like that—my sun has set."

Frederick reached out a sympathetic hand. "Don't say that, old girl."

Adelaide lifted his hand to her cheek. "This is really 'good-bye,' isn't it, Ricky? It seems rather queer to be saying it."

CHAPTER XXIII
SPRING COMES TO SHERWOOD

Jane was home again. Judy was better. Philomel sang. The world was a lovely place.

"Oh, but it's good to be back," Jane was telling Baldy at breakfast. The windows were wide open, the fragrance of lilacs streamed in, there were pink hyacinths on the table.

"It's heavenly."

Baldy smiled at her. "The same old Jane."

She shook her head, and the light in her eyes wavered as if some breath of doubt fanned it. "Not quite. The winter hasn't been easy. I'm a thousand years older."

"And with a wedding day ahead of you."

"Yes. Do you like it, Baldy?"

He leaned back in his chair and surveyed her. "Not a bit—if you want the truth—I shall be jealous of Mr. Frederick Towne."

"Silly. You know I shall never love anybody more than you, Baldy."

She was perfectly unconscious of the revelation she was making, but he knew—and was constrained to say, "Then you don't really love him."

"Oh, I do. He's much nicer than I imagined he might be."

"Oh, well, if you think you are going to be happy."

"I know I am—dearest," she blew a kiss from the tips of her fingers. "Baldy, I'm going to have a great house with a great garden—and invite Judy and the babies—every summer."

"Towne's not marrying Judy and the babies. He's marrying you. He won't want all of your poor relations hanging around."

"Oh, he will. He has been simply dear. I feel as if I can never do enough for him."

She was very much in earnest. Baldy refrained from further criticism lest he cloud the happiness of her home-coming. The thing was done. They might as well make the best of it. So he said, "Do you always call him 'Mr. Towne'?"

"Yes. He scolds, but I can't say Frederick—or Fred. He begs me to do it—but I tell him to wait till we're married and then I'll say 'dear.' Most wives do that, don't they?"

"I hope mine won't."

"Why not?"

"I shall want my wife to invent names for me, and if she can't, I'll do it for her."

Jane opened her eyes wide. "Romance with a big R, Baldy?"

"Yes, of course. I should want to be king, lover, master—friend to the woman who cared for me. That's the real thing, Janey."

"Is it?" But she did not follow the subject up;

she drew another cup of coffee for herself, and asked finally, "When is Evans coming back?"

"Not for several days. He will go to Boston when he finishes with New York."

"I see. And he's much better?"

"I should say. You wouldn't know him."

He rose. "I must run on. We're to dine at Towne's then?"

"Yes. Just the five of us. It seems funny that I haven't met Cousin Annabel. But she's able to take her place at the head of the table, Mr. Towne tells me. He told me, too, that she wants to meet me. But I have a feeling that she won't approve of me, Baldy. I'm not fashionable enough."

"Why should you be fashionable? You are all right as you are."

"Am I? Baldy, I believe my stock has gone up with you."

"It hasn't, Janey. You were always a darling. But I didn't want to spoil you."

"As if you could," she smiled wistfully. "Sometimes I have a feeling, Baldy, that I should like life to go on just as it is. Just you and me, Baldy. But of course it can't."

"Of course it can, if you wish it. You mustn't marry Towne if you have the least doubt."

"I haven't any doubts. So don't worry." She stood up and kissed him. "Briggs will come out for me—and we are all to see a play together afterward."

"Edith told me."

"Baldy," she had hold of the lapel of his coat, "how are things going with—Edith?"

"Do you mean, am I in love with her? I am."

"Are you going to marry her?"

"God knows."

She looked up at him in surprise. "What makes you say it that way? Has she told you she didn't care?"

"She has told me that she does care. But do you think, Janey, that I'm going to take her money?"

He patted her on the cheek and was off. She went to the top of the terrace and watched him ride away. Then she walked in the little shaded grove behind the house. Merrymaid followed her and the much-matured kitten. There was a carpet underfoot of pine needles and of fragrant young growth. Several of her old hens scratched in the rich mould—and their broods of tiny chicks answering the urgent mother-cry were like bits of yellow down blown before a breeze.

Jane picked a spray of princess-pine and stuck it in her blouse. Oh, what an adorable world! Her world. Could there be anything better that Frederick Towne could give her?

Baldy's words rang in her ears—"Do you think I am going to take her money?"

Yet she was taking Frederick Towne's money.

She wished it had not been necessary. Each day it seemed to her that the thought burned deeper: she was under obligations to her lover that could be repaid only by marriage. And they were to be married in June.

Yet why should the thought burn? She loved him. Not, perhaps, as Baldy loved Edith. But there were respect and admiration, yes, and when she was with him, she felt his charm, she was carried along on the whirling stream of his own adoration and tenderness.

Yet—there were things to dread. She would have to meet his friends. Be judged by them. There would be formal entertaining. Edith had said once that the demand of society on women was really high-class drudgery. "Much worse than washing dishes."

Jane didn't quite believe that. Yet there must be a happy medium. Her dreams had had to do with a little house—a little garden.

She went back to her own little house, and found a great box of roses waiting. She spent an hour filling vases and bowls with them. Old Sophy coming in from the kitchen said, "Looks lak dat Mistuh Towne's jes' fascinated with you, Miss Janey."

"Aren't the roses lovely, Sophy?" Jane wanted to tell Sophy that Mr. Towne would some day be her husband. But she still deferred the announcement of her engagement.

"I've told one or two people," Frederick had said.

"Whom?"

"Well, Adelaide. She's such an old friend. And I told Annabel, of course. I don't see why you should care, Jane."

"I think I'm afraid that when I go into a shop someone will say, 'Oh, she's going to marry Frederick Towne, and see how shabby she is.'"

"You are never shabby."

"That's because I made myself two new dresses while I was at Judy's. And this is one of them."

"You have the great art of looking lovely in the simplest things. But some day you are going to wear a frock that I have for you." He told her about the silver and blue creation he had bought in Chicago. "Now and then I take it out and look at it. I've put it in your room, Jane, and it is waiting for you."

She thought now of the blue and silver gown, as Sophy said, "Miss Jane, I done pressed that w'ite chiffon of yours twel it hardly hangs together."

"I'll wear it once more, Sophy. I'm having a sewing woman next week."

With the old white chiffon she wore a golden rose or two—and sat at Frederick's right, while on the other end of the great table, Cousin Annabel weighed her in the balance.

Jane knew she was being weighed. Cousin Annabel was so blue-blooded that it showed in the veins of her hands and nose—and her hair was dressed with a gray transformation which quite overpowered her thin little face with its thin little nose.

As a matter of fact, Cousin Annabel felt that Frederick had taken leave of his senses. What could he see in this short-haired girl—who hadn't a jewel, except the one he had given her?

Jane wore Towne's ring, hidden, on a ribbon around her neck. "Some day I'll let everybody see it," she had said, "but not now."

"You act as if you were ashamed of it."

"I'm not. But Cinderella must wait until the night of the ball."

It was while they were drinking their coffee in the drawing-room that the storm came up. It was one of those cyclonic winds that whip off the tops of the trees and blow the roofs from unsubstantial edifices. The thunder was a ceaseless reverberation—the lightning was pink and made the sky seem like a glistening inverted shell.

Cousin Annabel hated thunder-storms and said so. "I think I shall go to my room, Frederick."

"You are not a bit safer up there than here," Towne told her.

"But I feel safer, Frederick." She was very decided about it. What she meant to do was to sit in the middle of her bed and have her maid give her the smelling salts. She would be thus in a sense fortified.

So she went up and Baldy and Edith wandered across the hall to the library, where Edith insisted they could observe other aspects of the storm.

Jane and her lover were left alone, and presently Frederick was called to the telephone.

"I'm not sure that it's safe, sir, in this storm," Waldron warned.

"Nonsense, Waldron," Towne said, and stepped quickly across the polished floor.

Thus it happened that Jane sat by herself in the great drawing-room of the Ice Palace, while the wind howled, and the rain streamed down the window glass, and all the evil things in the world seemed let loose.

And she was afraid!

Not of the storm, but of the great house. She was so small and it was so big. Her own little cottage clasped her in its warm embrace. This great mansion stood away from her—as the sky stands away from the desert. All the rest of her life she would be going up and down those great stairs, sitting in front of this great fireplace, presiding at the far end of Frederick's great table—dwarfed by it all, losing personality, individuality, bidding good-bye forever to little Jane Barnes, becoming until death parted them the wife of Frederick Towne.

She sat huddled in her chair, panting a little, her eyes wide.

"Silly," she said with a sob.

The sound of her voice echoed and reëchoed, *"Silly, silly, silly."*

The noise without was deafening—the wind shook the walls. She stood up, her hands clenched, then ran swiftly into the hall.

A thundering crash and the lights went out.

She heard Frederick calling, "Jane, Jane!"

She called back, "I'm here," and saw the quick spurt of a match as he lighted it, holding it up and peering into the dark.

"There you are, my dearest." He lighted another match and came towards her, as Waldron, with a brace of candles, appeared in one door and Baldy and Edith in another.

Frederick lifted Jane in his strong arms. "Why, you're crying," he said; "don't, my darling, don't."

Then Baldy came up and demanded, "What's the matter, Kitten? You've never been afraid of storms."

She tried to smile at him. "Well, I've gone through such a lot lately." But Baldy wasn't satisfied. A Jane who dissolved into tears was a disturbing and desolating object. He glowered at Frederick, holding him responsible.

At this moment Waldron reappeared to say that Briggs had pronounced the streets impassable. Branches had been blown down—and there was other wreckage.

"That settles it," Frederick said. "You two
young things may as well stay here for the night. Jane's not fit to go out
anyhow."

"Oh, I'm all right," she protested.

Edith suggested bridge, so they played for a while. The big room was
still lighted by the candles, so that the shadows pressed close. Jane was very
pale, and now and then Frederick looked at her anxiously.

"You and Edith had better go up," he said at last. "And you must have
Alice get you some hot milk—I'll send Waldron with a bit of cordial to set
you up."

She shook her head. "I don't want it."

"But I want you to have it." There was a note of authority which almost
brought her again to tears. She hated to have anyone tell her what she should
do. She liked to do as she pleased. But later, when the glass of cordial came
up to her, she drank it.

She did not go to sleep for a long time. Edith sat by the bed and talked
to her. "I shouldn't," she apologized; "Uncle Fred told you to rest."

Jane curled up among her pillows, and said rebelliously, "Well, I don't
have to obey yet, do I?"

"Don't ever obey." Edith, in her winged chair with her Viking braids
and the classic draperies of her white dressing-gown, looked like a Norse
goddess. "Don't ever obey, or you'll make a tyrant out of him."

"But I hate—fighting."

"You won't have to fight. I do it because it's my temperament. But you
can manage him—by letting things go a bit—and coaxing will do the rest—
—"

"I don't want to manage—my husband," said Jane.

"All women do———"

"Would you want to manage—Baldy?"

Edith flushed. "That's different," she evaded.

"Not different. You know you wouldn't go through life with him,
pulling wires, making a puppet of him—of yourself—you want
comradeship—understanding. You'll flare up now and then. Baldy and I
do. But—oh, we love each other." Jane's voice shook.

Edith looked at her thoughtfully. "Jane, are you happy?"

"I ought to be———"

"But are you?"

"I'm tired, I think. I don't know. Ever since I came home I've been
nervous. Perhaps it is the reaction."

"Jane, I'm going to say something. Don't marry Uncle Fred unless you're—sure. I went through all that with Del. And you see how little I knew of what I had in my heart to give——" She stopped, her lovely face suffused with blushes. "I've learned—since then. And you mustn't make my—mistake. And, Jane dear," she leaned over the younger girl like some splendid angel, "don't

worry about material things. Baldy and I will want you always with us——"

Jane sat up. "Are you going to marry Baldy?"

"I am," sighing a little, "some day, when his ship comes in. He isn't willing to share my cargo—yet."

"He loves you," said Jane, "dearly."

Edith bent down and kissed her. "I know," she said, "and my heart sings it."

When Edith went away, they had not touched again on the question of Jane's marriage. Jane, lying awake in the dark, reflected that of course Edith could not know of her debt to Frederick. No one knew except Baldy.

In the morning Towne had gone when Jane came down. She and Edith had had breakfast in their rooms—and there had been a great rose on Jane's tray, with a note twisted about the stem—"To my golden girl." Her lover had called her up by the house telephone, and had told her he was leaving for New York at noon. "A telegram has just come. I'll see you the moment I get back."

Jane had a sense of relief. She would have three days to herself. Three days at Sherwood—with the blossoming trees, and the mating birds, and Merrymaid and the kitten, and old Sophy with her wise philosophy—and Baldy on the other side of the little table—and Philomel singing....

Briggs took her out at noon, and Sophy came in to say, "Mr. Evans called you-all up. He's back

fum New York. He say he'll come over to-night."

That was news indeed! Old Evans! Jane got into the frock of faded lilac gingham and went about the house singing. Three days! Of freedom!

It was after lunch that she told the old woman, "I'm going down in the Glen—there should be wild honeysuckle—Sophy."

Sophy surveyed her. "The whole place is chock-full of flowers, Miss Janey. And I'll miss my guess effen dey ain' mo' of 'em dis afternoon."

"But—wild honeysuckle, Sophy? The florists haven't that for me, have they?"

So Jane put on a wide-brimmed hat, and away she went down the long road with the pines on each side of it—the wide creek, which washed in shallow ripples over the brown stones, or eddied in still pools under the great old willows.

There were bees in the Glen and butterflies, and a cool silence. On the other side of the creek were pasture, and cattle grazing. But no human creature was in sight. Jane, walking along the narrow path, had a sense of utter peace. Here was familiar ground. She felt the welcome of inanimate things—the old willows, the singing stream, the great gray rocks that stuck their heads above the edges of the bank.

On the slope of the bank she saw the rosiness of the flowers she sought. She climbed up, picked the
fragrant sprays and sat down under a hickory tree to make a bouquet. From where she sat she could view the broad stream and a rustic bridge just at a turn of the path.

And now, around the turn of the path, came suddenly a man and two boys. They carried fishing-rods and stopped at a jutting rock to bait their hooks. One of the boys went out on the bridge and cast his line. His voice came to Jane clearly.

"Mr. Follette, there's a thing I hate to do, and that's to bait my hook with a worm. I'd much rather put on something that wasn't alive. Why is it that everything eats up something else?"

Jane peered down at the man poised on the rock. It *was* Evans! He was winding his reel against a taut line. "I've caught a snag," he said; "look out, Sandy, there's something on your hook."

As they landed the small catch with much excitement, Jane was aware of the strong swing of Evans' figure, the brown of his cheeks, the brightness of his glance as he spoke to the boys.

He gave the death stroke to the silver flapping fish with a jab of his knife-blade, and the boy on the bridge complained, "There you are, killing things. I don't like it, do you? Everything we eat? The woods are full of killing. It is dreadful when we think of it."

"It is dreadful." Evans sat down on the rock and looked across at the boy on the bridge. "But there are more dreadful things than death— injustice,
and cruelty, and hate. And more than all—fear. And you must think of this, Arthur, that what we call a violent death is sometimes the easiest. An old animal with teeth gone, trying to exist. That's dreadfulness. Or an old

person racked by pains. Much better if both could have been dead in the glory of youth.”

He had always had that quick and vivid voice, but this certainty of phrase was a resurrection. He spoke without hesitation. Sure of himself. Sure of the things he was about to say.

“You boys needn’t think that I don’t know what I am talking about. I do. When I came back from France there was something wrong. I was afraid of everything. I lived for months in dread of my shadow. It was awful. Nothing can be worse. Then, one night I came to see that God’s greatest gift to man is—strength to endure.”

He flung it at them—and their wide eyes answered him. After a moment Arthur said, huskily, “Gee, that’s great.”

Sandy sighed heavily. “I saw a picture the other day of a boy who wanted to play baseball, and he had to hold the baby. I reckon that’s what you mean. Most of us have to hold the baby when we want to play baseball.”

The others laughed, then young Arthur said, “It looks to me as if life is just one darned thing after another.”

“Not quite that.” Evans stood up. “I’m afraid
I’m an awful preacher,” he apologized, “but you will ask questions.”

“Most grown-ups don’t answer them,” said Arthur, earnestly; “they just say, ‘Be good and let who will be clever.’”

“They’d better say ‘Be strong.’” Evans was reeling in his line. “We must be getting towards home. Do you see those shadows? We’ll be late——”

He stopped suddenly. There had been the crack of a twig and he had turned his eyes towards the sound. And there, poised above him, her eyes lighted up, her hands held out to him, her hat off, the warm wind blowing her bobbed black hair, blowing, too, the folds of the lilac frock back from her slender figure, stood Jane ... *Jane....*

He went charging up the bank towards her.

“My dear,” he said, “my dear.”

That was all. But he was there, holding her hands, devouring her with his eyes.

Then he dropped her hands. “I thought you were a ghost,” he said, a little awkwardly. “I called you up this morning and Sophy said you were in town.”

“I came out at noon. The day was so perfect. I had to see the Glen.”

“It is perfect. When I found you were out, I got the boys. I am taking a half-holiday after my trip.”

He was talking naturally now, smiling up at her

as she stood above him. She found herself trembling, almost afraid to speak again lest her voice betray her. She had been more shaken than he by the encounter. She wondered at his ease.

She was to wonder more, as he walked home with her. The presence of the boys barred, of course, personalities. But Evans' clear eyes met hers without a shadow of self-consciousness. He asked her about her journey, about Judy, about the babies, about Bob. The only subject on which he did not touch was her marriage with Frederick Towne.

And so it happened that, woman-like, as they walked alone at last after the boys had left them in the little pine grove back of the house, that Jane said, "Evans, you haven't wished me happiness."

"No," he said, and his eyes met hers squarely. "I think you might spare me that, Jane."

She flushed. "Oh," she said, "I'm sorry."

He laid his hand for a moment on her shoulder. "Don't be sorry, little Jane. But we won't talk about it. That's the best way for both of us—not to talk."

He stayed to dinner, stayed for an hour or two afterward—fitting himself in pleasantly to former niches. Jane could hardly credit the change in him. It was, she decided, not so much a resurrection of the body as of the spirit. His hair was gray, and now and then his eyes showed tired, his shoulders sagged. But there was no trace of the old timidity, the old withdrawals. He was interested, responsive, at times buoyant. The things she had loved in him years ago were again there. *This man did not think dark thoughts!*

When he went away, she and Baldy stood together on the terrace in the warm darkness and watched him.

"He still limps a little," Jane said.

"Yes. Shall we go in now, Jane?"

"No. Let's sit on the steps and see the moon rise."

They sat side by side. "When is Towne coming back?" Baldy asked.

"In three days."

Tree-toads were shrilling in monotonous cadence—from far away came the plaintive note of a whippoorwill. But there was another plaintive note close at hand.

"Jane, you're crying," Baldy said, sharply. "What's the matter, dear?"

He put his arm about her. "What's the matter?"

"Baldy, I don't want to get—married. I want to stay with you—forever——"

"You shall stay with me."

She sobbed and sobbed, and he soothed her. "Little sister, little sister," he said, "you are crying too much in these days."

She sat up, wiped her eyes with his handkerchief, smoothed her hair with shaking hands. "It is rather silly, Baldy."

"Nothing of the kind, Janey. I knew the whole thing was a mistake."

She stopped him with a touch of her hand on his arm. "Don't," she said, "it isn't a mistake, Baldy. I was just a bit—low—in my mind——"

"Do you think I am going to let you marry Towne?"

There was a long silence. The bird in the Glen said, "Whippoorwill—whippoorwill," in dull reiteration, the tree-toads shrilled, the rising moon drew a line of gold across the horizon.

At last Jane spoke. "Dearest, I must marry him. There's no way out. He's done so much for me—and some day, perhaps, I'll love him."

CHAPTER XXIV
HAUNTED

It was after the day when she had met Evans in the Glen that Jane began to be haunted by ghosts.

There was a ghost who wandered through Sherwood on moonlights, a limping, hesitating ghost who said, "You're wine, Jane. I must have my daily sip of you."

And there was a ghost who came in a fog and said, "You are a lantern, Jane—held high."

And that ghost in the glow of the hearth-fire—"You are food and drink to me, Jane. Do you know it?"

Ghosts, ghosts, ghosts; holding out appealing hands to her. And always she had turned away. But now she did not turn. Over and over again she lent her ears to those whispering words, "Jane, you are wine.... Jane, you are a lantern.... You are food and drink, Jane...."

Well, she was having her punishment. She had not loved him when he needed her. And now that she needed him, she must not love him.

She hardly knew herself. All the years of her life she had seen things straight, and she had tried to live up to that vision. She saw them straight

now. She did not love Frederick Towne. She had no right to marry him. Yet she must. There was no way out.

Towne was aware of a difference in her when he returned from New York. She was more remote. A little less responsive. Yet these things caused him no disquiet. Her crisp coolness had always constituted one of her great charms. "You are tired, dearest," he told her. "I wish you would marry me right away, and let me make you happy."

They were lunching at the Capitol in the Senate restaurant. Frederick was an imposing figure and Jane was aware of his importance. People glanced at him and glanced again, and then told others who he was. Some day she would be his wife, and everybody would be telling everybody else that she was the wife of the great Frederick Towne.

The attentive waiter at her elbow laid toast on her plate, and served Maryland crab from a silver chafing-dish. Frederick knew what she liked and had ordered without asking her. But the delicious food was tasteless. She had been afraid Frederick would say something about an immediate marriage, and now he was saying it.

"Oh," she told him, earnestly, "you promised I might wait until Judy could come on. In June."

"I know. But it will be very hot, and you'll have a whole lifetime in which to see Judy."

"But not at my wedding. She's my only sister."

"I see," but his voice showed his annoyance;

"but it seems as if your family have demanded enough of you. Can't you think a bit about yourself—and me?"

She pressed her point. "Judy is like my mother. I can't be married without her and the babies."

"If the babies come, you'll be looking after them until the last moment, and it will be a great strain on you, sweetheart."

"Oh, it won't be. I adore babies."

His quick jealousy flared. "I don't," he said, with a touch of sulkiness. "I'm not fond of children."

She ate in silence. And presently he said repentantly, "You must think me a great boor, Jane. But you don't know how much I want you."

He was like a repentant boy. She made herself smile at him. "I think you are very patient, Mr. Towne."

"I am not patient. I am most impatient. And when are you going to stop calling me Mr. Towne?"

"When I can call you—husband."

"But I don't want to wait until then, dearest."

"But 'Frederick' is so long, and 'Fred' is so short, and 'Ricky' sounds like a highball." She had thrown off her depression and was sparkling.

"Nobody calls me 'Ricky' but Adelaide. I always hated it."

"Did you?" She was demure. "I might say 'my love,' like the ladies in the old-fashioned novels."

He laughed delightedly. "Say it."

She acquiesced unexpectedly. "My love, we are invited to a week-end with the Delafield Simms, at their new country place, Grass Hills."

"Are we?" Then in a sudden ardent rush of words, "Jane, I'd kiss you if the world wasn't looking on."

"The reporters would be ecstatic. Headlines."

"I am tired of headlines. And what do you mean about going to Delafield Simms?"

"They are asking a lot of his friends. It is his wife's introduction to his old crowd. Much will depend on whether you and Edith will accept. And it was Edith who asked me to—make you come——"

She gave him the truth, knowing it to be better than diplomacy. "I told her that I couldn't make you. But perhaps if you knew I wanted it——" She paused inquiringly.

He leaned towards her across the table. "Ask me, prettily, and I'll do it."

"Really?" She laughed, blushed and did it. "Will you go—my love?"

"Could I say 'no' to that?" He radiated satisfaction. "Do you know how charming you are, Jane?"

"Am I? But it is nice of you to go. I know how you'll hate it."

"Not if you are there. And now, who else are asked?"

"Oh, Mrs. Laramore and Eloise Harper and a lot of others. Lucy says she'll be like a fish out of water, but Delafield has made up his mind that his friends shan't think that he's ashamed of her."

When their ices came and their coffee, Frederick said, "I've got to spend a half-hour in a committee room. Shall I take you up to the Senate Gallery?"

"No—there's nothing interesting, is there? I'll wait in Statuary Hall."

Jane loved the marble figures that circled the Hall. Years ago there had not been so many. They had been, then, perhaps, more distinctive. As a child, she had chosen as her favorites the picturesque Colonials, the frontiersmen in leather tunics and coonskin caps. She had never liked the statesmen in stiff shirts and frock coats, although she had admitted their virtues. Even the incongruous classic draperies were more in keeping with the glamour which the past flung over the men who had given their best to America.

But it was Fulton who had captured her imagination, with his little ship, and Pere Marquette with his cross, the peace-loving Quaker who had conquered; adventurer, pioneer, priest and prophet—builders all of the structure of the new world.

She wondered what future generations would add to this glorious company. Would the Anglo-Saxon give way to the Semite? Would the Huguenot yield to the Slav? And would these newcomers hold high the banner of national idealism? What

would they give? And what would they take away?

There were groups of sightseers gathered about the great room—a guide placing them here and there on the marble blocks. The trick was to put someone behind a mottled pillar far away, and let him speak. Owing to some strange acoustic quality the sound would be telephoned to the person who stood on the whispering stone.

Years ago Jane had listened while a voice had come echoing across the hollow spaces of the great Hall, "My country—right or wrong—my country——"

Another ghost! The ghost of a boy, patriotic, passionately devoted to the great old gods. "Of course they were only men, Jane. Human. Faulty. But they blazed a path of freedom for those who followed...."

When Frederick came, he found her standing before the prim statue of Frances Willard.

"Tired, sweetheart?"

"No."

"I stayed longer than I expected."

"It didn't seem long. I have had plenty of company."

He was puzzled. "What do you mean?"

"All these." Her hand indicated the marble men and women.

He laughed. "Great old freaks, aren't they?"

Freaks!

Gods!

Well, of course, it all depended absolutely on the point of view.

"I like them all," she said, sturdily, "even the ones in the hideous frock coats."

"Surely not, my dear."

"Yes, I do. They may be bad art, but they're good Americans."

His laugh was indulgent. "After you've been abroad a few times, you won't be so provincial."

"If being provincial means loving my own, I'll stay provincial."

"Travel broadens the mind, changes the point of view."

"But why should I love my country less? I know her faults. And I know Baldy's. But I love him just the same."

As they walked on, he fell into step with her. "We won't argue. You are probably right, and if not, you're too pretty for me to contradict."

His gallantry was faultless, but she wanted more than gallantry. There had been the vivid give and take of her arguments with Evans. They had had royal battles, youth had crossed swords with youth. And from their disagreements had come convictions.

She had once more the illusion of Frederick as a feather cushion! He would perhaps agree with her always!

And her soul would be—smothered!

CHAPTER XXV
AGAIN THE LANTERN

It was the morning of the day that she was going to the Delafield Simms, and Jane was packing her bag. She felt unaccountably depressed. During this week-end her engagement would be announced. And when Judy came they would be married in the Sherwood church.

And that would be the end of it!

Her lover had planned the honeymoon with enthusiasm, "Dieppe, Jane, Avignon—the North Sea. Such sunsets."

Jane felt that she didn't care in the least for sunsets or trips abroad. She was almost frightened at her indifference to the wonders of a world of which Frederick talked continually. Oh, what were mountains and sea at a time like this? Her heart should beat high—the dawns should be rosy, the nights full of stars. But they were not. Her heart was like a stone in her breast. The mornings broke gray and blank. The nights were dark. Her dreams were troubled.

She knew now what had happened to her. She had let herself be blinded by a light which she had thought was the sun. And it was not even the

moon! It was a big round artificial brilliance which warmed no one!

Life with Frederick Towne would be just going up and down great stairs, eating under the eye of a stately butler, riding on puffy cushions behind a stately chauffeur, sitting beside a man who was everlastingly and punctiliously polite.

Oh, half the fun in the world was in the tussle with hard things. She knew that now. Life in the little house had been at times desperately difficult. But it had been like facing a stiff breeze, and coming out of it thrilled with the battle against the elements.

Yet how could she tell these things to Frederick? He was complacent, comfortable. She was young and he liked that. He never dreamed that he might seem to her somewhat staid and stodgy. For a moment, in Chicago, he had been lighted by almost youthful fires. But in these days of daily meetings, she had become aware of his fixed habits, his fixed opinions, the fixed programs which must be carried out at any cost.

She had found, indeed, that she had little voice in any plans that Frederick made for her. When he consulted her on matters of redecorating the big house he brought to the subject a wealth of technical knowledge that appalled her. Jane knew what she liked, but she did not know why she liked it. But Frederick knew. He had the lore of period furniture at his fingers' ends. Rugs and tapestries—paintings

and porcelains! He had drawings made and water-color sketches, and brought them out to Jane. She had a feeling that when the house was finished it would be like some exquisitely ordered mausoleum. There would be no chintzes, no pussy-cats purring, no Philomel singing!

As for clothes! Frederick's mind dwelt much on the subject. Jane was told that she must have an ermine wrap, and one of Persian lamb. Most of her things would be made in Paris—there was a man over there who did things in just the right style for her—picturesque but not sophisticated. Frederick was already having certain jewels set appropriately. Gray pearls and emeralds—he had even gone to the point of getting samples of silk and chiffon that she might see the smoke-gray and jade color-scheme he had in mind for her.

Samples!

A man's mind shouldn't be on clothes. He should have other things to think of.

There was Evans, for example. He had described the other night the boys' club he was starting in Sherwood. "In the old pavilion, Jane. It will do as it is in summer, and in winter we'll enclose it. And we are to have a baseball team, and play against the surrounding towns. You should see my little lads."

She and Baldy had been much interested. The three of them had put their heads together as they sat on the porch of the little house, with the moon

whitening the world, and the whippoorwill mourning far away in the swamp.

They had planned excitedly, and every word they had said had been warm with enthusiasm. They had been flushed, exultant. It would be a great thing for Sherwood.

That was the kind of thing to live for, to live with. Ideas. Effort. She had always known it. Yet for a moment, she had forgotten. Had thought of herself as—Curlylocks.

She flung up her hands in a sort of despair. There was no way out of it. She was bound to Frederick Towne by the favors she had accepted from him. And that settled it.

She went on feverishly with the packing of her shabby suitcase. She rather glorified in its shabbiness. *At least it is mine own*, was her attitude of mind.

As she leaned over it, the great ring that Frederick had given her swung back and forth on its ribbon. She tucked it into the neck of her frock but it would not stay. At last she took it off and was aware of a sense of freedom as if she had shed her shackles. It winked and blinked at her on the dresser, so she shut it in a drawer and was still aware of it shining in the darkness, balefully!

Briggs was not to come for her until four in the afternoon. She decided to go over to Castle Manor and talk to Mrs. Follette. She would take some strawberries as an excuse. The strawberries in

the Castle Manor garden were never as perfect as those which Jane had planted. Evans said it was because Jane coaxed things into rosiness and roundness. But Jane had worked hard over the beds, and she had had her reward.

Carrying a basket, therefore, of red and luscious fruit, Jane went through the pine grove along the path that led to the Castle Manor. Under the trees was a green light which she breasted as one breasts the cool waters of the sea. Her breath came quickly. In a few short weeks she would be far away from this sweet and silent spot, with its sacred memories.

Leaving the grove, she passed the field where the scarecrow reigned.

She leaned on the fence. With the coming of spring, the scarecrow had been decked in gay attire. He wore a pink shirt of Evans' and a pair of white trousers. His hat was of straw, and as he danced in the warm south breeze he had an air of care-free jauntiness.

Jane found herself resenting his jaunty air. She felt that she had liked him better in his days of appealing loneliness. She had resented, in like manner, the change in Evans. He, too, had an air of making a world for himself. She had no part in it, apparently. She was, in effect, the Peri at the gate!

And she wanted to be in his world. Evans' world. She didn't want to be left out. Yet she

had chosen. And Evans had accepted her decision. She had not thought it would be so hard to have him—accept.

His interests seemed now to include everything but Jane. He was doing many things for the boys of Sherwood, there was his work in town, the added responsibility he had assumed in the affairs of the farm.

"She's such an old darling, Jane. Doing it with her duchess air. But she's not strong. I'm trying to make her let things go a bit. But she's so proud of her success. I wish you could see her showing Edith Towne and her fashionable friends about the dairy. With tea on the lawn afterward. You must come over and join in the fun, Jane."

"I am coming," Jane had told him, "but my days have been so filled."

He had known who had filled them. But he had ignored that, and had gone on with his subject. "The idea I have now is to keep bees and sell honey. The boys and I have some books on bee culture. They are quite crazy about it."

It was always now the boys and himself. His mother and himself. And once it had been himself and Jane!

Leaning on the fence, Jane spoke to the scarecrow. "I ought to be glad but I am not."

The scarecrow bowed and danced in the breeze. He had no heart, of course. He was made of two crossed sticks....

Jane found Mrs. Follette on the wide porch. She was snowy and crisp in white linen. She wore a black enamel brooch, and a flat black hat which was so old-fashioned that it took on a mid-Victorian stateliness.

"My dear child," she said, "stay and have lunch with me. Mary has baked fresh bread, and we'll have it with your berries, and some Dutch cheeses and cream."

"I'd love it," Jane said; "I hoped you'd ask me. We are going at four to Delafield Simms for the week-end. I shall have to be fashionable for forty-eight hours, and I hate it."

Mrs. Follette smiled indulgently. "Of course, you don't mean it. And don't try to be fashionable. Just be yourself. It is only people who have never been anybody who try to make themselves like others."

"Well," said Jane, "I'm afraid I've never been anybody, Mrs. Follette. I'm just little Jane Barnes."

Her air was dejected.

"What's the matter with you, Jane?" Mrs. Follette demanded.

Jane clasped her hands together. "Oh, I want my mother. I want my mother." Her voice was low, but there was a poignant note in it.

Old Mary came out with the tray, and when she had gone, Mrs. Follette said, "Now tell me what's troubling you?"

"I'm afraid."

"Of what?"

"Oh, of Mr. Towne's big house, and—I think I'm a little bit afraid of him, too, Mrs. Follette."

"Why should you be afraid?"

"Of the things he'll expect of me. The things I'll expect of myself. I can't explain it. I just—feel it."

Mrs. Follette, pouring ice-cold milk from a silver pitcher, said, "It is a case of nerves, my dear. You don't know how lucky you are."

"Am I lucky?" wistfully.

"Of course you are lucky. But all girls feel as you do, Jane, when the wedding day isn't far off. They wonder and wonder. It's the newness—the——"

"'Laying flesh and spirit ... in his hands ...'" Jane quoted, with quick-drawn breath.

"I shouldn't put it quite like that," Mrs. Follette said with some severity; "we didn't talk like that when I was a girl."

"Didn't you?" Jane asked. "Well, I know you were a darling, Mrs. Follette. And you were pretty. There's that portrait of you in the library in pink."

"I looked well in pink," said Mrs. Follette, thoughtfully, "but the best picture that was ever done of me is a miniature that Evans has." She buttered another slice of bread. She had no fear of growing fat. She *was* fat, but she was also

stately and one neutralized the other. To think of Mrs. Follette as thin would have been to rob her of her duchess rôle.

Jane had not seen the miniature. She asked if she might.

"I'll get it," said Mrs. Follette, and rose.

Jane protested, "Can't I do it?"

"No, my dear. I know right where to put my hand on it."

She went into the cool and shadowy hall and started up the stairs, and it was from the shadows that Jane heard her call.

There was something faint and agitated in the cry, and Jane flew on winged feet.

Mrs. Follette was holding on to the stair-rail, swaying a little. "I can't go any higher," she panted; "I'll sit here, my dear, while you get my medicine. It's in my room on the dresser."

Jane passed her on the stairs, and was back again in a moment with the medicine, a spoon, and a glass of water. With her arm around the elder woman she held her until the color returned to her cheeks.

"How foolish," said Mrs. Follette at last, sitting up. "I almost fainted. I was afraid of falling down the stairs."

"Let me help you to your room," Jane said, "and you can lie on the couch—and be quiet——"

"I don't want to be quiet, but I'll lie on the couch—if you'll sit there and talk to me."

So with Jane supporting her, Mrs. Follette went up the rest of the flight, and across the hall—and was made comfortable on a couch at the foot of her bed.

Jane loved the up-stairs rooms at Castle Manor. Especially in summer. Mrs. Follette followed the southern fashion of taking up winter rugs and winter curtains and substituting sheer muslins and leaving a delightful bareness of waxed floor.

"Perhaps I can tell you where to find the miniature," Mrs. Follette said, as Jane fanned her; "it is in Evans' desk set back under the row of pigeon-holes. You can't miss it, and I want to see it."

Jane crossed the hall to Evans' room. It faced south and was big and square. It had the same studied bareness that made the rest of the house beautiful. There was a mahogany bed and dresser, many books, deep window-seats with faded velvet cushions.

Evans' desk was in an alcove by the east window which overlooked Sherwood. It was a mahogany desk of the secretary type, and there was nothing about it to drain the color from Jane's cheeks, to send her hand to her heart.

Above the desk, however, where his eyes could rest upon it whenever he raised them from his writing, was an old lantern! Jane knew it at once. It was an ancient ship's lantern that she and Baldy had used through all the years, a heritage from some sea-going ancestor. It was the lantern she had carried that night she had found Evans in the fog!

Since her return from Chicago she had not been able to find it. Baldy had complained, "Sophy must have taken it home with her." But Sophy had not taken it. It was here. And Jane knew, with a certainty that swept away all doubts, why.

"You are a lantern, Jane, held high...."

She found the miniature and carried it back to Mrs. Follette. "I told you you were pretty and you have never gotten over it."

She had regained her radiance. Mrs. Follette reflected complacently that girls were like that. Moods of the moment. Even in her own day.

She spoke of it to Evans that night. "Jane had lunch with me. She was very tired and depressed. I told her not to worry. It's natural she should feel the responsibility of the future. Marriage is a serious obligation."

"Marriage is more than that, Mother."

"What do you mean?"

"Oh, it's a great adventure. The greatest adventure. If a woman loved me, I'd want her to fly to me—on wings. There'd be no fear of the future if Jane loved Towne."

"But she does love him. She wouldn't marry him for his money."

"No, she wouldn't," with a touch of weariness. "It is one of the things I can't make clear to myself. And I think I'd rather not talk about it, Mother."

They were in Mrs. Follette's room. She had told her son about her heart attack, and he had been anxious. But she had been quite herself after and had made light of it. "I shall have Hallam over in the morning," he had insisted, and she had acquiesced. "I don't need him, but if it will make you feel better."

Evans told her "good-night" presently and went into his own room. It was flooded with moonlight. He curled up on the cushions of the window-seat, with his arms around his knees and thought of Jane. He did not know that she had been that day in his room. Yet she was there now—a shadowy presence. The one woman in the world for him. The woman who had lighted his way. Who still, thank God, lighted it, though she was not his and would never be.

In a few short weeks she would be married. Would go out of his life—forever. Yet what she had been to him, Towne could never take away. The little Jane of Sherwood whom Evans had known would never belong absolutely to her husband. Her spirit would escape him—come back where it belonged, to the man who worshipped her.

He stood up, struck a match and lighted the low candle in the old lantern. It would burn dimly until he was asleep. Night after night he had opened his eyes to see it burning. It seemed to him that his dreams were less troubled because of that dim lantern.

CHAPTER XXVI
THE DISCORDANT NOTE

Lucy was still to Eloise Harper the stenographer of Frederick Towne. Out of place, of course, in this fine country house, with its formal gardens, its great stables, its retinue of servants.

"What do you do with yourselves?" she asked her hostess, as she came down, ready for dinner, in revealing apricot draperies and found Lucy crisp in white organdie with a band of black velvet around her throat.

"Do?" Lucy's smile was ingenuous. "We are very busy, Del and I. We feed the pigs."

"Pigs?" Eloise stared. She had assumed that a girl of Lucy's type would affect an elaborate attitude of leisure. And here she was, instead, fashionably energetic.

They fed the pigs, it seemed, actually. "Of course not the big ones. But the little ones have their bottles. There are ten and their mother died. You should see Del and me. He carries the bottle in a metal holder—round,"— Lucy's hand described the shape,—"and when they see him coming they all squeal, and it's adorable."

Lucy's air was demure. She was very happy.

She was a woman of strong spirit. Already she had interested her weak husband beyond anything he had ever known in his drifting days of bachelorhood. "After dinner," she told Eloise, "I'll show you Del's roses. They are quite marvellous. I think his collection will be beyond anything in this part of the country."

Delafield, coming up, said, "They are Lucy's roses, but she says I am to do the work."

"But why not have a gardener?" Eloise demanded.

"Oh, we have. But I should hate to have our garden a mere matter of— mechanics. Del has some splendid ideas. We are going to work for the flower shows. Prizes and all that."

Delafield purred like a pussy-cat. "I shall name my first rose the 'Little Lucy Logan.'"

Edith, locking arms with Jane, a little later, as they strolled under a wisteria-hung trellis towards the fountain, said, "Lucy's making a man of him because she loves him. And I would have laughed at him. We would have bored each other to death."

"They will never be bored," Jane decided, "with their roses and their little pigs."

They had reached the fountain. It was an old-fashioned one, with thin streams of water spouting up from the bill of a bronzed crane. There were goldfish in the pool, and a big green frog leaped from a lily pad. Beyond the fountain the wisteria roofed a path of pale light. A peacock walked slowly towards them, its long tail sweeping the ground in burnished beauty.

"Think of this," said Jane, "and Lucy's days at the office."

"And yet," Edith pondered, "she told me if he had not had a penny she would have been happy with him."

"I believe it. With a cottage, one pig, and a rose-bush, they would find bliss. It is like that with them."

The two women sat down on the marble coping of the fountain. The peacock trailed by them, its jewels all ablaze under the sun.

"That peacock makes me think of Adelaide." Edith swept her hand through the water, scaring the little fishes.

"Why?"

"In that dress she had on to-night—bronze and blue and green tulle. I will say this for Adelaide, she knows how to dress."

"Does she ever think of anything else but clothes?"

"Men," succinctly.

"Oh."

"Women like Adelaide," Edith elucidated, "want to look well, and to be admired. They live for it. They wake up in the morning and go to bed with that one idea. And the men fall for it."

"Do they?"

"Yes. Adelaide knows how to play on the keys of their vanity. You and I don't—or won't. When our youth goes, Jane, we'll have to be loved for our virtues. Adelaide will be loved for the part she plays, and she plays it well."

She laughed and stood up. "I am afraid your announcement to-morrow will hurt her feelings, Jane."

"She knows," Jane said quietly. "Mr. Towne told her."

"Really?" Edith stopped, and went on in a lower tone, "Speaking of angels—here she comes."

Adelaide, in her burnished tulle, tall, slender, graceful as a willow, was swinging along beneath the trellis. The peacock had turned and walked beside her. "What a picture Baldy could make of that," Edith said, "'The Proud Lady.'"

"Do you know," Jane's voice was also lowered, "when I look at her, I feel that it is she who should marry your uncle."

Edith was frank. "I should hate her. And so would he in a month. She's artificial, and you are so adorably natural, Jane."

Adelaide had reached the circle of light that surrounded the fountain. "The men have come and have gone up to dress," she said. "All except your uncle, Edith. He telephoned that he can't get here until after dinner. He has an important conference."

"He said he might be late. Benny came, of course?"

"Yes, and Eloise is happy. He had brought her all the town gossip. That's why I left. I hate gossip."

Edith knew that pose. No one could talk more devastatingly than Adelaide of her neighbor's affairs. But she did it, subtly, with an effect of charity. "I am very fond of her," was her way of prefacing a ruthless revelation.

"I thought your brother would be down," Adelaide looked at Jane, poised on the rim of the fountain, like a blue butterfly,—"but he wasn't with the rest."

"Baldy can't be here until to-morrow noon. He had to be in the office."

"What are you going to do with yourself in the meantime, Edith?" Adelaide was in a mood to make people uncomfortable. She was uncomfortable herself. Jane, in billowing heavenly blue with rose ribbons floating at her girdle, was youth incarnate. And it was her youth that had attracted Towne.

The three women walked towards the house together. As they came out from under the arbor, they were aware of black clouds stretched across the horizon. "I hope it won't rain," Edith said. "Lucy is planning to serve dinner on the terrace."

Adelaide was irritable. "I wish she wouldn't. There'll be bugs and things."

Jane liked the idea of an out-of-door dinner. She thought that the maids in their pink linen were like

rose-leaves blown across the lawn. There was a great umbrella over the table, rose-striped. "How gay it is," she said; "I hope the rain won't spoil it."

When they reached the wide-pillared piazza, no one was there. The wind was blowing steadily from the bank of clouds. Edith went in to get a scarf.

And so Jane and Adelaide were left alone.

Adelaide sat in a big chair with a back like a spreading fan; she was statuesque, and knew it, but she would have exchanged at the moment every classic line for the effect that Jane gave of unpremeditated grace and beauty. The child had flung a cushion on the marble step, and had dropped down upon it. The wind caught up her ruffles, so that she seemed to float in a cloud.

She laughed, and tucked her whirling draperies about her. "I love the wind, don't you?"

Adelaide did not love the wind. It rumpled her hair. She felt spitefully ready to hurt Jane.

"It is a pity," she said, after a pause, "that Ricky can't dine with us."

Jane agreed. "Mr. Towne always seems to be a very busy person."

Adelaide carried a little gauze fan with gold-lacquered sticks. When she spoke she kept her eyes upon the fan. "Do you always call him 'Mr. Towne'?"

"Of course."

"But not when you're alone."

Jane flushed. "Yes, I do. Why not?"

"But, my dear, it is so very formal. And you are going to marry him."

"He said that he had told you."

"Ricky tells me everything. We are very old friends, you know."

Jane said nothing. There was, indeed, nothing to say. She was not in the least jealous of Adelaide. She wondered, of course, why Towne should have overlooked this lovely lady to choose a shabby child. But he had chosen the child, and that settled it as far as Mrs. Laramore was concerned.

But it did not settle it for Adelaide. "I think it is distinctly amusing for you to call him 'Mr. Towne.' Poor Ricky! You mustn't hold him at arms' length."

"Why not?"

"Well, none of the rest of us have," said Adelaide, deliberately.

Jane looked up at her. "The rest of you? What do you mean, Mrs. Laramore?"

"Oh, the women that Ricky has loved," lightly.

The winds fluttered the ribbons of Jane's frock, fluttered her ruffles. The peacock on the lawn uttered a discordant note. Jane was subconsciously aware of a kinship between Adelaide and the burnished bird. She spoke of the peacock.

"What a disagreeable voice he has."

Adelaide stared. "Who?"

"The peacock," said Jane.

Then Eloise and Edith came in, and presently the men, and Lucy and Del from a trip to the small porkers, and Adelaide going out with Del to dinner was uncomfortably aware that Jane had either artlessly or artfully refused to discuss with her the women who had been loved by Frederick Towne!

The dinner was delicious. "Our farm products," Delafield boasted. Even the fish, it seemed, he had caught that morning, motoring over to the river and bringing them back to be split and broiled and served with little new potatoes. There was chicken and asparagus, small cream cheeses with the salad, heaped-up berries in a Royal Worcester bowl, roses from the garden. "All home-grown," said the proud new husband.

Jane ate with little appetite. She had refused to discuss with Adelaide the former heart affairs of her betrothed, but the words rang in her ears, "The women that Ricky has loved."

Jane was young. And to youth, love is for the eternities. The thought of herself as one of a succession of Dulcineas was degrading. She was restless and unhappy. It was useless to assure herself that Towne had chosen her above all the rest. She was not sophisticated enough to assume that it is, perhaps, better to be a man's last love than his first. That Towne had made it possible for any woman to speak of him as Adelaide spoke, seemed to Jane to drag her own relation to him in the dust.

The strength of the wind increased. The table was sheltered by the house, but at last Delafield decided, "We'd better go in. The rain is coming. We can have our coffee in the hall."

Their leaving had the effect of a stampede. Big drops splashed into the plates. The men servants and maids scurried to the rescue of china and linen.

The draperies of the women streamed in the wind. Adelaide's tulle was a banner of green and blue. The peacock came swiftly up the walk, crying raucously, and found a sheltered spot beneath the steps.

From the wide hall, they saw the rain in silver sheets. Then the doors were shut against the beating wind.

They drank their coffee, and bridge tables were brought in. There were enough without Jane to form two tables. And she was glad. She wandered into the living-room and curled herself up in a window-seat. The window opened on the porch. Beyond the white pillars she could see the road, and the rain-drenched garden.

After a time the rain stopped, and the world showed clear as crystal against the opal brightness of the western sky. The peacock came out of his hiding-place, and dragged a heavy tail over the sodden lawn.

It was cool and the air was sweet. Jane lay with her head against a cushion, looking out. She was lonely and wished that Towne would come.

Perhaps in his presence her doubts would vanish. It grew dark and darker. Jane shut her eyes and at last she fell asleep.

She was waked by Towne's voice. He was on the porch. "Where is everybody?"

It was Adelaide who answered him. "They have motored into Alexandria to the movies. Eloise would have it. But I stayed—waiting for you, Ricky."

"Where's Jane?"

"She went up-stairs early. Like a sleepy child."

Jane heard his laugh. "She is a child—a darling child."

Then in the darkness Adelaide said, "Don't, Ricky."

"Why not?"

"Do you remember that once upon a time you called me—a darling child?"

"Did I? Well, perhaps you were. You are certainly a very charming woman."

Jane, listening breathlessly, assured herself that of course he was polite. He had to be.

Adelaide was speaking. "So you are going to announce it to-morrow?"

"Who told you?"

"Edith."

"Well, it seemed best, Adelaide. The wedding day isn't far off—and the world will have to know it."

A hushed moment, then, "Oh, Ricky, Ricky!"

"Adelaide! Don't take it like that."

"I can't help it. You are going out of my life. And you've always been so strong, and big, and brave. No other man will ever match you."

When he spoke, his voice had a new and softer note. "I didn't dream it would hurt you."

"You might have known."

The lightning flickering along the horizon showed Adelaide standing beside Towne's chair.

"Ricky"—the whispered words reached Jane—"kiss me once—to say 'good-bye.'"

CHAPTER XXVII
FLIGHT

Young Baldwin Barnes, on Saturday morning, ate breakfast alone in the little house. He read his paper and drank his coffee. But the savor of things was gone. He missed Jane. Her engaging chatter, the spirited challenge, even the small irritations. "She is such a darling-dear," was his homesick meditation.

Oh, a man needed a woman on the other side of the table. And when Jane was married, what then?

Edith!

Oh, if he might! If Philomel might sing for her! Toast and poached eggs! Nectar and ambrosia! His little house a castle!

"But it isn't mine own," the young poet reminded himself; "there is still the mortgage." He came down to earth, cleared the table, fed the pussy-cats. Then he went down to the post-box to get the mail.

The Barnes' mail was rarely voluminous, rarely interesting. A bill or two, a letter from Judy—some futile advertising stuff.

This morning, however, there was a long envelope. In one corner was the name of the magazine to which, nearly six months before, Baldy had sent

his prize cover design. The thing had almost gone out of his thoughts. He had long ceased to hope. Money did not miraculously fall into one's lap.

He tore open the envelope. Within was a closely typed letter and a pale pink check.

The check was for two thousand dollars. He had won the prize!

Breathless with the thought of it, deprived of strength, he sat down on the terrace steps. Merrymaid and the kitten came down and angled for attention, but Baldy overlooked them utterly. The letter was astounding. The magazine had not only given him the prize but they wanted more of his work. They would pay well for it—and if he would come to New York at their expense, the art editor would like to talk it over!

Baldy, looking up from the pregnant phrases and catching Merrymaid's eye upon him, demanded, "Now, what do you think of that? Shall I resign from the office? I'll tell the world, I will."

Oh, the thing might even make it possible for him to marry Edith. He could at least pay for the honeymoon—preserve some sense of personal independence while he worked towards fame. If she would only see it. That he must ask her to live for a time—in the little house. He'd make things easy for her,—oh, well, the thing could be done—it could be done.

He flew up the steps on the wings of his delight. He would ride like the wind to Virginia—find

Edith, in a rose-garden, fling himself at her feet! Declare his good fortune! And he would see her eyes!

Packing his bag, he decided to stop in Washington, and perpetrate a few extravagances. Something for Edith. Something for Jane. Something for himself. There would be no harm in looking his best....

He arrived at Grass Hills in time for lunch. His little Ford came up the drive as proudly as a Rolls-Royce. And Baldy descending was a gay and gallant figure. There was no one in sight but the servants who took his bag, and drove his car around to the garage. A maid in rose linen said that Mr. and Mrs. Simms were at the stables. Miss Towne was on the links with the other guests, and would return from the Country Club in time for lunch at two o'clock. Miss Barnes was up-stairs. Her head had ached, and she had had her breakfast in bed.

"Will you let her know that I am here?"

The maid went up and came down again to say that Miss Barnes was in the second gallery—and would he go right up.

The second gallery looked out over the river. Jane lay in a long chair. She was pale, and there were shadows under her eyes.

"Oh, look here, Janey," Baldy blurted out, "is it as bad as this?"

"I'm just—lazy." She sat up and kissed

him. Then buried her face in his coat and wept silently.

"For heaven's sake, Jane," he patted her shoulder, "what's the matter?"

"I want to go home."

He looked blank. "Home?"

"Yes." She stopped crying. "Baldy, something has happened—and I've got to tell you." Tensely, with her hands clasped about her knees, she rehearsed for him the scene between Adelaide and Frederick Towne. And when she finished she said, "I can't marry him."

"Of course not. A girl like you. You'd be miserable. And that's the end of it."

"Utterly miserable." She stared before her. Then presently she went on. "I stayed up-stairs all the morning. Lucy and Edith have been perfect dears. I think Edith lays it to the announcement of my engagement to-night. That I was dreading it. Of course it mustn't be announced, Baldy."

He stood up, sternly renouncing his dreams. "Get your things on, Jane, and I'll take you home. You can't stay here, of course. We can decide later what it is best to do."

"I don't see how I can break it off. He's done so much for us. I can't ever—pay him——"

In Baldy's pocket was the pink slip. He took it out and handed it to his sister. "Jane, I got the prize. Two thousand dollars."

"Baldy!" Her tone was incredulous.

He had no joy in the announcement. The thing had ceased to mean freedom—it had ceased to mean—Edith. It meant only one thing at the moment, to free Jane from bondage.

He gave Jane the letter and she read it. "It is your great opportunity."

"Yes." He refused to discuss that aspect of it. "And it comes in the nick of time for you, old dear."

Their flight was a hurried one. A note for Lucy and one for Towne. A note for Edith!

Jane was not well was the reason given their hostess. The note to Towne said more than that. And the note to Edith was—renunciation.

Edith coming home to luncheon found the note in her room. All the morning she had been filled with glorious anticipation. Baldy would arrive in a few hours. Together they would walk down that trellised path to the fountain, they would sit on the marble coping. She would trail her hand through the water. Further than that she would not let her imagination carry her. It was enough that she would see him in that magic place with his air of golden youth.

But she was not to see him, for the note said:

"Beloved—I make no excuse for calling you that because I say it always in my heart—Jane has made up her mind that she cannot marry your uncle. So we are leaving at once.

"I can't tell you what the thought of these two days with you meant to me. And now I must give them up. Perhaps I must give you up, I don't know. I came with high hopes. I go away without any hope at all. But I love you."

Edith read the note twice, then put it to her lips. She hardly dared admit to herself the keenness of her disappointment.

She stood for a long time at the window looking out. Why had Jane decided not to marry Uncle Frederick? What had happened since yesterday afternoon?

From Edith's window she could see the south lawn. The servants were arranging a buffet luncheon. Little tables were set around—and wicker chairs. Adelaide, tall and fair, in her favorite blue and a broad black hat stood by one of the little tables. She was feeding the peacock with bits of bread. She made a picture, and Towne's window faced that way.

"I wonder——" Edith said, and stopped. She remembered coming in from the movies the night before and finding Adelaide and Towne on the porch. And where was Jane?

Towne did not eat lunch. He pleaded important business, and had his car brought around. But everybody knew that he was following Jane. Mystery was in the air. Adelaide was restless. Only Edith knew the truth.

After lunch, she told Lucy. "Jane isn't going

to marry Uncle Fred. I don't know why. But I am afraid it is breaking up your house party."

"I hope it is," said Lucy, calmly. "Delafield is bored to death. He wants to get back to his pigs and roses. I am speaking frankly to you because I know you understand. I want our lives to be bigger and broader than they would have been if we hadn't met. And as for you"—her voice shook a little—"you'll always be a sort of goddess blessing our hearth."

Edith bent and kissed her, emotion gripping her. "Your hearth is blessed without me," she said, "but I'll always be glad to come."

Towne, riding like mad along the Virginia roads, behind the competent Briggs, reread Jane's letter.

"I was not up-stairs last night when you came. I was asleep in the window-seat of the living-room, just off the porch. And your voice waked me and I heard what you said, and Mrs. Laramore. And I can't marry you. I know how much you've done for me,—and I shall never forget your goodness. Baldy will take me home."

Enclosed was a pink check.

Towne blamed Adelaide furiously. Of course it was her fault. Such foolishness. And sentimentality. And he had been weak enough to fall for it.

Yet, as he cooled a bit, he was glad that Jane had showed her resentment. It was in keeping with his conception of her. Her innocence had flamed against such sophistication. There might, too, be

a hint of jealousy. Women were like that. Jealous.

As they whirled through Washington, Briggs voiced his fears. "If we meet a cop it will be all up with us, Mr. Towne."

"Take a chance, Briggs. Give her more gas. We've got to get there."

With all their speed, however, it was four o'clock when they reached Sherwood. Towne was still in the clothes he had worn on the links. He had not eaten since breakfast. He felt the strain.

He stormed up the terrace, where once he had climbed in the snow. He rang the bell. It whirred and whirred again in the silence. The house was empty.

CHAPTER XXVIII
IN THE PINE GROVE

It was on the way home that Jane had said to Baldy: "I feel like a selfish pig."

"Why, my dear?"

"To take your precious prize before it is cold. It doesn't seem right."

"It isn't a question of right or wrong. If things turn out with these new people as I hope, I'll be painting like mad for the next two months. And you'll have your work cut out for you as my model. They like you, Jane. They said so."

He had driven on steadily for a time, and had then said, "I never wanted you to marry him."

"Why not, Baldy?"

He turned his lighted-up eyes upon her. "Janey—I wanted you to have your—dreams——"

She had laid her hand on his arm in a swift caress. "You're a darling——" and after a while, "Nothing can take us from each other, ever, Baldy."

Never had they drawn closer in spirit than at this moment. But they said very little about it. When they came to the house, Baldy went at once to the garage. "I'll answer that letter, and put in

a good afternoon looking over my sketches." He did not tell her how gray the day stretched ahead of him—that golden day which had started with high hopes.

Jane changed to a loose straight frock of orange cotton, and without a hat, feeling actual physical freedom in the breaking of her bonds, she swung along the path to the little grove. It was aromatic with the warm scent of the pines, and there was a cool shade in the heart of it. Jane had brought a bag of stockings to mend, and sat down to her homely task, smiling a little as she thought of the contrast between this afternoon and yesterday, when she had sat on the rim of the fountain and watched Adelaide and the peacock. She had no feeling of rancor against Adelaide. She was aware only of a great thankfulness.

She was, indeed, at the moment, steeped in divine content. Here was the place where she belonged. She had a sense of blissful escape.

Merrymaid came down the path, her tail a plume. The kitten followed. A bronze butterfly floated across their vision, and they leaped for it—but it went above them—joyously towards the open blue of the sky. The two cats gazed after it, then composed themselves carefully like a pair of miniature lions—their paws in front of them, sleepy-eyed but alert for more butterflies, or for Jane's busy thread.

And it was thus that Towne found her. Convinced that the house was empty, he had started

towards Baldy's studio. Then down the vista of the pine grove, his eye had been caught by a spot of golden color. He had followed it.

She laid down her work and looked up at him. "You shouldn't have come."

"My dear child, why not? Jane, you are making mountains of molehills."

"I'm not."

He sat down beside her. The little cats drew away, doubtful. "It was natural that you should have resented it. And a thing like that isn't easy for a man to explain. Without seeming a—cad——"

"There isn't anything to explain."

"But there is. I have made you unhappy, and I'm sorry."

She shook her head, and spoke thoughtfully. "I think I am—happy. Mr. Towne, your world isn't my world. I like simple things and pleasant things, and honest things. And I like a One-Woman man, Mr. Towne."

He tried to laugh. "You are jealous."

"No," she said, quietly, "it isn't that, although men like you think it is. A woman who has self-respect must know her husband has her respect. Her heart must rest in him."

He spoke slowly. "I'll admit that I've philandered a lot. But I've never wanted to marry anyone but you. I can promise you my future."

"I'm sorry. But even if last night had never

been—I think I should have—given you up. I had begun to feel that I didn't love you. That out there in Chicago you swept me off my feet. Mr. Towne, I am sorry. And I am grateful. For all your kindness——" She flushed and went on, "You know, of course, that I shan't be happy until—I don't owe you anything...."

He laid his hand on hers. "I wish you wouldn't speak of it. It was nothing."

"It was a great deal."

He looked down at her, slender and young and infinitely desirable. "You needn't think I am going to let you go," he said.

"I'm afraid—you must——"

He flamed suddenly. "I'm more of a One-Woman man than you think. If you won't marry me, I won't have anyone else. I'll go on alone. As for

Adelaide——A woman like that doesn't expect much more than I gave. That's all I can say about her. She means nothing to me, seriously, and never will. She plays the game, and so do I, but it's only a game."

He looked tired and old. "I'll go abroad to-morrow. When I come back, perhaps you'll change your mind."

"I shall never change it," she said, "never."

He stood up. "Jane, I could make you happy." He held her hand as she stood beside him.

She looked at him and knew that he could not. Her dreams had come back to her—of Galahad—of

Robin Hood ... the world of romance had again flung wide its gates....

After Towne had gone she sat for a long time thinking it over. She blamed herself. She had broken her promise. Yet, he, too, had broken a promise.

She finished mending the stockings, and rolled them into compact balls. The little cats were asleep—the shadows were stretched out and the sun slanted through the pines. She had dinner to get, for her return had been unexpected, and Sophy had not been notified.

She might have brought to the thought of her tasks some faint feeling of regret. But she had none. She was glad to go in—to make an omelette—and cream the potatoes—and have hot biscuits and berries—and honey.

Planning thus, competently, she raised her eyes—to see coming along the path the two boys who had of late been Evans' close companions. She spoke to them as they reached her. "Can't you stay a minute? I'll make you some lemonade."

They stopped and looked at her in a way that startled her. "We can't," Arthur said; "we're going over to the Follettes. We thought we might help."

She stared at them. "Help? What do you mean?"

Sandy gasped. "Oh, didn't you know? Mrs. Follette died this morning...."

CHAPTER XXIX
JANE DREAMS

Evans had found his mother at noon, lying on the couch at the foot of her bed. He had stayed at home in the morning to help her, and at ten o'clock she had gone up-stairs to rest a bit before lunch. Old Mary had called her, and she had not answered. So Evans had entered her room to find that she had slipped away peacefully from the world in which she exaggerated her own importance. It would go on without her. She had not been neighborly but the neighbors would all come and sympathize with her son. And they would miss her, because she had added to the community some measure of stateliness, which they admired even as they resented it.

Evans had tried to get Baldy on the telephone, but could not. Jane was at Grass Hills. He would call up at long distance later. There was no reason why he should spoil for them this day of days.

So he had done the things that had to be done in the shadowed house. Dr. Hallam came, and others. Evans saw them and they went away. He moved in a dream. He had no one to share intimately his sorrow—no sister, no brother, no one,

except his little dog, who trailed after him, wistful-eyed, and with limping steps.

The full force of the thing that had happened did not come to him at once. He had a feeling that at any moment his mother might sweep in from the out-of-doors, in her white linen and flat black hat, and sit at the head of the table, and tell him the news of the morning.

He had had no lunch, so old Mary fixed a tray for him. He did not eat, but drank some milk. Then he and Rusty took up their restless wandering through the silent rooms. Old Mary, true to tradition, had drawn all the blinds and shut many of the windows, so that the house was filled with a sort of golden gloom. Evans went into his mother's little office on the first floor, and sat down at her desk. It was in perfect order, and laid out on the blotter was the writing paper with the golden crest, and the box of golden seals. And he had laughed at her! He remembered with a pang that they would never again laugh together. He was alone.

He wondered why such things happened. Was all of life as sinister as this? Must one always find tragedy at every turn of the road? He had lost his youth, had lost Jane. And now his mother. Was everything to be taken away? Would there be nothing left but strength to endure?

Well, God helping him, he would endure to the end....

He closed the desk gently and went out into the darkened hall. As he followed its length, a door opened at the end. Black against the brightness beyond, he saw the two lads. They came forward with some hesitation, but when they saw his tired face, they forgot self-consciousness.

"We just heard. And we want to help." Sandy was spokesman. Arthur was speechless. But he caught hold of Evans' sleeve and looked up at him. His eyes said what his voice refused.

Evans, with his arms across their shoulders, drew the boys to him. "It was good of you to come."

"Miss Barnes said," again it was Sandy who spoke, "that perhaps we might get some pine from the little grove. That your mother liked it."

"Miss Barnes? Is she back? Does she know?"

"We told her. She is coming right over."

Baldy drove Jane in his little car. As she entered she seemed to bring the light in with her. She illumined the house like a torch.

She walked swiftly towards Evans, and held out her hand. "My dear, I am so sorry."

"I thought you were at Grass Hills."

"We came back unexpectedly."

"I am so glad—you came."

He was having a bad time with his voice. He could not go on....

Jane spoke to the boys. "Did you ask him about the pine branches? Just those, and roses from the garden, Evans."

"You always think of things——"

"Baldy will take the boys to the grove, and do any errands you may have for him." She was her calm and competent self—letting him get control of his emotion while she directed others.

Baldy, coming in, wrung Evans' hand. "The boys and I will get the pine, and Edith Towne is coming out to help. I called her up to tell her——"

Baldy stopped at that. He could not speak here of the glory that encompassed him. He had said, "*If death should come to us, Edith! Does anything else count?*" And she had said, "*Nothing.*" And now she was coming and they would pick roses together in the garden. And love and life would minister to a greater mystery....

When Baldy and the boys had gone, Jane and Evans opened the windows and pulled up the shades. The house was filled with clear light, and was cool in the breeze.

When they had finished, Jane said, "That's all, I think. We can rest a bit. And presently it will be time for dinner."

"I don't want any dinner."

They were in the library. Outside was an amethyst twilight, with a young moon low in the sky. Evans and Jane stood by the window, looking out, and Jane asked in a hushed voice, "You don't want any dinner because she won't be at the other end of the table?"

"Yes." His face was turned from her. His hands were clinched. His throat was dry. For a moment he wished he were alone that he might weep for his mother.

And then Jane said, "Let me sit at the other end of your table."

He turned back to her, and saw her eyes, and what he saw made him reach out blindly for her hand—sympathy, tenderness—a womanly brooding tenderness.

"Oh, Evans, Evans," she said, "I am not going to marry Frederick Towne."

"Why not?" thickly.

"I don't love him."

"Do you love me, Jane?"

She nodded and could not speak. They clung together. He wept and was not ashamed of it.

And standing there, with his head against her breast, Jane knew that she had found the best. Marriage was not a thing of luxury and soft living, of flaming moments of wild emotion. It was a thing of hardness shared, of spirit meeting spirit, of dream matching dream. Jane, that afternoon, had caught her breath as she had come into the darkened hall, and had seen Evans standing between those slender lads. So some day, perhaps, in this old house—his sons!